ALL SHE NEEDS

SEATTLE WHALERS HOCKEY ROMANCE

ALL SHE NEEDS

Emily Bunney

4 Horsemen Publications, Inc.
1497 Main St. Suite 169
Dunedin, FL 34698
4horsemenpublications.com
info@4horsemenpublications.com

Edited by J.M. Paquette

Ebook ISBN: 978-1-64450-274-7
Audiobook ISBN: 978-1-64450-273-0
Print ISBN: 978-1-64450-272-3

Dedication

I'm dedicating this book to my wonderful mum.
She's been a constant support to me through the
good times and the bad. When I told her I had
written a book, she was so proud. I love you, mum. I
couldn't have done any of this without you.

Table of Contents

PROLOGUE

Bugs

For as long as I've known Cameron, I've wanted her. And tonight, I finally get what I need, what I crave. Sure, I've been happy in the Friend Zone if it means we can hang out, but the deep, throbbing need to get my hands on her curves has been my daily obsession.

Looking down at her sweet, sleeping face fills me with so much emotion it makes my chest hurt. I'm not going to lie—the caveman inside is beating his chest and wants to shout about his conquest from the rooftops. But along with that, there's a protectiveness that makes me want to hold her to me, to be all she needs.

Obviously, I'm sated after the incredible sex we've just had. She was so uninhibited which surprised me. Cam has always had a gentle, kind nature, except when she's at work and then she's all business. When she gave me that sizzling look at Matt and Mila's housewarming party and told me she wanted me, I couldn't get us out of there fast enough.

Part of me knew this could ruin our friendship forever, but that part wasn't in charge as her soft, full lips crashed against mine. I couldn't think straight as I gripped her slim hips and guided her movements on top of me. And my mind was completely blown when she came apart beneath me, moaning and writhing in so much pleasure I released with such power I saw stars.

Cam shifts in my arms and snuggles in deeper, hooking her long leg over mine, but she doesn't wake. I can feel my eyelids drooping and the steady rhythm of her breathing is lulling me to sleep. However, I don't want to miss a second of this time with her. If this is it, if this one incredible night is all I get, then I'm going to hold on to each precious moment.

This is the last thought I have before sleep finally claims me.

And when I wake the next morning, I'm alone.

Cameron

"Don, your three o'clock is here," I say into the intercom, smiling pleasantly at the sports agent sitting on the sectional couch in my office. She smiles back and busily scrolls through her phone.

"Just give me a minute, Cam. I'm finishing up with an email," Don replies in his warm, deep baritone. As the General Manager of a successful NHL franchise, he's always running from one meeting or email to another.

"Can I get you something to drink while you wait, Trixie?" I ask, rising from my chair. Trixie is one of my favorite agents, and her firm represents many of our top players, including our Captain, Warren "Bugs" Parker. She looks like a classic English rose with her porcelain skin, chic business suit that barely contains her curvy hourglass figure, and blonde hair cut in a stylish choppy bob. However, as soon as she opens her mouth, she releases a deluge of colorful British slang that I struggle to understand and would make most hardened hockey players blush.

1

She's awesome.

"No, I'm fine. Thanks, love," she replies. She once told me she's from East London, but I couldn't tell you how her accent is any different from any other part of London or England for that matter. "I've just had a cuppa with one of my football players. What is it with you Yanks and your fucking terrible tea? He actually tried to microwave the water! What a wanker." She scrunches up her freckled nose and grimaces.

I chuckle and shake my head. "I can't help you with that. I'm strictly a coffee drinker."

As we continue to discuss tea versus coffee, Don opens his office door and greets Trixie, who stands and shakes his hand. They share some polite small talk and disappear into his office; I know not to disturb them now. It's that time in the season when some of our players are involved in contract negotiations, so there's a never-ending parade of agents and managers going through this office.

The Whalers have made it to the Stanley Cup play-offs, and the buzz around the office is electric. We start the first series against Vancouver in a few days, so not only am I wrangling a myriad of meetings, I must also get myself and Don to all the away games.

In fact, that reminds me. I need to head down to the Coaching Floor to liaise with Mila, the Head Coach's Assistant, to get the travel itinerary. We have home ice advantage for the first two games against the Vikings, so there's no hurry, but I feel like getting out of the office while I can.

Coffee with Mila feels like a good idea; we've not caught up since her housewarming over a week ago, and I have some important things to talk to her about. Namely the hot night I had with my best friend. Oh, did I mention he happens to be the team captain?

A slideshow of our sweaty encounter flashes through my mind and heats my core, causing me to involuntarily clench my thighs together. Goddamn it, it's been a week, and my sex flashbacks are just as strong as ever.

Trying to shake my arousal away, I hit the divert button on my desk phone, grab my cell and my purse, and head toward the elevator.

As I round the corner to the lobby, I come face to face with a wall of muscles in navy and gold. I expel a loud oof as I bounce off the obstacle, then feel large hands grip my biceps to steady me. The scent of warm man and spicy cologne invades my senses, and I know exactly who it is.

"Shit, Cam. I almost knocked you on your ass." Warren's deep voice vibrates through my body as he continues to hold my arms even though I've found my balance.

"You need to watch where you're going, you big tree," I grumble, wriggling free from his grasp and stepping back. Ever since he had his hands on me, I find it impossible to be too close to him.

Concern and hurt shadow Warren's ridiculously handsome face as he rubs the dark beard that covers his chin, cheeks, and neck. Like most NHL players, he refuses to shave or cut his hair during the playoffs, and I must admit, the rough look suits him. His fern green eyes drop as he thrusts his hands into the pockets of his team sweatpants and rocks on his heels, looking uncomfortable.

"Umm, I was actually looking for Trixie," he mumbles at his sneakers. "I heard she was in with Don."

Oh, this is so awkward.

I hate that I seem to have a brain freeze every time I see Warren now. I no longer see my best friend; I just see the look he had on his face when he saw me naked for the first time. Ugh, I'm mortified.

I cough to clear the lump in my throat and say, "Trixie's just gone in to see Don, so they might be a while. You can wait in my office if you like. I'm just heading out."

Quickly, I scoot around him and literally sprint toward the elevator which, to my immense relief, is just opening. I hear Warren calling "Sawyer, wait!" as the doors slide shut, and I slump against the wall, struggling to get my breathing under control. Oh god, it's so awkward. I slap my hand to my forehead and cringe, flashbacks of our night assaulting my brain as I deal with the fact that Warren has seen me naked.

What the fuck was I thinking, sleeping with him? We had a great friendship before, although I've always known that he's attracted to me. I gave in to my loneliness and horniness and detonated an awkward bomb all over our friendship.

The ping of the elevator arriving at the Coaching Floor snaps me out of my pity party, and I smile at the Goaltending Coach as we pass. I feel like it's time to come clean to my best girlfriend and get some advice. Mila has experience dating one of the players. She's just moved in with Matt Landon, our center, after a very tumultuous start to their relationship. They tried the friend thing after an anonymous one-night stand, and it ended up becoming a serious relationship. As much as it worked for them, I don't think that's what I want with Warren. We were great as friends, and I want that back. I miss talking to him when funny stuff happens and the long runs we go on. I've always been a bit of a loner—my mom was my best friend—so when she died, I found it difficult to make friends and let people in. But with Warren, I clicked instantly; I can't even explain what it was that drew me to him. Yes, we have similar interests and sense of humor, and we share the sadness of losing a parent, but it's more than that: he feels safe and like home. That is priceless to me, and the thought of losing that over a one-night stand makes my stomach twist up in knots.

Thankfully, Mila is in her office. "Hi, you got time for coffee?" I ask in my cheeriest voice, leaning through her door.

She looks up from peering at her laptop, her long red hair up in a loopy bun. "Hey, Cam." She leans back in her office chair, rubbing her eyes. "I could use a break. I swear I need glasses; this screen is fuzzy as shit."

"No shame in that." I laugh, waggling my own glasses at her. I couldn't face putting my contacts in this morning, so I went for the easy option.

"I fear if I get them, Matt will have all these sexy secretary fantasies." She giggles, locking her laptop, diverting her phone, and grabbing her purse and cell.

"Ewwww, that's a visual I could really do without, thanks." I grimace. "It's bad enough wondering what weird shit Beth and Nate will get up to next, let alone you as well."

Mila's former roommate is also dating one of the Whalers, and to say the pair of them are experimental in their sex life is an understatement. I'm still scarred from the time Beth wore vibrating panties to our favorite bar and had an orgasm right next to me.

It's a pleasant spring day, and for a change in Seattle, it's not raining. We walk out of the arena complex toward our favorite coffee shop, and I suddenly have a craving for a massive, sticky chocolate something to go along with my confession.

Once we've placed our order, we find a free table at the back and settle in, first talking about the excitement for the upcoming playoffs before getting into the juicy stuff.

"I have a question." Mila smirks, ripping apart her warm croissant and smearing it in apricot jelly. "I lost track of you after the karaoke thing at our party. Where'd you go?"

My coffee cup comes to a stuttering halt in front of my face, and latte sloshes onto my sweater.

"Oh shit," I curse, dabbing at the liquid with my napkin. Mila's curious amber eyes bore into me. When the spilled latte is cleaned up, I huff out an exasperated breath and roll my eyes. "From the look on your face, you know exactly what happened."

Mila's eyebrows shoot up, and she attempts to look innocent, but I know she knows about Warren and me.

"I've heard something interesting, I will admit. I would like to hear it from you though." Mila sits back in her chair and crosses her arms. "And after you tell me, I'm gonna give you shit for holding out on me for so long."

I blow out a breath so the strands of light brown hair lift off my face and take a long drink of coffee, preparing myself.

"Warren and I slept together," I confess, searching Mila's face for shock, but all I find is a quest for more details.

"Annnnnnd …" she says, making a "keep going" gesture with her hand, popping another bite of flaky pastry into her mouth.

"If you know, why are you asking me?" I sigh. "Obviously, Matt's told you everything."

"No, all I got out of him was that it happened. He muttered something about bro code and stomped off into the shower. Even a blow job didn't get the deets out of him." Mila smirks, blushing pink at her naughty confession.

"Ugh, TMI." I stare at my untouched chocolate brownie, suddenly not hungry for it anymore.

Mila waits patiently, picking up flakes of croissant from her plate with her finger and popping them into her mouth.

As I wonder what to say next, I am flooded with memories of Warren's lips, tongue, and fingers on me. Stroking and licking me into a frenzy before finally taking me with a raw passion that still makes my toes curl and my panties flood with desire.

Mila chuckles. "I can tell from the dreamy look in your eyes that it was awesome, but I'm confused. What happened? Why aren't you together? I thought it would be the push you both needed to make a go of it."

"Look, I was lonely, horny, and there was all that love in the room with Nate winning Beth back. And he looked sexy as fuck dancing around to The Backstreet Boys, then he was grinding up against me. I'm only human!" By the time I get to the end of my speech, my voice is all weird and high-pitched.

"So it was that good?" Mila asks with a naughty smirk.

I feel my cheeks blush red, and I have to concentrate really hard on stirring my coffee. Finally, I look up at her. "It was incredible," I admit quietly.

After a triumphant giggle, Mila asks, "And you both agreed it was just a one-night thing?"

"Sort of," I whisper shyly, remembering the way we ripped at each other's clothes when we got to Warren's house, moving through the rooms until we landed on his bed. Warren did plenty of talking after that, but it was mostly the dirty variety.

"Oh, for fuck's sake, Cam. You're killing me," Mila huffs. "How did you leave it? I've seen the pair of you circling round each other since the party, and it's weird."

"I know! It's awkward," I confess, feeling slightly ashamed of the way I left things that night. "I kind of skipped out on him while he was sleeping."

I can still feel my heart beating out of my chest as I remember gathering my clothes and taking one last look at Warren's handsome, sleeping face. I felt like shit then, and I still feel like shit for doing that to him. But also for ignoring his texts and calls the next day. I was so confused and embarrassed, I suddenly had all these conflicting feelings for a man who had always been just a friend. When he persisted, I finally had to make up a bullshit excuse for not being able to talk, and I've been avoiding him ever since. Today's encounter at the elevator is the first time we've been in each other's company since it happened.

"Huh! I've been there, my friend." Mila hmphs. She did a similar thing after her one-night stand with Matt, only they'd not known each other. It was fate that brought them face to face at the Whalers.

"How did you deal with it?" I beg. I need someone to help me process this.

"Oh, honey. Our situation wasn't the same as what's going on with you," she consoles me. "We didn't know each other, but you and Bugs have a friendship already. Matt told me he's kind of hurt and confused that you're ghosting him. He thinks he's hurt you or done something wrong. The guy's all over the place."

I scowl at Mila and her hand suddenly flies to her mouth like she knows she's said too much. "I thought Matt didn't tell you the details?"

She giggles and blushes bright red. "I guess the blow job got *some* information out of him."

I finally laugh and roll my eyes. God, this is a fucked-up situation.

"What should I do? I miss him, Mila. I miss our friendship, but I don't know if we can be the same after sleeping together."

"But why do you want things to be the same?" she asks, cocking her head to the side. "Why don't you want to give a relationship with him a chance? You've admitted the sex was incredible, and you know you get along really well. What's the problem?"

And this is exactly what I've been wrestling with all week. On the surface, it seems so simple: Warren and I have a fantastic sexual connection, and on top of that, we actually get along, so why not become a couple?

I sigh heavily and cover my face with my hands, a sudden rush of emotions overwhelming me. A quiet, hitching sob escapes me, and I hear the scrape of Mila's chair as she scoots closer to me.

"Oh, honey. I didn't mean to upset you," she coos as she gently rubs my back, handing me a napkin.

"I'm sorry. I'm such a fucking mess." I sniff, lifting my glasses and dabbing my eyes, thankful the coffee shop isn't busy today.

Mila continues to soothe me with reassuring strokes. "I was so messed up after Richard cheated; he stole my confidence and made me feel completely undesirable. He was such an asshole toward the end and made me feel like it was my fault he strayed."

"What a dick," Mila growls. "My ex was the same. Why do they do that?"

I laugh a little bitterly. "I don't know? It seems like every man I let into my life ends up screwing me over in some way. My 'sperm donor' father was the first."

"But Warren isn't like that. He adores you."

"And that's what makes it so scary," I blurt. "What if he ends up growing tired of me like all the others? My dad didn't want anything to do with me, the first guy I seriously dated couldn't hack it when my mom got sick and bailed, and then Richard. I can't add Warren to that list. I value our friendship too much. We work as friends—I know that. It's safe, and I know how that relationship works."

Mila sighs and hugs me tightly. "I'm so sorry you've had so much heartbreak, honey. I totally understand why you're scared."

Suddenly she releases me, a huge smile on her face.

"Come over tonight. I'll call Beth, and we'll work this out. It's Champagne Tuesday after all." Mila grabs her phone and starts typing out a text to Beth to make arrangements, and I finally tear into my brownie, slightly more hopeful that my new girl squad will help me figure out this mess.

2

Bugs

I've been sitting on the couch in Cam's office for thirty minutes, and neither she nor Trixie have made an appearance. I can hear Trixie's loud, filthy laugh through Don's door, so it sounds like whatever negotiations they're having are going well. I just thank god I'm not the subject of their talk; my contract is airtight for another three years, so I can sleep easy at night. I do, however, want to talk to her about the new ad campaign she's negotiating for me with a luxury sportswear brand.

Also, I thought if I came up here, I could take the opportunity to talk to Cam about why the fuck she's been ghosting me. I know confronting her at work isn't the smartest idea I've ever had, but she won't answer my calls or texts, and whenever we're in close proximity at work, she makes damn sure there are other people around. I understand what happened was unexpected. I've been in the Friend Zone so long, it took me a few moments to fully understand what she needed. The hooded, lustful look in her eyes and the way she kept biting her lip as she waited for me to respond to her proposal had thickened my cock to painful proportions. And then she just about ended me.

"I need you, Warren. Just for tonight … please."

Then that was that; I grabbed her hand, and we drove back to my place for the best night of my life. Her soft, satiny skin and wet needy pussy, the way she keened and moaned as I licked her center. When she finally came apart, she pulled at my hair and bucked her hips in complete abandon.

I shift uncomfortably on the couch as the recollection of that night gives me a semi, not a good look in sweatpants. However, the sour memory of waking up alone and the shut out that followed takes care of it. I don't understand what I did wrong, and not knowing is driving me crazy. I'm happy to go back to being friends, but I can't suggest this to Cam if she continues to ignore me.

"It was lovely doing business with you, Don."Trixie's loud voice jolts me from my thoughts, and I watch as the pair come out of his office. "I'll get the office to send the papers over to you ASAP."

"Always a pleasure, Trixie. I only feel slightly eviscerated by you today." Don chuckles, smiling warmly at her before he notices me. "Parker. Can I help you with something?"

I jump to my feet and run my hand over my face. My playoff beard is still at that early itchy stage, and it's bugging the shit out of me.

"No, sir. I'm just waiting for Trixie," I reply, nodding at my agent and manager.

"Good. Well, I'll leave you to it." Don looks at Cam's empty desk and pulls his cell phone out of his pocket. "I'm sure I'll see you again soon, Trixie." He waves absent-mindedly at us and disappears back into his office.

"What can I do for you, love?" Trixie asks, glancing briefly at her smart watch. "I've got a meeting in an hour across town, and traffic's a bitch at this time of day. Can we walk and talk?"

"Sure." I just about get the word out before Trixie takes off toward the elevators at a hell of a pace for a woman in high heels. I jog to catch up, then match her speed as we walk along the corridor. "I just wanted to check on the progress of the sportswear deal. I'm planning on spending the summer working on my cabin, so I just wanted to check when I needed to be around."

"Don't you worry about that, love. The campaign is for their spring collection, so they won't need you until you're back in Seattle for training camp." Trixie smirks at me as we reach the elevators. "You know you could've asked me that question over the phone, right?"

"I know, but I thought it would be nice to catch up," I reply. Trixie knows me too well to fall for a line of bull-shit like that.

Her eyebrow shoots up in a perfect arch. "Bollocks!" she blurts, slapping the call button on the elevator. "I know you, Bugs. There's no way you'd sit on a couch for half an hour waiting to ask me that one question. You were waiting for the lovely Cameron to come back, weren't you?"

I feel heat burn my cheeks, and I rub the back of my neck nervously. "Am I that fucking transparent?"

Trixie slaps me lightly on the cheek and laughs. "Don't worry, love. I won't tell a soul. We should have dinner some time, and you can tell me all about it." The elevator arrives and she strides inside. "Later, lover boy."

I puff out my cheeks, exasperated at the situation. If I continue to wait around for Cam to come back, I'm bordering on pathetic. The vibration of my phone in my pocket saves me from further procrastination.

[MATT: Where the fuck are you, Cap? We're waiting in the gym. You're late, and Coach is pissed.]

"Fuck!" I sprint for the stairs. No point in waiting for the elevator and making myself even later.

"We have two days before the start of the playoffs," Coach Casey says, skating back and forth in front of us, a Whalers beanie covering his steel grey hair. "Obviously, I don't need to tell you how important it is that we take full advantage of playing the first two games on home ice."

There's a deep rumble of agreement from the semi-circle of players surrounding him, all of us having taken a knee after a brutal scrimmage game. Each one of us is dripping with sweat, our muscles flooded with lactic acid but pumped up at the prospect of fighting our local rivals in the first round of the Stanley Cup playoffs.

"We've prepared all season for this, and I want each and every one of you to have your head in the game." Coach comes to a halt in front of me, and I feel his hard green eyes bore into me. "Whatever shit you've got going on in your personal lives—pregnant wives, strained relationships, a sick fucking dog—I want you to leave it off the ice."

I can feel a blush creeping up my neck, and I clench my jaw. I know he's addressing the team, but he must have noticed my distraction, and I'm pissed at myself. I'm the captain and as such should lead by example. I can't get at the guys for being distracted by their personal lives if I'm doing that very thing.

Coach continues to give us his pep talk, and he runs down the schedule for the next four days. After the two home games, we're on the plane to Vancouver for the next two games. If we start well, we could take the series with no more games and be fresh for the second round.

"Parker, a word," Coach barks at me, and suddenly I realize the rest of the guys are getting up and heading to the locker room. I'm still on my knee, lost in a daydream.

"Sure thing, Coach." I rise and we begin to skate slowly round the rink while the equipment team clears the pucks and goals away.

"What's going on, son? You seem distracted."

Okay, straight to the point.

"You know that the guys look to you for leadership, especially the younger ones, and if you're floating around with your head up your ass, it's gonna give off the wrong signal." Coach stops skating and we face each other. He's not pissed, thank fuck, but he is serious.

I huff out a breath and take my helmet off, stuffing it under my arm. "It's nothing, Coach. I'm fully committed to beating the shit out of Vancouver and progressing to the second round." I pull myself up to my full height, which is even more enormous in all my gear. "I've got my shit together; this is not a problem."

Coach seems to relax a little, and he slaps me on the shoulder. "Good to hear. You and Landon make a good team as Captain and Assistant Captain. I'd hate to ruin that dynamic because you're distracted."

"One hundred percent not distracted," I confirm as we reach the gate and leave the ice.

"Excellent. Now hit the showers and remind the guys that it's straight home for a good meal and bed. I don't want any of those yahoos out on the town tonight because they have a free day tomorrow."

"Sure thing." I smirk. We've had a few issues with the rookies being a little too into the Seattle party scene. Knox in particular has been in trouble more than the rest. He's a hell of a winger, but the kid needs to get a handle on his partying before Coach benches his ass.

By the time I hit the showers, most of the guys are drying off and dressing, except for Matt who takes a ridiculous amount of time washing his hair. Dude is worse than any woman I've ever known.

"What did Coach want?" he asks, rinsing shampoo from his hair.

"He thinks I'm distracted and just wanted to make sure I have my head in the game," I grumble, turning on the water, allowing the stream to cocoon me in heat.

I hear Matt chuckle through the noise of the shower, so I scrub my hands over my face to push away the water and glare at him.

"Don't be a dick, man," I growl, grabbing my body wash and squirting way too much into my hand.

Matt continues to laugh. "I'm sorry, but that's bad if Coach has noticed you mooning around here like a lovesick puppy."

"I'm not fucking mooning. I'm confused and pissed off."

"Okay, good." Matt turns the water off in his cubicle and grabs his towel. "What do you intend to do about it? Because I'm with Coach on this one; if you go into the playoffs with your head up your ass, we're gonna crash and burn."

"I know, I know." I sigh, turning my shower off as well, wrapping the towel round my waist, and slipping into my sliders. "I need to talk to Cam, but she's still ghosting me. We crossed paths today, and she practically ran away from me."

We walk into the locker room and begin to dress; all the other guys have already left and just the equipment team are left.

"I know we're supposed to head straight home tonight, but why don't you come over and we can grill out? I've got some T-bones that I need to use," Matt suggests, pulling on his jeans and buttoning them up.

"I don't know, man. Coach is pretty insistent we head straight home," I reply, pulling on my hoodie.

"Come on. You know that's to stop the younger guys going out and partying too hard." Matt grabs his duffel. "If he finds out, we can say we were talking strategy."

"Okay, fine. I'll follow you out there." I zip up my duffel and follow him out of the locker room.

"And just think—you can always pump Mila for info on Cam. I'm sure the two of them have already put this situation to rights." He chuckles, pushing through the door.

3

Cameron

The pop of the champagne cork and Mila's excited screech makes me almost jump out of my skin and drop the plate of cheese and crackers.

"For fuck's sake, Beth! Give a girl some warning before you do that." I gasp, delivering the snacks to the coffee table intact.

"Sorry, babe." Beth laughs, pouring the gushing fizz into the awaiting flutes, flicking her platinum bob. "I guess I blew my load a bit prematurely." A naughty smirk creases her bright red lips, and she winks at me.

I roll my eyes at her sexual innuendo and flop down onto the couch, grabbing a fat grape from the plate and popping it into my mouth.

"Stop being gross, Bee." Mila chuckles, taking her champagne flute from Beth and joining me on the couch.

"I can't help it. When you date a younger guy, you have to keep all your sexual feelings right at the surface. I never know when Nate will want to ravish me."

From the lusty look in her eyes, I'd say she enjoys it as much as Nate does.

"Ugh, enough about you," Mila chides, slapping her friend's thigh. "We've dealt with enough of your relationship drama. This is about Cam and Bugs."

"So, you did fuck him at the housewarming party then?" Beth asks while chomping on a piece of cheese.

I feel my cheeks burn, and I concentrate really hard on my drink. I love Beth—she's kind and caring—but I still get embarrassed by her frank and explicit sex talk. I notice a pink stain on Mila's cheek, and I know she feels it too.

"Well, not at the party," I reply. "But yes, that night we went home together."

Beth takes a grape, leaning forward and resting her elbows on her knees. "Who made the first move: you or Bugs? I need all the information before I can help you."

I huff out a breath and curl my legs underneath me, setting my untouched drink down, ready to spill the beans about one of the most incredible nights of my life. Beth and Mila listen in greedy silence, eating up the details I give them. I obviously don't give them *all* the details because some things are private.

"That sounds really hot," Beth breathes, eating more crackers. "I mean, if I wasn't already banging the hottest Whaler, Bugs would definitely be on my list."

"Um, I beg to differ," Mila pipes up. "Matt is the hottest Whaler. Did you see his picture in the team charity calendar?"

"No, Nate's hotter," Beth butts in, waving her glass around, sloshing champagne on the rug. "Have you seen his …"

"Girls, please!" I yell, holding my hands up. "Can we argue about your boyfriends later? I have an issue here."

Mila and Beth freeze, looking suitably chagrined. "Sorry," they say in unison like naughty children.

At that moment, we hear the front door open, and the sound of male voices echoes through the large foyer. I feel a shiver crawl up my spine as I recognize Warren's voice immediately.

Mila's eyes become impossibly wide, and she flies off the couch to intercept the horribly awkward scene that's about the play out. I feel like my heart is ready to beat through my ribcage as Beth flaps about, trying to fluff up my hair, pulling my glasses off and flinging them behind me.

"Will you get off me?" I hiss, slapping her hands away, but also subconsciously straightening my sweater and sitting up a little taller.

Mila comes barreling back into the room with an apologetic look on her face, followed by Matt and then Warren, who looks about as uncomfortable as I feel. What the fuck is going on? Is this some sort of intervention set up by my supposed best friends?

"This is a pleasant surprise, ladies," Matt says cheerfully, clapping his large, tattooed hands together. "We're gonna go out on the deck and get the grill on if you wanna stay for food."

"Would love to," Beth says. "Although I feel like a fifth wheel, so can I call Nate?"

"Sure thing, babe. Just tell him to keep it on the DL. We're not supposed to be hanging out with the playoffs starting on Thursday," Matt replies, pulling Mila into a breathtaking kiss before disappearing into the kitchen.

Warren and I exchange an awkward head nod, and he follows Matt out of the room.

While Beth makes a call to Nate, I stomp over to a blushing Mila and grab her arms. "What the heck, Mila? Did you guys set this up?"

"Of course not," she gasps. "I swear, Cam. I had no idea Matt would invite Bugs over. Coach made it clear to the guys that they should stay home tonight."

"Oh god, I have to leave," I grumble, grabbing my glasses.

"No, please don't," Mila begs. "This could be a blessing in disguise. Matt said that Coach has even picked up on the fact that Bugs is distracted. You need to sort this out before the playoffs start."

The enormity of the situation suddenly lands square on my shoulders. Shit, our awkwardness around each other can't affect the team. I have to pull on my big girl panties and deal with it.

"Okay, okay. Take Beth into the kitchen and send Warren in." I sigh, feeling butterflies take off in my stomach. I don't have the first clue what to say to him. I hope he talks first.

"What's going on?" Beth asks, sliding her phone back into her pocket, looking between Mila and me.

"Cam's going to talk to Bugs, so we need to make ourselves scarce," Mila says, pulling Beth toward the kitchen.

I begin to pace, wringing my hands as the voices from the kitchen float around me, and finally I hear Beth yell, "Just get your ass in there and sort this out, you big idiot!"

Moments later, a very sheepish looking Warren stalks into the room, his hands buried deeply in his pockets, his green eyes downcast. As I take in his appearance, I notice for the first time that the energy that usually crackles around him is gone. He looks exhausted.

The feeling of guilt and responsibility hits me like a puck to the gut, and I have to catch my breath. My selfish need for a night filled with orgasms has not only caused my friendship with this man to implode; it's also the reason he's distracted from his goal. We've talked plenty about his dream of leading his team to a Stanley Cup win, and he's on the way to achieving this.

I need to fix this, and I need to fix this now.

"Hey, Warren," I say despite the massive dry lump clogging my throat.

"Hey, Sawyer," he replies, locking his fern green eyes on me, the familiar use of my last name suddenly confirming that things will be okay.

We stand and look at each other for what feels like an age, neither of us wanting to start this awkward as fuck conversation.

"I'm sorry I've been avoiding you …" I begin.

"This is shit …" Warren says at the same time, and suddenly we crack up into peals of laughter, and the weight lifts from my shoulders slightly.

"Fucking hell, Sawyer. What happening to us?" He chuckles coming toward me, that devastating grin firmly in place.

"I'm sorry this got weird." I sigh, taking a deep breath, inhaling Warren's spicy scent, and quickly realizing my mistake. They say smell is one of the strongest stimulants of memory, and suddenly I'm back in his bedroom, under his huge, muscular body while he rolls against me, bringing me more pleasure than any man has before.

My center floods at the memory, and I have to take a small step back.

"Look Warren, I want us to clear the air," I say firmly. I need to take control of this conversation before he distracts me with that sexy, cocky grin. "Yes, we had a moment, but I don't want this to ruin our friendship, and I certainly don't want it to distract you from the playoffs."

"I agree about the friendship thing," Warren replies, closing that small distance between us. I have no room to step back any farther because my legs are pressed up against the couch. "I've missed you this week. I went for a run the other morning, and it didn't feel the same without you chatting my ear off the whole time." He smirks.

"Jerk!" I playfully punch his arm like I used to before I knew what it felt like to fall asleep wrapped up in them. "Look, I suggest we just forget about what happened and go back to being friends."

But Warren is right up in my space, and my senses are overwhelmed by his scent, his big, warm body, and his intense green eyes. "I'm never gonna forget it happened, Cameron," he whispers in a husky voice. "But for the sake of our friendship, I'll store it away in the spank bank."

I let out an embarrassed breath and press my hands against his chest to move him back, happy that we seem to be making our way back to normal. "Don't be gross."

Warren winks at me and pinches my cheek, something he knows I hate. "Good to have you back, Sawyer."

I slap his hand away and huff out a breath. "Let's go find the others before they die of curiosity."

"Sure thing, babe." He puts his muscular arm around my shoulders, and we walk into the kitchen. On the surface, things are back to normal. However, as my body tingles at his proximity, I know—for me— things will never be quite the same again.

Bugs

The sweat burns my eyes as I take off down the rink, the biscuit at my stick. I can sense the Vancouver wingers bearing down on me as I head for the goal. A quick look to my left and I see Matt in exactly the right position. We've skated this play a million times, and I'm running on pure muscle memory. I wind my stick back and pass the puck across the clear ice, skimming past the stick of a Vancouver player by mere inches.

Matt collects my pass and sails round the back of the net, confusing the goalie who assumes he'll go for the top shelf. However, as he appears on the goalie's offside, he hooks the puck into the net, and the red-light flares.

Fuck YEAH! An overtime goal and that's game four of the first series. We're through to the second round. I join the dog pile that's forming at center ice, and the Seattle fans who've traveled to Canada are going crazy. All the players on the bench jump the boards and join our celebrations, slapping helmets and butts, raising our sticks in tribute to the die-hard fans, our coaches, and our GM. Jesus, there's no feeling like it.

Once I'm free from the pile of hot, sweaty dudes, my eyes wander to the GM's box where I know Cam will be. I can see her leaping around like a crazy person, waving her arms like she's trying to get my attention. I raise my stick in the air and point it at her, winking and smirking. It feels right to share this moment with her; she is my best friend, after all.

And that's what I continue to tell myself despite the fact that my cock is trying to stir inside my cup. I'm proud of us for trying to get back to normal after our one-night stand, but I'm not going to lie; it's not easy. I've had a taste of her now, and that's not something I'm going to forget easily.

The locker room is a riot of loud rock music, jerseys, and equipment flying around and jubilant roars of triumph. Thor is standing up on the bench by his cubby, completely butt-ass naked, hammering his chest, yelling some sort of Swedish battle cry. This is part of the addiction of playing professional ice hockey— the team camaraderie, working together with your buddies to achieve a common goal. There's really no feeling like it.

Even Coach Casey joins us in our celebrations; he hates the Vancouver coach with a passion, and this win must mean a lot to him. I've got no idea where the rivalry stems from, but it's always a tense time when our teams meet.

"The bus leaves in thirty minutes, so get your asses ready," Coach yells through the mayhem. "If any of you miss the plane, you're on your own."

"And don't forget—my place for the celebration party tomorrow night," I shout, already in my suit. I have to do press with Coach, so I hustled through my cool down and shower.

Another roar of deep male voices echoes around the locker room, and I follow Coach out to the waiting press. I'm fucking buzzing, and all I can think about is sharing this with Cam.

We've been in the air for half an hour, and I'm sitting up at the front of the plane with the coaches because the guys are getting pretty rowdy in the back. I'd love nothing more than to sit back there, drink a beer, play some cards, and celebrate the win, but I have responsibilities as captain. I'll have a meeting with Coach Casey tomorrow after the team debrief, so I want to have my notes ready before I get home and collapse. It's not even the hockey that tires me out in the playoffs; it's the goddamn traveling.

It looks like we'll be up against Dallas in the second round if the series goes in their favor tomorrow. Obviously, the game will be on at my party, so we can see what we're up against in the second round.

"That was a hell of a game, Cap." I look up from my iPad where I'm reviewing game footage to see Cameron standing in front of me. Her light brown hair is in a tight ponytail, not a hair out of place as usual, and her dark brown eyes are crinkled in a smile.

"Thanks, Sawyer," I reply, closing my iPad and patting the seat next to me. "Sit down and tell me more about how fucking awesome I am."

Cam rolls her eyes and sits, kicking off her heels and tucking her long legs under her. I love how graceful she is—a lean, athletic body, small pert breasts that fit perfectly in my palms. She has great legs having run track at school and college, and they're by far her best physical feature. I'm a leg and ass man, and when we first met, that was what I noticed. She was wearing patterned yoga pants that hugged every inch, and I remember popping an embarrassing boner when we were introduced.

However, as we got to know each other, this was quickly overtaken by her extreme kindness, wit, and compassion. We began to talk when we shared the treadmills in the gym and soon, we progressed to running together in a variety of locations around Seattle. It was nice to have someone other than my teammates to work out with, and our friendship grew from there.

That is until we almost fucked it up. Even though she came on to me, I still take full responsibility for what happened. I've always had more than friendly feelings for Cam, and when she basically offered herself to me the night of Matt and Mila's housewarming, I should've said no. I should've been strong and told her it was a bad idea. But I was weak and horny, and I let myself have a taste of what I wanted.

But as we sit together on the flight back to Seattle and shoot the shit, it feels almost like we're back to normal. Sure, my palms are a bit sweaty sitting this close to her. The smell of her light, flowery perfume infiltrates my senses, reminding me of the morning after we made love when it still lingered on my pillowcase. My dick has been half hard since she sat down, and every time her raspy laughter fills the cabin, it twitches uncontrollably.

Shit, I need to get a handle on this if there's any chance of our friendship surviving.

Thankfully, the flight is a short one, and as we disembark the plane at the private airport, we make our way through the press pack and into the terminal. Of course, as captain, I stand and talk to the press, have my photo taken, and talk about our hopes for the second round. I notice a few of the other guys are also talking. They're much more willing to do this when we're returning on a win, and I feel proud of each and every one of them.

Once we're in the terminal, we grab our bags and head off to the cars. I drove here alone this time, even though I usually share a ride with one of the guys on my line. As I'm walking toward my truck, I see Cam standing next to her red Jeep, kicking aggressively at the tire.

"What's up, Sawyer?" I ask, approaching her in the deserted parking lot.

"Stupid flat tire," she grumbles, kicking it again and grimacing as she obviously hurts her toe.

"Need some help changing it?" I ask, dumping my duffel and removing my suit jacket.

"I would if I had a goddamn spare," she replies sheepishly.

"What? You don't have a spare?" I ask, gobsmacked that the ever-organized Cameron Sawyer doesn't have a spare tire.

"No! That was my spare, okay!" Cam snaps. "I got a flat last month and put the spare on, but I haven't had a chance to get a new one." Her shoulders bunch up around her ears, and her jaw ticks with anxiety. I can read the signs that she's getting stressed, so I try to calm the situation. I know how this must be making her feel; she likes order and control, and I'm sure she's in major meltdown mode right now.

"Okay, no problem," I say, in the kind of voice I use to calm my crazy twin nephews when they're having a tantrum. "Look, I can take you home and pick you up in the morning, go get a tire, and then bring you back to change it. No problem."

I see the tension slowly release from her shoulders as her breathing regulates. "Thank you, Warren. I hate that I've been so careless."

"Hey, it's a crazy time. I'm sure Don has you all twisted up in knots with the playoffs. It's no wonder you forgot to get a new tire." I pull her into an awkward hug and gently rub her back. Before, this would have just been a friendly gesture, but now there's that electrical charge between us. The memory our bodies have of being joined so perfectly together is intoxicating, so I let go of her and step back, running my hands through my messy dark hair.

"C'mon, Sawyer. I'm tired. Let's go."

With a shy smile, Cam retrieves her bags from the trunk, and we head off toward my truck. "Thanks, Warren. I know you could do without this."

"Hey, what are friends for?" I put my arm around her shoulder and pull her into my body, kissing the top of her head.

Cameron

I'm such a freaking idiot. I knew I was on borrowed time with that spare tire, but it's been so crazy these last few weeks. I haven't had a chance to catch my breath, let alone take time to go to the mechanic to get it replaced.

When I walked up to my Jeep and saw it leaning limply on the flat, I felt the anxiety rise in my throat. Most of the players had already left and it was late at night, so I looked around the deserted parking lot to check who was still there. And of course, I noticed Warren's expensive truck parked on the other side of the lot. That's just typical!

Thankfully, when he noticed me freaking out next to my vehicle, he was sweet and helpful and didn't chirp my ass too hard over the fact I didn't have a spare.

And now we're driving through the rainy Seattle night toward my house on the outskirts of town. Warren is being so kind because my place is in the opposite direction to his; he could have easily put me in an Uber and gone home to sleep. But that's not his style.

"You okay, Sawyer?" He glances over at me, his face illuminated by the passing streetlights. "You're quiet. Don't dwell on the tire. Everyone makes mistakes."

I huff out a breath and cross my arms. He knows better than anyone that I hate making mistakes, and I do everything in my power to avoid them.

"It's just one mistake after another with me at the moment," I mutter under my breath, shooting him a look, and I immediately see his jaw tighten.

Shit, that was uncalled for. He obviously thinks I'm talking about our little tryst. "I didn't mean us …" I begin.

"It's fine," he growls, keeping his eyes fixed on the road, hitting the turning light a little hard as we come to my street. "We both agreed it was a mistake. I just didn't think you'd keep bringing it up."

"I'm sorry. I'm just pissed at myself about…" I desperately try to backpedal, but Warren pulls up outside my house and kills the engine.

"Don't sweat it. The garage opens at eight, so I'll pick you up at seven-thirty."

I can tell by his tone that the conversation is over, and I should probably go.

"Thanks for the help and the ride. I really appreciate it," I say quietly as I open the door. I slide out of the seat and retrieve my bag from the back. Before I close the door, I state, "And I don't think what happened between us was a mistake. It was the best night of my life. I just value our friendship too much to muddy the waters. Goodnight."

I go to slam the door, but his voice stops me. "Sawyer, wait."

Opening the door fully, I wait for him to speak again.

"Look, I'm sorry. I don't think it was a mistake either. And for the record, I thought it was pretty fucking incredible as well." I smile shyly at his complement. "But I also get that now is a terrible time to start up a relationship. I hope once the playoffs are done, we can have a serious conversation about us."

"Warren, I …"

"I know you have reasons to be cautious," he interrupts. "We've talked enough about your shitty dad and that fucking douchewaffle ex. I understand. But please just agree to talk about it when we have the time."

I take a deep breath; I do owe him that much. The sincerity on his handsome face just about kills me. "Okay, I can do that."

"Awesome. Now get your butt in the house and get some rest." He smiles warmly at me, and I return it freely.

As he drives away, I unlock my door and am immediately greeted by purring and chattering around my ankles. I flick on the hall light and look down to see the sleek dappled coat and huge amber eyes belonging to my Bengal cat Gatsby.

"Hey there, Mr. G." I dump my bag and bend to pick him up, but he shoots out of reach and stands by his food dish, looking at me like I'm an asshole. I know for a fact my neighbor fed him a little over two hours ago, so he can't possibly be hungry. He's just making his point that I'm a bad mommy for leaving him again. He'll be aloof and stand-offish for a while, but I guarantee that by morning we'll be spooning in bed together.

As I unpack and put on a load of laundry, I eventually give in to my guilt and take Gatsby's treats down from the high cabinet. Bengals are intelligent, and when I first got him, I made the mistake of leaving his treats on the counter. I came home one day to find an empty container on the floor, a huge pile of cat vomit, and a sleeping Gatsby. From that day on, I kept his treats in the cabinet so he couldn't get to them.

"C'mon, Mr. G," I coo, rattling the container. "I give in. Come and get a treat, and then we'll head to bed." I take a meaty treat out, but the smell of it causes my stomach to roll with nausea. Oh Jesus, that's disgusting. I feel the bile rise quickly, and I have to dash to the sink before I vomit all over my kitchen floor. By the time I've finished retching, my stomach hurts, and I'm light-headed.

What the fuck was that? I swill my mouth directly from the faucet.

I thought the tuna baguette I ate on the flight had a slightly funny taste. I hope it hasn't given me food poisoning. That would be a scheduling disaster for the next series. Gatsby is still swirling around my feet, yowling for his treat, so I hold my nose and grab a couple from the container, tossing them onto the floor before sealing the container and putting it away.

"That's enough for you," I tell him as I take a bottle of water out of the fridge and check the front door is locked and the alarm is set again before heading upstairs to bed. I'm so bone tired. I really hope I'm not going to be up all night being sick.

As predicted, Gatsby follows close behind, jumping on the bed and circling, settling down to sleep as I go about my bedtime routine, nervously sipping the water. Thankfully, my queasy feeling seems to have passed, and I put it down to being overtired after all the travelling.

I manage to keep my exchange with Warren in the back of mind until I'm lying in the dark. Then it's all I can think about. I was such a brat, letting my annoyance about the tire spill out all over him. If our friendship is going to continue, I can't keep throwing our night together in his face. It's not fair to either of us. Plus, it keeps that night at the forefront of my mind and as I lay here in bed with my cat, I feel so lonely I can almost taste it.

5

Bugs

"**H**ere's to Round Two of the Stanley Cup, baby!" Knox yells before downing his shooter and cannonballing into my heated outdoor swimming pool.

Everyone around the pool cheers and yells, following him in, some of them still fully clothed.

The party at my house has been going strong for several hours, and it's just about to hit fifth gear. The deck and the pool area are teeming with players, coaches, and their significant others. I've also spotted a few of the team puck bunnies in their barely-there bikinis. Most of them are hanging off Knox and the other rookies, so I leave them to it.

After making sure things aren't getting too crazy by the pool, I head inside to my cinema room where I find the guys from my line watching the Dallas game. The Diamonds are up by two goals, and there's still a period left to play so it's still wide open.

Matt and Mila are sharing one of the loveseats, arms and legs wrapped around each other, Matt's lips permanently fused to her neck while he keeps one eye on the game. Nate and Beth are making out like teen-agers in the back row of the cinema-style seating while the rest of us try to ignore their moans and groans.

Thor, our goalie, and the wingers, Ford and Brett, are the only ones who seem interested in the game, so I join them at the front and try to ignore all the coupling going on. I crack open a cold beer from the fridge and listen to the intermission round up.

"How're they looking?" I ask the guys.

"Pretty tight," Thor rumbles, sipping his neat vodka. "Their goalie is a fucking unit. He's new, yes?"

"Yeah, he was a trade from the Russian league," Ford replies, looking toward the back of the room when Beth lets out a particularly loud whimper. "Jesus, it's like a porno shoot in here."

I chuckle and call over my shoulder, "Kid, give it a fucking rest, will you? You're giving Ford a chubby!"

"Fuck you!" Ford yells, throwing a handful of pret-zels at me, which I easily bat away.

A minute later, an extremely hot and disheveled Nate and Beth appear from the back of the room, both of their faces red and blotchy from all the kissing. They take a seat in one of the other loveseats, Beth sitting on Nate's lap, just as the door opens, and I see a familiar tall slender silhouette in the doorway.

"This is where you're all hiding." Cam laughs as she comes in and greets the girls with cheek kisses and the guys with fist bumps.

"Hey, Warren," she says quietly as she sits down next to me, crossing her long toned legs. This causes the skirt she's wearing to ride up a little, and I have to force my eyes back to the screen as the puck drops for the final period.

"How's the tire working out for you?" I ask, desperate for something to say that doesn't involve me putting my hand on her thigh.

Cam laughs quietly. "Yeah, it's good. Thanks. It does everything it's supposed to do."

Fuck, this is awkward. Why can't we just talk and laugh like we used to? Thankfully, the Dallas game starts with a goal by the opposing team, so everyone's attention is fixed on our possible next opponents. Sitting this close to Cam is a special kind of torture; her floral perfume fills my nose and the warmth of her thigh pressing against mine is causing a situation in my jeans. She keeps crossing and uncrossing her legs, and I swear to god, it takes a Herculean effort not to pull her into my lap and kiss her soft pouty lips.

So much for just being friends. At least when I crushed on her from afar, I had no idea what it felt like to kiss her, to slide my tongue into her sweet, wet pussy, to make love to her. But now I do know, and it's killing me.

The sound of pissed off hockey players brings me back from my reverie. Shit, it's now a tie game with ten minutes of the period left. Dallas is the best of the two teams for us to face, so I just hope they get the goal they need to win the series.

As word spreads about the tie game, the room starts to fill up with players and coaches. By the time the buzzer sounds for the end of the game, it's standing room only. And as I hope, Dallas gets the win.

"I guess we need to kick some Diamond ass," Thor roars, standing up and ripping his shirt open. "I don't know about you, but I'm fucking ready!" He beats his massive fists against his hard chest, and the entire room erupts into howls and cheers.

"We were born ready, baby!" Brett yells, jumping up on his seat and fist-pumping the air. Shit, it looks like I'll need to shut this party down before things get out of hand. Our schedule has just moved up by a few days because Dallas secured their series in four games. We do have home ice advantage against them for the first two games, but it'll start sooner than anticipated. I'm sure Coach Casey is sending out texts as we speak telling us to haul our asses in for training tomorrow.

It looks like most of the team are still in the room, so I jump up onto my seat and blow a loud whistle to get their attention.

"Listen up, Whalers. We have our next opponents, so it's time to get back in the game," I shout as the last few people give me their attention. "So as awesome as this party is, I'm shutting it down!"

I'm immediately pelted with boos and pretzels, but I continue. "Coach will no doubt call us in for training tomorrow, and we need to be fresh and ready to go. Get yourselves home, get yourselves sober, and no after parties." I look directly at Knox. "If I hear of any shady shit going down, people will be skating suicides until they puke. Everyone understand?"

"YES, CAP!" comes the resounding reply, and slowly people start to disperse, arranging car shares and Ubers. As I climb down from the chair, I see Cam furiously typing away on her phone.

"Everything okay, Sawyer?" I ask as people pass by, saying goodbye.

"Yeah, all good," she says absently. "Just Don with his never-ending list of things to prepare for the next series."

I look over and see Mila in a similar situation, obviously receiving a flurry of messages from Coach Casey.

"Anything I can do?" I ask, putting my hand on her shoulder, enjoying the way she leans into me slightly.

"No, it's fine," Cam replies, looking over at Mila. "Do you have the training schedules? Don wants to check them over."

"Sure, hang on." Mila jumps up from Matt's lap and joins Cam so they can talk about it.

Matt gets up and walks over to me, rolling his eyes. "I guess the party's over." He chuckles, shooting the girls an amused look.

I laugh and slap him on the shoulder. "C'mon, man. She's got a job to do just like us. You can help me get these meatheads in their Ubers and then clean up this mess."

"Sure, why not?" Matt huffs. "Let's move on out people! Get your Ubers ordered and go straight home." He starts herding people out of the cinema room, and I begin to consider how I'm going to get all the goddamn crushed pretzels out of my carpet.

6

Cameron

I'm so exhausted I don't even know what to do next. Mila is typing away on her iPad with her earbuds in having just devoured her room service cheeseburger. I'm still just looking at my bowl of chicken noodle soup. For some reason, I can't bring myself to eat it. I've had a weird stomach flu for the last couple of weeks, and some days I just can't face eating. I guess the stress of the Stanley Cup is really getting to me this season.

My brain is whirling with everything I have to do here in Dallas, and I'm struggling to prioritize and find solutions. This is usually the kind of situation I thrive on; I love troubleshooting, but for some reason I just can't order my thoughts.

"Are you okay, babe?"

I look up and see Mila has taken her earbuds out, and she's looking at me with concern in her eyes. We decided to share a room on this road trip so we could get work done, and she wouldn't disturb Matt's sleep pattern.

"Yeah, I'm just brain dead." I release a deep breath. "I think I'll go for a run now that it's cooler."

"Want some company?" she asks, looking less than enthusiastic about her offer.

I let out a loud, surprised laugh. "Really?" I know for a fact Mila hates running with a passion, so her offer to accompany me is sweet but unnecessary.

She giggles. "No, not really, but I thought I'd try to be supportive."

"Thanks, but I'll be okay. I'll just run around the block a few times to clear my head." I stand up from my chair, get my yoga pants and sports bra out of my suitcase, and change.

Within ten minutes I'm pounding along the sidewalk, my running playlist blasting my ears, pushing me forward. I feel so free when I run; it's always been my thinking space. And despite the myriad of work tasks I should be thinking about, all I can concentrate on is Warren.

The Whalers have had a terrible start to the second-round playoffs, losing both home games to Dallas. Their new Russian goalie has proven to be an impenetrable wall and despite Thor doing his best to keep their goals out of the webbing, each game one slipped through. We managed to win the first game in Dallas last night, but only following a brutal overtime where the Dallas captain was sent to the penalty box for hooking Knox while he was on a breakaway. Of course, it ended in a fight when the hot-headed rookie threw his gloves off and charged the Dallas player into the boards. Thankfully, we scored during the power play and took game three.

Warren has taken the losses hard, and I can see him becoming more and more frustrated. He's been completely focused on leading his team, so we haven't had much time to hang out. I make a mental note to sit with him during a team meal so we can touch base.

However, even though we haven't really seen much of each other, I can't ignore the stolen glances he throws my way. They're filled with the same smoldering intensity he had that night, sucking me in and making my heart stutter in my chest. Sometimes I wonder if I'm being a complete idiot. I have this incredible man who obviously has feelings for me, we know we're more than compatible in bed, and we have a great time as friends. What would be so bad about taking this relationship to a romantic place?

No. Now is absolutely the wrong time to let these thoughts into my head. I need to focus on my job, and Warren needs to play the best hockey of his life. But the promise of the talk we're going to have once the playoff madness ends still lingers in the back of mind.

As I turn the corner and run back toward the hotel, I speed up and sprint the last part. I draw the warm Texas air into my lungs and feel my muscles burn, coming to a stop by the front doors. I pace around, my hands on my hips as I attempt to regulate my breathing and prevent the sudden wave of nausea from taking hold.

"That was a fast two hundred feet, Sawyer. Think you could do that on skates?"

I gasp and snap my head round and see Warren leaning up against the wall in his athletic shorts and Whalers hoodie. His hair is wet like he's just showered, and he has a bottle of water in his hand. There are dark circles under his eyes. With his scruffy hair and beard, he looks like a wild mountain man. It's kind of hot.

"What are you doing out here?" I ask breathlessly, wiping my sweaty forehead with the back of hand, swallowing down the bile that chooses that moment to rise up my throat.

"I needed some air. I can't look at those fucking four walls all night," he grumbles. "Also, Mila dropped by, so I thought I'd give her and Matt some 'couple time.'" He uses air quotes and rolls his eyes.

I chuckle and raise my eyebrows. The disadvantage of Matt and Mila not sharing a room on this road trip is that they need somewhere to hook up. This means that either Warren or I get kicked out of our room for an hour or two.

"You can't stand out here all night. Come on. We can hang out if you want," I offer, gesturing for him to follow me. He gives me a wary, questioning look, but shrugs and follows me into the lobby. It's deserted at this hour, so we head to the elevators, and Warren shoots a text off to Matt telling him where he is.

"You look tired," I state once we're in the elevator.

"You don't look so hot yourself." He laughs, scrubbing his hand over his scruffy face. His playoff beard is filling out nicely.

"Thanks." I playfully slap his arm. "Are you sleeping?"

I know from previous conversations that he struggles to turn his brain off when he's stressed. I can relate.

"I'm getting a few hours at night so I try to nap if I can."

The elevator reaches my floor, and we walk down the corridor toward my room. It's quiet so we avoid talking again until we're safely inside. It wouldn't go down well with Don or Coach Casey if Warren is seen going into my room in the middle of the night. They don't have a game tomorrow, but as captain, he needs to be setting an example.

"Why don't you find us a movie to watch?" I suggest. "I need a shower after my run."

I notice a strained look pass quickly across Warren's face, but he nods and searches for the remote. I grab my sleep shorts and tank top and disappear into the bathroom. I quickly undress and dive into the hot shower, washing the sweat from my hair and body.

After I dress, I comb out my damp hair and let it fall in brown waves around my shoulders.

"What movie did you choose?" I ask, walking out of the bathroom.

But I stop short.

Warren is laying on my bed, his thick arms folded behind his head and his long legs stretched out and crossed at the ankle, his feet bare. His broad chest rises and falls steadily, and his eyes are closed, his dark lashes resting on his cheeks. I'm always amazed at how so many guys have naturally long, thick eyelashes. Life's just not fair.

I stand and watch him sleep for a few moments; he's so incredibly masculine but beautiful at the same time. He looks much younger when he's asleep, and I suddenly get a flashback to the night we spent together. I did this very same thing just before I snuck out of his house; I watched him sleep and marveled at his youth and beauty.

There's absolutely no way I'm going to wake him up, so I sneak over and grab my cell. I fire off a text to Mila, telling her to spend the night in Matt's room, so she doesn't come back and we have to wake Warren up. He needs his rest, and if he has to do it here, then so be it.

Suddenly, my own tiredness overwhelms me, and I crawl under the covers next to Warren. He didn't get into the bed, so I feel comfortable lying next to him. In fact, it feels warm and safe. As I turn off the lamp, Warren sighs and rolls away from me, and I quickly drift off.

Bugs

In my dream, I'm skating through a field of wild-flowers, which is impossible, but dreams can be all sorts of crazy. The smell of the flowers is making me hard, and when I plow to a stop, I spray petals into the air like confetti. As they clear, I see Cameron lying among the flowers, her light brown hair spread out around her head like a halo. She's covered in petals, but only covering her most tempting places, like the chick in that *American Beauty* film.

Slowly, Cam reaches out her hand and beckons to me, a naughty smile on her plump lips. She doesn't need to ask me twice, and I fall on top of her, my hockey gear suddenly gone, my naked skin pressing against hers as I fill my hands with her supple breasts.

She moans and arches her back, her hard puckered nipples rubbing against my calloused palms.

"Warren, Warren," Cam moans into my mouth, her needy voice makes my dick ache.

As always seems to be the case when getting to the best bit of a sexy dream, I start to wake up just as it gets good. However, as certain parts of the dream evaporate, others come into sharp focus—like the smell of flowers, the feeling of Cam under me and her breasts beneath my hands.

My eyes fly open, and I focus on the deep brown pools of Cam's confused expression. The room is grey with predawn light, but I can still see her eyebrows knot together, silently asking what the fuck is going on.

My mind computes several problems at once; in the night I seem to have crawled under the covers, I'm lying on top of Cam with my thigh between her legs, and my rock hard dick pressing into her stomach. But the most inappropriate thing is the way my hands are still covering her small, perky tits. Under her tank top. Skin to skin.

Oh fuck.

I can feel her chest rising and falling rapidly beneath my hands, but I can't seem to move, and she doesn't seem to be making any attempt to shove me off.

"Warren?" Her quiet voice is both questioning and needy.

I realize that I want her so badly it hurts, and unless I'm mistaken, Cam wants me too. She drags her tongue across her lower lip and bites it, looking at me with hooded eyes. Before I can stop myself or consider the consequences, I press my lips softly to hers. Cam sighs against my lips and opens to accept my tongue, tilting her head to the side to allow me to deepen the kiss.

Jesus, I forgot how intoxicating her taste is. She moves her tongue in perfect unison with mine as we begin to speed out of control, my hips taking on a life of their own, grinding against her. My hands continue to massage her breasts, rolling her hard nipples between my fingers while her hands explore my back and shoulders.

Just as Cam's fingers glide under the front of my T-shirt, grazing my abs, I hear the click of the keycard engaging the lock, and I freeze. Cam also freezes, and then in the blink of an eye, she pushes me off and pulls the covers over her head. She makes a small squeaking sound, and I feel like a total douche. I quickly roll away from her just as Mila comes in.

I listen to her sneak around, then I decide that in order to avoid any weirdness with Cam, I should get up and leave.

"Hey Mila," I whisper, sitting up and scrubbing my hand over my face. I immediately realize this is a mistake because I can smell Cam's scent all over it. "I'm just leaving. I must've passed out last night and Cam didn't wake me."

Mila looks up from digging around in her suitcase. "Oh, hey. I didn't wake you, did I?"

"No, I need to get up anyway and fit a workout in before team breakfast." I discreetly check that my hard on has gone down enough that I won't scare Mila half to death, and I swing my legs out of bed, stand, and stretch. Cam is still buried under the blankets, playing possum.

"Everything okay here?" Mila asks as I pull on my sneakers, and when I look up, she's smirking, and her eyebrows are almost lost in her hairline.

"Yup," I reply non-committedly, sneaking past her to the door. The look on Mila's face tells me that she suspects *something* went down, but I don't say anything else other than a whispered goodbye as I slip out of their room.

"Morning, Cap." The words hit me square in the balls, and I feel them shrivel.

Shit, I'm rumbled.

I spin around and see Knox standing outside his door with the biggest shit-eating grin on his face and a breakfast burrito in his hand. I need to think quickly–do I make something up or style this out?

"You shouldn't eat that shit, rookie. Your body's a machine, and you won't be young forever," I grumble, stomping past him toward the elevator.

"Sure thing, Cap." He smirks. "See you later."

Goddamn it, that little piece of gossip will be all over the locker room by the time we hit the ice this morning for a scrimmage game. I shake my head and stab at the call button. How could I be so stupid … again? God knows what Cam must have thought, waking up with me all over her. But as I replay the memory again to check all the details, I wasn't mistaken about the heat in her eyes and her hands and lips on me. She wanted it as much as I did.

I ride the elevator down to the lobby to grab some breakfast, balling my fists and letting out a strangled groan. Now is not the time to get all twisted up about my feelings for Cam or her possible feelings for me.

I need to shut this shit down and focus on getting through this series. My team needs me with my head one hundred percent in the game, so I make a vow to myself.

I'm going to stay away from Cameron Sawyer until this is all over.

7

Cameron

I manage to hide under the blanket until Mila showers, dresses, and gets ready to head down to meet Coach Casey for their breakfast briefing.

"Don't think for a second I'm not gonna ask you about this little situation later." She chuckles just before I hear the door open and close behind her.

I guess my fake sleeping act isn't fooling Mila, so I fling the comforter off and puff out a frustrated breath. I'm frustrated that yet again I was helpless to resist Warren's weight on top of me and his lips on mine. I'm frustrated that Mila walked in and probably saw everything. But most of all I'm frustrated that Warren got me wet and horny and then left me unsatisfied. My nipples, the same nipples he was tweaking, are still hard and achy, and I feel slick between my legs.

Slowly, I slide my hand down my body and slip them under the waistband of my shorts, through the short curls and into my wet folds. Catching my breath, I close my eyes and conjure up Warren's face hovering above me in the pale dawn light. His eyes are so dark they seem almost black, his handsome face half covered in a dark, scruffy beard. As my fingers begin to move over my swollen clit, I think about the way his firm lips press to mine, his urgent tongue sliding and roaming in my mouth. Then I think back to our night together, the way he used that talented tongue to make me come on his face several times.

With these erotic memories playing out in my head, I hurtle toward my climax, reaching under my tank top to rub my breasts, feeling desperate to come.

Suddenly, Don's shrill ringtone blares from my phone, and I completely lose my orgasm. As hard as I try to ignore it and finish, I know for a fact there's no coming back from that clit killer. So, I groan and roll over to grab my cell, just missing Don's call.

"Shit," I curse. He's going to be pissed now. I quickly return the call, and Don asks me to meet him at his makeshift office in one of the board rooms in thirty minutes. With a serious case of lady blue balls, I throw myself into the shower and get ready for my day. All thoughts of Warren and his sexy kisses need to be shelved. I've got a job to do.

Several hours later, I finally come up for air and head to the conference room that's been set up for the Whalers to use. It's a place to hold team meetings, hang out, and eat away from the prying eyes of the public. There are several couches around large TVs with games consoles attached, ping pong and foosball tables and various other activities to keep the players and coaches occupied during their downtime.

As I enter, I see several players at the hot buffet, loading up their plates with lean protein, pasta, veggies, and fruit. My stomach gurgles loudly. In my hurry to get to Don, I didn't manage to eat breakfast, but instead of being hungry, I feel slightly nauseated by the smell of all that food. I'm probably too hungry. I didn't eat my soup last night, so it's been about eighteen hours since I had anything substantial to eat. And with the weird stomach flu I've been battling, it's no wonder my appetite is all over the place. I decide to head to the buffet and grab some soup and crackers. If that goes well, I'll get myself a plateful.

"Cam, over here!" I hear Mila call from a small table in the corner, so I make my way through the sea of players, greeting many on my way. I plop down next to Mila and unscrew the lid of my water bottle, taking a long draw as I feel her eyes on me. I know what's coming: the Spanish Inquisition. My stomach lurches again as the water hits it, and I open the packet of crackers and begin to cautiously nibble them.

"Jesus, Cam. I'm dying here. What happened between you and Bugs last night?" Mila finally whispers, looking like she's about ready to explode.

I slowly eat the dry cracker and take another swig of my water, washing it down, feeling slightly better.

"He fell asleep while we watched a movie, and I know he's not been sleeping, so I didn't want to wake him," I reply innocently, but I can feel my cheeks heating up.

"So, when I came in this morning, I didn't see him on top of you while you got busy?" she smirks, spearing a chunk of chicken salad, cocking her eyebrow.

I press my lips into a thin line as my stomach churns and bile rises in my throat, but I manage to fight it down and answer her.

"We may have had a little under the covers action, but it was in the heat of the moment, and you totally cockblocked us, so thanks for that," I mumble, eating another cracker.

"Oh, babe. I'm sorry. I didn't mean to embarrass you." Mila reaches over and squeezes my hand. I'm sure it feels as clammy as a dead fish because that's suddenly how I feel all over.

Warren and the rest of his line pick that moment to walk into the conference room, laughing loudly and goofing around as they head to the buffet to load up after practice. Mila's head snaps up at the sound of her man, and a ridiculous smile spreads across her face. She appears to motion to Matt and then makes a shooing gesture with her hand; I guess she's telling him to sit somewhere else while we finish our conversation.

"Are you sure you're okay?" Mila asks, sensing how uncomfortable I am.

"I don't know." I sigh and it's completely true. I have no idea how to feel at the moment. "I can't seem to shake this stomach flu, and I'm so tired all the time. I just need a vacation."

"I hear that. Do you want to get out of here?" Mila asks.

"I need to go anyway. Don has a conference call this afternoon, and I still have some prep to do," I mumble, side-eyeing the guys as they laugh and load up their plates.

"But you haven't eaten anything?" she says, her eyes and voice full of concern.

"I'm not hungry." I stand up and toss my empty water bottle in the recycling bin. "I'll see you later."

I rush off before Mila can say anything else. I feel shitty for blowing her off, but I just want to get to the end of this away series with a win under our belt and my feelings for Warren under control.

Who knows if either of those things are possible? I have a feeling the next few weeks are going to put many of us to the test.

8

Bugs

T he steak sizzles on the grill as I flip it for the last time. Thor likes his black and blue, so I barely show it the heat before I whip it off onto a board to rest while I finish the others. The afternoon is hot so most of my linemates are sunning themselves beside my infinity pool, drinking their hard-earned beers.

It's been two days since our disastrous exit from the Stanley Cup, and we're all still walking wounded, both physically and emotionally. Matt's sore from taking a puck to the skate, a huge purple bruise blooming over his foot and ankle. Nate's sporting a split lip, black eye, and stitches in his eyebrow after that fight with the Dallas captain, and Thor's voice is still gruff and croaky after taking a puck to the throat during his last heroic save before going off injured.

My own body is a wreck; I'm covered in bruises with aching muscles and swollen joints. But it's my head that's totally fucked. I'm furious that we fell apart as a team once the injuries started, and we let our-selves get drawn into stupid penalties and pointless fights. Knox completely lost his shit and let himself and the rest of his linemates down. I'm pretty sure he's going to have a deeply uncomfortable meeting with Coach Casey and Don before he's allowed to go on his summer break.

The other thing that's fucking with my head is a certain tall willowy brunette who invades my thoughts at every possible moment. Since our brief tryst in her hotel room, we've hardly managed to exchange two words. When I invited my line over for a barbecue, I told Nate and Matt to bring their women in the hope that would encourage Cam to accept my invitation. However, I got a text saying they had a spa day planned, so we ended up having a "guys only" day.

Returning my attention to the steaks, which are about to go from perfect to overdone, I remove them from the grill just in time and transfer them to the resting board.

"Okay, guys. Head inside and load up on sides, then come and get your steak," I call, wiping sweat from my face with the dishcloth that I've looped into my apron strings.

"Finally!" Thor croaks, hefting his massive body from the sun lounger, leading the rest of the guys into the kitchen where they start loading their plates with couscous, greens, baked potatoes, and crusty sourdough rolls. As I dollop a huge amount of sour cream onto my potato, I thank god I can mostly eat what I want for a few months. I love food and I love to cook, so having to follow the nutritionist's strict diet during the season is very limiting. I tried to avoid getting all the pre-cooked meals the other guys favor, but after a continued battle,

I relent and accept the weekly delivery of bland crap. I made peace with this by promising that during the off-season I would cook for myself every day.

Once we retrieve our steaks and refresh our beers, we sit around my outdoor dining table and eat in relative silence; even the usually chatty Ford is quiet and pensive while he eats. I know how much all of them are hurting because I feel the same. But I also know it's my job to snap them out of their sour moods.

"What's everyone got planned for the off-season?" I ask, hoping to start a positive conversation.

I hear a few grunts and finally Nate starts. "Beth and I are taking that vacation to Hawaii I got at the auction, and then I might go back to Oklahoma for a few weeks." He looks slightly tense mentioning his home. His mom died suddenly a few months ago, and he's trying to reconcile his relationship with his father.

"How're things going with your dad?" Matt asks, taking a swig of beer.

"Not bad actually. He came to a few games, and we try to talk on the phone once a week. It's still kinda weird, but we're both trying …" He trails off and digs into his steak; the conversation is obviously over.

"You going home, man?" I ask Thor. He usually goes back to Sweden for part or all of his summer break.

Our big goalie finishes his mouthful and nods his head. "Yeah, my brother's getting married, so I'll be heading home at some point."

"Hey, that's exciting," I reply, remembering that Thor is the youngest of four brothers and apparently now the last single one.

"It will be as long as my Mor doesn't get on my case about being single. She's already asked me if I'm bringing a date." He puffs out a breath that flips up his long blonde hair off his forehead. All of us are still sporting our playoff look complete with scruffy beards and shaggy hair.

"Who knows, man? You might meet a cute little milkmaid while you're back home." Brett snorts.

Thor groans and rolls his icy blue eyes. "Dude, you need to be a bit more culturally aware. We don't have milkmaids in Sweden."

"So, what about you, Cap?" Ford asks in his slow Southern drawl. "You gonna mope around Seattle waiting for Cam to give you another chance?"

This elicits a few smirks from the guys, and a growl of frustration from me. "No, smart ass. I'm flying up to Edmonton to see my dad. Then I'm collecting my dog and holing up in my cabin for the summer." The more I describe my plans, the more I want to start them as soon as possible. "I plan to finish building my deck. I've already bought a hot tub which I'm having delivered so that's my motivation to finally get it finished."

Ford's comment does, however, remind me that Cam and I still have to have our "talk." She's been super busy with Don since we left the playoffs because he's planning on spending most of the summer in Australia, so we still haven't had a chance to catch up. I was hoping if she came today we could talk, but that idea's shot to shit. Perhaps I can invite her up to the cabin for a long weekend?

"Sounds good if not a bit lonesome." Ford's reply brings me back into the conversation. "You should throw a party when it's finished so we can check out your carpentry skills."

I snort out a laugh and nod. "Sure, why not? I'll hit you all up when it's ready."

"But seriously, Cap. Don't spend too much time alone this summer. Maybe it's time for a little holiday romance." Brett winks at me and the guys laugh, clinking their beers together.

"Here's to Cap's summer of love," Matt cheers and I flip him off, standing to retrieve the New York cheesecake before they can chirp me any further about my pathetic love life.

Cameron

The feeling of floating weightlessly in calm warm water is beyond heaven. I look up at the bright blue sky and allow my entire body to slowly relax. This spa day is an amazing idea.

I've been so unbelievably stressed with the Stanley Cup finals, the horrendous loss, and the aftermath. Don took the loss badly, and he's been like a bear with a sore head around the office, snapping at agents and managers who come in to negotiate for their clients. Thank god he's off to Australia for a month to visit his wife's family; hopefully, he'll be able to unwind during the off-season and come back a happier man.

His trip also offers me a rare month off work. I haven't taken any vacation time all year, and when Don told me about his plans, he offered me an extended vacation.

I was kind of reluctant at first. We're not busy during the summer, but there are still things to do and people calling in. Don assured me he could do business from Australia just as well as he could do it in Seattle.

In the end, he threatened to fire me if I didn't take up his offer, so I accepted and began to think about how I'll spend my summer. I guess the reason I'm so reluctant to accept the time off is because I have nothing to do and no one to spend my time with. There's no way I'm third wheeling with Matt and Mila or Nate and Beth; that's just pathetic. And things with Warren are still up in the air; there just hasn't been an opportunity for us to hang out and talk because I've been so busy at work, and he's been licking his wounds. I hope we can manage to get together before he goes to Canada. I really don't want to spend the whole summer in limbo.

"Cam! Our mud ritual starts in ten minutes," Beth calls from her lounger, stirring me from my contemplation. I lift my head and turn over, swimming slowly to the edge of the pool and hauling myself out.

"What is this mud thing again?" I ask as I dry myself with a towel and wrap the fluffy terry cloth robe around my body.

"It's fabulous," Beth enthuses, taking off her sunglasses and peering up at me. "First, we cover ourselves in special mud that will draw the toxins out of our skin and exfoliate. Then, we sit in the steam to help it work, and after, we wash it off and slather ourselves in lotion. It's awesome."

Beth is a makeup artist and has just wrapped her first Hollywood movie, so I trust her when she says this is going to make my skin look and feel amazing. Lately,

I've felt so run down and tired, I'm breaking out in spots all the time, so I need this pamper session desperately. My stress has even started affecting my periods which have never been particularly regular. Over the last few months, I've only had a few spotty ones. I used to get the same issue when I was a teenager, and I had a big test or track meet, so I'm used to my period just showing up when it feels like it.

"You've no idea how much I need this." I sigh while Beth and Mila put their robes on over their bikinis and gather their e-readers and towels.

"C'mon, let's get dirty." Mila laughs, putting her arms around me.

Twenty minutes later, we're laughing and slinging mud around like little kids. We must look hilarious, covered from head to toe in sticky, grey goop.

"Why does it smell so eggy?" Mila moans, scrunching up her nose while applying a layer to her face with her fingertips.

"The mud is brought in from the foothills of a volcano, so I think it's the sulphur," Beth replies, tapping the buttons on the steam room control panel to get it started. "Now we have to steam for ten minutes to help draw out all the toxins."

She opens the glass door, and we're greeted with a billowing cloud of steam. The heat smacks me right in the face. I'm not sure how long I'll last in there, but I'll give it a go.

Once we're seated on the tiled benches, sweating away, Mila asks Beth, "Are you looking forward to your vacation?"

"Oh, I'm so ready for Hawaii." She moans, reclining on her bench.

"I bet Nate can't wait," Mila replies. "Matt and I are going down to Tampa in a few weeks. His sister is coming home from France for a visit, so his parents are really excited to see her."

"What about you, Cam?" Beth inquires. "What are you doing with your month off?"

Ugh, I've been dreading this question. I'm going to sound so tragic when I tell them I've got no plans, I've got no one to do anything with, and I'm probably going to spend the summer holed up in my house binge-watching *Downton Abbey*, sleeping until noon, and eating Chinese takeout with my cat.

"I don't know. I might just book somewhere last minute," I mutter, desperate for a change of subject.

"What's Bugs up to?" Beth pushes, giving me a knowing smile.

I was wrong. This is the question I've been dreading.

"He's off to Canada in a few days as far as I know," I reply, feeling my chest tighten at the thought of him being gone all summer.

"Did you guys have that talk yet?" Beth pushes, earning her an elbow in the ribs from Mila.

"Umm, no ... we ... we."

Oh Jesus, why can't I catch my breath?

Suddenly, the steam is oppressive and stifling. I need some air. I lurch to my feet and push open the glass door, feeling the immediate relief of cool air in the tiled wet room. I take in several huge gulps of air, but all that does is make me light-headed and dizzy. I slump onto the bench and put my head between my knees.

"Hey!" Mila cries bursting out of the steam room. "What the hell happened?" I don't look up, but I can see her muddy legs in front of me followed by Beth's. Hands begin to rub my back as I feel vomit rise in my throat, and I make a dash for the sink, emptying the contents of my stomach into it.

Beth makes a disgusted noise, and I hear Mila tell her to shut up as I heave and vomit again. I'm past caring that I have an audience; I just need to stop feeling like this. I grip the side of the basin so hard my knuckles turn white as my empty stomach heaves and wretches.

"Babe, are you okay?" Mila asks, rubbing my back and holding my stringy wet hair out of the way. From my other side, Beth hands me a bottle of water which I accept with shaky hands, taking a tentative sip.

"I think the steam was too much," I whisper, deeply embarrassed about the mess I've made in the pristine spa basin.

"Take a seat and sip your water. We'll deal with this." Mila guides me to the bench while Beth turns on the faucet and makes another noise of displeasure. The mud drying on my skin is beginning to itch, and I feel uncomfortable and freaked out. Gently, Mila continues to rub my back while I wait for the room to stop spinning.

"What's going on, Cam?" she asks kindly. "Are you sick?"

I take a deep breath and sip my water. "I don't know. I've had this stomach flu that just comes and goes. I think the steam got to me. I didn't eat breakfast either."

"Okay, let's rinse off and get out of here," Beth says, turning on the showers and testing the temperature.

"We can stop by the drugstore on the way home if you need something to settle your stomach."

"Thanks, girls. I'm so sorry to ruin the day," I reply, my eyes filling with tears. I let out a gasping sob and bury my muddy face in my hands.

"Jesus, Cam. Anyone would think you're knocked up…" Beth jokes, but the way she stops short makes me raise my head to gape at her.

"Oh shit, you're not, are you?" she chokes out, shock written all over her face.

"I … um … no?" I stammer, feeling sick and dizzy all over again.

"Cam, seriously, could you be?" Mila asks, kneeling in front of me.

"Oh god, I don't think so. I've only had sex with Warren, and we used protection."

"It's not one hundred percent effective." Mila stands up, and suddenly she's all about taking charge. "Get in the shower. We'll go to the drugstore and get a test. Then at least you'll know."

I feel completely out of control which I hate. Mila's ready to take charge of this situation. For once, I'm thankful to have someone guide me through this situation that's unfolding before me.

Who knew five minutes could feel like an eternity?

Beth and Mila sit on my bed while I pace the width of my bedroom waiting for the result of the test. The girls convinced me to splash out on a packet of the fancy digital kind that even tells you how many weeks along you are. Now if the test can just tell me what to do if it's positive that would be great.

"What the hell am I gonna do if it's positive?" I ask, still pacing, while time moves slower than I thought possible.

"What do you want to do?" Beth asks.

"If I knew that, I wouldn't be asking," I snap back, feeling like a douche for snapping at my friend who's just trying to be helpful. "I'm sorry, Bee. I'm just freaking out here."

Beth stands up and envelops me in a warm hug. "I know. And don't worry. I'm not that easily offended. If yelling at me helps you get through this, then you go for it." She holds me at arm's length and then kisses my cheek.

The beep of Mila's alarm makes us all jump and signals that my life might be about to change forever.

"Do you want me to look?" Mila asks, standing up.

"No! I need to do this," I blurt, holding up my hand. "Just give me a minute, okay?"

My friends nod and give me encouraging smiles as I disappear into the bathroom and close the door. The pregnancy test stick is sitting on the edge of my vanity like a small incendiary device ready to blow up my life.

I can do this. I've been alone since I was nineteen when my mom passed away from cancer. I'm a strong, independent woman, and if the test is positive, I'll deal with it. I can't even begin to think about how I'll tell Warren. Or Don. How do I tell my boss that I got knocked up by the captain of his hockey team?

I need to stop spiraling and look at the damn test. If it's negative, then this is all conjecture, and I can just get drunk with my girls and move on with my life.

Taking a deep, cleansing breath, I reach out and grab the stick and stare at the result.

Ten weeks pregnant.

Shit!

9

Bugs

"**U**ncle Warren, push me higher!" one of my twin nephews squeals from the swing in my dad's backyard. His little butt almost smacks me in the face as he swings back toward me, but my hockey reflexes kick in, and I get my hands in front and push him again before he knocks me on my ass.

Need to keep my fucking head in the game and not daydream about Cam while I'm in charge of these little guys. My sister would happily skin me alive if anything happened to them.

"And me. And me!" the identical boy screams as he whooshes past me on the other swing, his bright red hair flying around his freckled face.

Jesus, I'm being tag teamed by these pint-sized hellions. I don't know how April does it on her own. Her husband Patrick is in the military and is often away on maneuvers, so she spends a lot of time at our dad's place. I remember the summer she had the boys; dad and I built this playset in the backyard. It's a castle playhouse with a swing set and a slide. The twins love it, and now that they're four, they basically live out here during the summer. Their mom draws the line at them sleeping out here, though.

"Hey, boys. I'm back, and I've got Timmy's." My sister April appears through the side gate holding up grease-stained fast-food bags and a tray of takeout cups.

I've only been in Edmonton for a day, and she's already plying me with all the good things Canada has to offer.

"There'd better be a crispy chicken stack and tenders in that bag, sis," I reply, grabbing the back of the twins' swings to slow their trajectory as they squirm to get to their cheese and ham melts.

"Of course! You've had the same order since you were seven. Even when you were a scrawny string bean, you could put away more food than should've been humanly possible." She laughs, unbagging the food on the patio table. "Boys, go inside and wash up."

"Yes, momma," they reply in perfect unison, dashing into the house just as my dad comes out.

"Easy boys," he growls as the twins whizz past him, a proud grandpop look on his face. Bob Parker is the gentlest soul you could ever wish to meet. He's worked his whole life as a builder, so on the exterior he's weather worn and rugged. However, on the inside, he's a soppy old geezer who tears up if one of his grandsons draws him a picture.

"C'mon, daddy. Come and get your burger," April says, indicating the food she's laying out on the table. "And please don't feed it to Juneau again. It took me ages to get the dog vomit out of the rug last time." She points an accusing finger at my dad, and he holds up his hands in surrender, chuckling.

At the sound of his name, my Alaskan Malamute lifts his black and white head and whines, fixing his crystal blue eyes on the tempting buffet.

"Juneau, stay!" I command in my best dog dad voice, and he whines again but stays put, resting his big head on his paws. Being the sucker I am, I'll save him one of my chicken tenders and sneak it to him later.

The twins reappear like mini hurricanes, and April hands them their sandwiches so they can eat in their fort, Juneau trotting after them in the hope they drop him a crumb or two.

"Do you have all the timber you need for the deck?" my dad asks as we tuck into our food.

"Yep, the order's in and should be delivered the day after tomorrow," I reply with a mouthful of crispy chicken.

"Good, good. Did you go to Larry like I suggested?"

"Yep, he gave me a real good deal. Are you still coming up in a few weeks to check my work?" I smirk, making my sister giggle as well.

"Don't be a fucking smart ass," he grumbles, but I know there's no real anger behind his words. Despite his rough words, his eyes twinkle.

"Dad, language!" April hisses, even though the boys are preoccupied playing some sort of game that involves wooden swords and chasing Juneau around the yard.

"Sorry, honey." He pats her hand and looks back at me. "To answer your question, yes, I will be coming up to check your work. I don't want you taking out half your hockey team with shoddy carpentry when you have a party and the thing collapses."

"Sure thing, dad." God, I love this man. He raised my sister and me alone for the most part. Our mother died shortly after I was born, so I have no memory of her, only my dad and April. She's ten years older than me, so from a young age she was a mini mom to me. April made so many sacrifices; she went to community college so she could stay at home and help dad raise me, driving me to hockey practice and away games when she should've been out partying with her college friends.

I'll never forget everything they did to help me reach the NHL. When I signed my first multi-million-dollar deal, I tried to buy dad a new house which he quickly refused. He did let me clear his mortgage and buy him a new pickup, but that was it. April also refused my offer to buy her a house, so instead I set up a trust fund for each of the twins. I didn't tell her how much I put in them, but put it this way, she and Pat will never have to save for college or help the boys buy their first car or house.

Once our food is finished my sister calls, "Bryan, Seamus, it's home time." Two freckly faces appear in the windows of the playhouse, then the whining starts.

"Momma, we're still playing," Seamus begs. He's the more dominant twin and always the one who tries to negotiate. I know for a fact he's in a no-win situation. My sister does not negotiate with small boys as I found out at their age.

"No Seamus, your daddy will be home soon, and he'll wanna see you before you go to bed," April replies in her stern mom voice. "Now get your butts over here and say goodbye to Warren and Grandpop."

"Yes, momma." They walk as slowly as humanly possible across the yard and hug my dad and me goodbye while April gathers up all the junk she seems to take with her everywhere.

"Pat has a day off tomorrow, so we'll stop by for breakfast to see you before you head off, eh?" April says as she pulls me in for a hug. We're both tall like our dad, so unlike most women, she doesn't get a face full of my chest.

"Sure thing," I reply, kissing her temple and high-fiving my nephews. "Laters, alligators."

"We're not alligators. We're boys," they chorus in unison. It's our little bit—the way we end every FaceTime or phone call. I don't see them half as often as I'd like so I try and make them feel as special as I can whenever we're together.

My dad and I walk my sister and the boys out to her minivan and wave them off.

"Do you want a beer?" dad asks as we amble back up the drive.

"Nah, I should take Juneau for a walk, and then I need to pack up the truck. I can still take your saw?"

"Sure, I'll bring it back when I come up." Suddenly, he stops and looks at me square in the eyes. "I'm so proud of you, son. I don't feel like I say it enough, so I wanted to make sure you know it."

Shit, my nose tingles, and my eyes get hot as the emotion radiates off my dad and hits me right in the chest. The fact is he tells me how proud he is every time we talk after every game I play. However, standing here in the fading light, on the driveway of my childhood home, it feels amazing. I've got no idea what it must be like to love someone unconditionally like my dad loves his family. I hope to have that one day with my own family.

10

Cameron

Three days.

Three days since I took a pregnancy test, and it came back positive.

Three days since I spoke to Mila or Beth despite their constant calls, texts, and visits to my door.

Three days since I slept, trying to come to terms with the fact I have a massive decision to make.

And judging by the smell in my bedroom, I'm three days past having a shower.

I've done nothing but stare at my laptop, googling everything I can about the stages of pregnancy. At ten weeks, my baby is developing ears and a jawbone complete with milk teeth. Its heart is fully formed and beats one hundred and eighty times a minute.

The fact that my baby has a heart made me sob uncontrollably for an hour and cemented my decision to keep it. As terrifying as it is to think about becoming a mom, it's inconceivable to me to end this pregnancy. For the millionth time since I found out, I rub my palm protectively across my flat belly and consider the future for me and my baby.

Despite losing my mom so young, she was the most wonderful mom in the world. It was always just the two of us; my father was never on the scene. He and my mom had a brief affair, and he had no interest in becoming a family, so she raised me alone. He earns the prize as the first man to abandon me, and I was angry at him for so long. I always thought it was my fault that he left us, that my very existence made him leave. But my mom made it clear that it was his choice to go and that I did nothing wrong; he'd hit the road months before I even came into the world and never once attempted to make contact with me. That only made me turn my vitriol toward him for leaving my mom pregnant and unsupported as she had no family worth speaking of. However, my mom was amazing, and she did the job of both parents with what seemed like natural ease.

When she was diagnosed with terminal skin cancer, we only had a few months left together. I came home halfway through my freshman year at college to care for her in her final weeks, and even though it was the most heart-breaking time of my life, it was also the most magical. She took the time to bestow all her wisdom on me and tell me all her funny stories and life lessons.

I still remember the morning she died so clearly, I can replay it in my mind like a movie. I'd got up early to fix her some pancakes because the day before she'd said her appetite had come back, and that's what she wanted for breakfast. As I entered her dark room and quietly drew the drapes, sunlight flooded the space, and when I turned around, she looked so beautiful and peaceful. Her colorful headscarf had slipped slightly in the night, revealing the wispy brown hair that was beginning to grow back after she quit chemo.

But as I looked at her, bathed in the very sunlight that caused her cancer, I knew she was gone. Her chest was still, and when I held her hand, it was cold and stiff. At that moment, I knew that I was alone in the world, the one person who'd loved me unconditionally my whole life was gone, and I had no idea how to cope. I was barely an adult, and I now had to deal with life on my own. A piece of my heart broke away that day; it's become the piece that I guard closely and never give away. I keep it especially for her, so I never forget that I was loved once.

After arranging her small funeral, I saw her attorney, had her will read, and sold our house, which was her wish. I went back to college because what else was I supposed to do? I had no immediate family, and as mom pointed out to me during one of our talks, I needed to get out in the world and start making my own memories.

My time at college seems like a dream, looking back on it now. I barely existed, moving from classes to my waitressing job and back to my room in the dorms in a zombie-like state. The guy I'd started dating at the beginning of freshman year didn't hang around once I left to take care of mom. At the time, I couldn't process the fact that he'd dumped me while my mom was dying of cancer, but once I returned to school, I had to let him know what a dick move that was. One day we had a very public argument in the quad and from then on, I gained an unfair reputation as a weird clinger who couldn't deal when a guy broke up with her. It made me sad that no one even asked to hear my side of the story.

It was a really lonely time, but once I started my junior year, I made the decision to snap out of my self-imposed solitude and put myself out there. So, I started trying to start conversations during classes, and I made a few tentative friendships. One such friendship led to an invitation to a frat party, and that's where I met Richard.

He was a math major and had plans to become a statistician after graduation; he was serious and focused, and I felt like he understood me. He'd lost his father to prostate cancer, so I knew he was someone I could talk to about my loss. We'd talk for hours in my cramped single bed, and we'd discuss our fears and our dreams for the future. For the first time since my mom died, I felt something close to safe and loved. However, I just couldn't give Richard my whole heart. That broken piece was locked securely away, and looking back now, perhaps that's why he cheated on me. I think deep down he knew I was holding out on him, so he decided to look elsewhere for his happily ever after.

And yet again, I was alone.

But by then, I was working for Don at the Whalers and Warren was part of my life. He was there for me when I ended things with Richard, supporting me with long runs and nights watching sappy movies while I cried into my popcorn. Warren never once asked anything in return, and I'll always love him for that. He could've easily taken advantage of my situation, but that's not his style; he's a good guy and that makes my current situation so difficult. He'll want to do the right thing by me and the baby, even if it traps him with me for the rest of our lives.

Looking back at how my life has turned out, I remember the box of letters I received during the reading of my mom's will. The attorney handed it to me, and when I opened it, it was filled with crisp white envelopes with my mom's loopy handwriting on the front. The first one I took out had "After my funeral" written on it. The next had "When you feel blue" and the next "Graduation Day." It looked like she'd tried to cover every possible life event. It made me smile because this was so typical of my mom. There's no way she would leave me in the world alone; even though she can't be with me in body, she certainly is in spirit.

Thinking about the letters, I haul myself out of bed and open my walk-in closet, reaching up to the top shelf. Getting a whiff of my own underarms, I decide that once I'm done here, I will definitely have a shower next.

After reaching around for a few moments, my fingers brush the box containing my mom's letters and I pull it down, returning to my bed. As I open it, I get the slight scent of her perfume, and my eyes fill with tears. God, I need my mom right now. Quickly I search through the box, coming across the one that reads "When you fall in love." I realize now that when I was with Richard, I never opened this letter. I guess that says it all really. I continue to sift through the letters to find the ones I'm looking for. One reads "You're pregnant (planned)" and the second one reads "You're pregnant (unplanned)."

I smile despite my sadness; I certainly know where I get my hyper-organization from.

Taking a deep breath, I rip open the second envelope and get another hit of my mom's perfume. I hold the paper to my nose and breathe in, images of my mom hugging me after a track meet or teaching me to flip pancakes flash through my mind, and I linger in the memories for a moment. Then I prepare to read and digest her advice.

Dearest Cammy,

Don't panic! I know you must be freaking out, but please take a breath.

Okay, now that you're calm, let's look at the facts. If you're reading this letter, then you've found yourself in a less than ideal situation. Obviously, I don't know the ins and outs, but I want you to consider a few things before you make any decisions:

1. How do you feel about it? Whatever you feel is okay. If you want to keep the baby or not, it's your decision.

2. Is the father in the picture? If not, you are a strong woman, and you can do this alone if you have to. I did it. Being your mom is the most precious gift in the world, and I don't regret going it alone for one second.

3. If he is in the picture, I will say one thing to you. You must tell him he's going to be a dad. He has a right to know, and he might just surprise you.

4. I know you've surrounded yourself with great friends—let them help you. Don't be alone in this.

I know you're probably avoiding everyone and hiding away, but please don't. Pull yourself together, be strong, and take that first step forward.

Whatever direction you decide to go in, I trust you to make the right decision for you at this point in your life. If I were there with you, I would give you this same advice with no judgement—just love.

I miss you so much, baby, and I would give anything to be there to help you with this.

All my love forever,

Mom

By the time I'm done reading, the ink on the paper is smudged as my tears fall from my chin. I quickly wipe my face and flop back into bed, keeping the precious letter away from my snotty nose. As usual, mom's come good with the advice. I feel slightly calmer, and my thoughts are falling into place.

As I wipe my eyes and blow my nose, I realize the next things I have to do are let Mila and Beth back in and then figure out how to tell Warren.

"One thing at a time, Sawyer," I tell myself as I climb out of bed and strip off my stinking leggings and T-shirt.

The hot, healing water feels incredible, and once I'm done showering, I dress in clean yoga pants and tank top and go out for a run. It's been days since I ran, and my muscles feel rested and desperate for exercise. Eventually, I hit my stride, and I cover my usual five miles with ease, using the time to plan my next steps.

When I get back to my house, I fire off a text to Beth and Mila and ask them to come over for lunch. Only Mila replies, reminding me that Beth and Nate have left for their vacation in Hawaii, but she'll be over in an hour and will bring dessert.

Realizing I only have Cheez Whizz and a questionable avocado in my fridge, I head out to the store and buy the ingredients for eggplant parmesan and set about preparing our lunch. For the first time since I discovered I'm pregnant, I feel a tiny glimmer of hope.

Mila arrives just as I take the bubbly, cheesy tray of eggplant out of the oven. I whip off my oven gloves and answer the door only to be enveloped in a warm hug.

"Don't you ever do that again, do you hear me?" she growls in my ear, holding the box of cannoli out to the side so as not to smoosh it between us.

"I'm sorry," I whisper, kissing her cheek and detaching myself from her embrace. "I had to spend some time alone to get my head straight. Come on in. Lunch is ready."

"It smells fantastic." Mila follows me into the kitchen where I've set the table with a large green salad and the eggplant along with a bottle of sparkling fruit water in place of the wine I really want.

While I put the cannoli in the fridge, Mila serves gooey slices onto our plates and pours the water into glasses.

"You're lucky you called today," Mila says as I join her at the table and take a gulp of water. My mouth is suddenly dry. "Matt and I head down to Tampa tomorrow." She gives me a shitty look, and I totally deserve it for shutting her out.

"I'm sorry," I offer again, serving myself some salad leaves. "Is Beth pissed as well?"

"Put it this way," she replies. "Nate virtually had to kidnap her to get her to go on vacation. She didn't want to go before we spoke to you, and obviously she couldn't tell Nate why. He got upset because he thought she was getting cold feet about the vacation and their relationship. It was typical Beth and Nate drama, but in the end, she went. Oh, and she told me to give you this if I saw you before she got back."

Mila seems to dig around in her jeans pocket, but when she pulls her hand out, she flips me off. I snort out a laugh and shake my head.

"I guess I deserve that."

Mila laughs as well. The slight air of tension in the room eases, and we begin to eat before our food gets cold. I'm happy that she's not pressing me to talk, and we eat in comfortable silence for a while.

Finishing first, Mila puts down her cutlery and folds her arms across her chest. "That's your grace period over, Cam. You need to talk to me."

I chew and swallow my last bite and push the plate away. "Okay." I look at my good friend and feel strangely calm about the words I'm about to say. "I'm going to keep the baby."

Mila's eyes fill with tears as she leaps up from her seat and pulls me into a clumsy hug. "We're having a baby?" she cries.

I laugh. "Yes, we are."

"I need to call Beth." She lets me go and pulls her phone out of her pocket and starts a FaceTime call. After a minute, Beth appears on the screen, obviously laying out in the Hawaiian sun.

"Hey, Mils. What's shaking?"

"I'm with Cam," Mila whispers. "Is Nate there?"

"No, he's at the gym. What's going on?" Beth sits up and pulls her sunglasses off.

Mila turns the phone, so we're both in the shot, and I wave gingerly at Beth who scowls.

"Hi, Bee. Sorry."

She lets out an exasperated huff. "Did Mila give you my message?" she asks, flipping me off as well.

"Yes, she did." I laugh and thankfully so does Beth.

"We were so worried about you," she scolds. "Are you okay?"

"I am. I've decided to keep the baby."

The ear-splitting squeal that comes out of the phone makes Mila flinch, and I see Beth bounce up and down on her sun lounger, her breasts jiggling in her tiny bikini.

"Oh my god, Cam. You're gonna be a mommy?" she cries.

"What the fuck?" I hear Nate's deep voice, and Beth's head whips around as he appears behind her.

"Oh shit," she gasps. "I'll take care of this. Call you back in a minute."

The call ends, and I feel my stomach try to reject the food I've just eaten. Shit, if Nate knows, he's bound to tell Warren before I get a chance to. Beth had better use every weapon in her arsenal to make sure Nate keeps quiet.

"Oh, that's so bad. So, so bad," I mutter, getting up to pace around.

"It's fine, babe. Beth will make sure Nate keeps quiet, even if she has to sit on his face." Mila laughs.

As her laughter dies, she suddenly gets all serious. "What do you intend to do about Bugs?"

Hearing my mom's advice in my head, I say, "I'm going to tell him, but make it clear he's under no obligation to be with me or be in the baby's life. I know how crazy his life is, and I wouldn't want him to feel that pressure."

"But what if he wants to be with you and the baby or be part of the baby's life?" she asks.

I suppose I should consider that possibility. I know Warren is a good man and would always want to do the right thing, but is it the right thing that we get together for the sake of raising our child? Surely that's not a good foundation for a long-term relationship. I know we could raise a baby together as friends, but what if he wants more? What happens then?

"I really don't know," I reply honestly. "I guess I won't know until I speak to him."

Mila's face falls, and she quickly starts typing a message on her phone. I begin to panic, thinking she's asking Warren to come over. But when she sees the terror on my face, she pats my arm. "I'm asking Matt something. Don't freak out. I have a feeling Bugs has already gone back to Canada for the summer. Matt said something about him heading out early."

Shit, that makes this even more complicated.

The ping of an incoming message takes Mila's attention, and she puffs out a breath and shakes her head.

"Yep, he's already back in Canada. Matt said he's spent a few days with his family in Edmonton, and he's driving to his cabin."

"Oh." My heart sinks. The thought of having to wait until the end of the summer to tell Warren about the baby is implausible. There's no way I'm dropping that bombshell over the phone. I'll be over halfway through the pregnancy by then, and there'll be no hiding it from anyone. That's not fair.

"Don't worry. I have a plan." Mila hugs me and gets to work on her phone while I sink into my chair, despair filling my heart once again.

11

Bugs

After a long, sweaty journey, I pull into the gravel driveway of my lakefront cabin and kill the engine. Juneau is panting next to me, so I know my first job is to get the poor dog some water. He's not built for the summer heat.

"C'mon, Juneau. Let's go!" I yell, jumping out of my pickup, my dog leaping over the center console after me. We run around the side of the house together, Juneau barking happily as we hit the sand. I kick off my sneakers, throw my cell into one of them, and charge straight into the cool water. It momentarily takes my breath away, but soon the shock disappears, and Juneau and I plough out into the lake.

I fucking love this place. The cabin was a condemned mess when I bought the land and it's taken me four summers to get it almost finished. The deck is the last piece of the puzzle to get it how I want it. I fully intend to retire up here one day.

Juneau and I mess around in the water for a little longer, but I realize it's getting late, and I need to unpack the truck and get the cabin out of mothballs. Once I'm back on the beach, I grab my cell and sneakers and head back to my truck to get my keys and unlock the place. Juneau follows me obediently, sniffing everything and remarking his territory while I unlock the back door, fire up the generator, and clear the water pipes. It takes me a few hours to get the place ready to live in again, then I unpack everything from the flatbed of my pickup and dump most of it by the front door to deal with tomorrow.

My sister sent me here with enough food to see me through a small apocalypse, so I put most of it in the chest freezer in the garage and put the rest of my groceries away. Thankfully, my dad left a six pack of beer in the fridge from his last fishing trip, so once I'm satisfied I've done as much unpacking as I need to do for now, I sit out on the small back porch with my dog and watch the sun set.

This is the life. I close my eyes as the sun disappears into the lake and let myself relax for the first time in months.

The next morning, the sun and the silence wakes me. Every time I come up here, I forget how fucking quiet it is. It always takes me a few days to acclimate and even longer to get into the habit of sleeping past sunrise.

After a long stretch and a few minutes scratching Juneau behind his ears, I get up and pull on my athletic shorts and sneakers. This day calls for a run along the beach followed by breakfast before the timber delivery arrives at noon.

I put Juneau's leash on and stuff a few poop bags in my pocket, and then we head off on our usual route along the beach toward the north shore of the lake. It's still early, so the swimmers and kayakers aren't out on the lake yet, and I have the place to myself. Unlike when I run in the city, I don't put my earbuds in because I like to listen to the sounds of the lake.

Because of this, I'm drawn to the angry shouts of a woman as I run past one of the cabins a few hundred feet along the beach from my own.

"GODDAMN FUCKING SHIT!"

My head swivels round, and I see a petite redhead on her deck in what looks like a towel, rattling the doorknob of her cabin. I tug on Juneau's leash to bring him to a stop, and I take in the scene before me. I'm torn between offering assistance or carrying on with my run. Will the woman be embarrassed if I approach her when she's only wearing a towel, or will she be grateful for the help?

I decide to be a gentleman and offer my assistance. "Morning! Can I help you?"

The redhead whips round and almost loses her towel in the process. I halt my approach and raise my eyes to the sky, so she knows I'm not checking her out.

"I heard you yelling and thought you might need some help," I clarify to make sure I don't come off like a creeper.

"Oh, I'm sorry for the colorful language. I seem to have locked myself out." The woman replies. I take a risk and lower my eyes to look at her; thankfully, her towel is firmly in place. Although it is extremely short and barely covers her ample tits.

I know that the cabin belongs to the Andersons, and they sometimes rent it out during the summer. I also happen to know they keep a spare key hidden in one of those fake pebbles by their hot tub.

"I can help, if you're happy for me to come up onto the deck?"

I realize I'm shirtless and sweaty, and at six feet four, I'm an imposing figure to a vulnerable, half naked woman, so she might tell me to take a hike.

The woman looks at me warily for a while, playing with her red curls, deciding whether to accept my offer. She must be in her mid-thirties and attractive in a cute, bouncy kind of way. Not really my type, but the words of my friends echo in my ears. Maybe I should have a summer fling.

"Can you leave the dog down there? I'm allergic," she says pointing at Juneau who whines as I tie him to the fence post.

"Sure. I'm Warren." I advance slowly up the path toward her deck and wave.

"I'm Nancy," she replies, going to wave back but remembering she's holding her small towel closed.

"I'm friendly with the Andersons, and I know they keep a spare key around here somewhere," I explain, searching the smooth pebbles around the base of the hot tub until I find the one that rattles. "There we go."

I crack the pebble open and hand her the key, seeing the relief wash over her face. Now that I'm closer, I notice she has freckles all over her face and body, her skin is pale and creamy, and her eyes are bright blue.

She's definitely cute, but I feel nothing in the way of attraction to her.

"Oh god, you have no idea how happy I am," Nancy gushes, grabbing the key and fitting it into the lock. "Thanks, Warren. I really owe you. But right now, I'm going into my house to die because I can't believe the captain of the Seattle Whalers just saw me in a towel!"

In a flash, Nancy slips into the house and slams the door in my face. I chuckle to myself and shake my head. Okay, I guess I won't be having a summer romance with her. Laughing, I jog back to the beach, untie a grumpy looking Juneau, and continue down the beach.

After our run, Juneau and I head home where he wolfs down his breakfast, and I take a shower. I cook myself an egg white omelet which I eat out on the porch, then I finish unpacking so I'm all set before the timber delivery arrives.

I'm about to finish putting fresh sheets on my bed when I hear the sound of the timber truck pulling up the driveway. I fling the last pillow on the bed and head outside to meet Larry and start my summer project.

"Your dad asked me to drop by in a few days to see how you're getting on," Larry chuckles as he pulls his thick gloves off and wipes his sweaty hands on his overalls.

I bark out a laugh and shake my head. Typical dad. "That old bastard. I guess he doesn't trust me not to fuck this up." I laugh good naturedly.

"Nah, he just doesn't want you killing yourself with a saw or a nail gun." Larry slaps me hard on the arm and heads back to his truck. "You have my number if you need anything."

"Thanks, man." I wave Larry off as he reverses back up the drive, and I'm left alone with an intimidating pile of timber. Shit, I think it may be more than a one-man job. I might have to ask around in town to see if any of the local carpenters can help me out.

I know one job I can get started today is digging out the holes for the support posts, so I go to the garage and find the shovel and the wheelbarrow. Despite the heat of the afternoon, I feel good about the hard physical work I'm about to engage in. I love to push myself. I always have, and I'm not happy unless I can say I've given a job one hundred percent effort. That goes for hockey, and it sure as shit goes for building this deck.

After going into the house to find the plans I had drawn up, I measure the plot with builders' lines and mark the ground with spray paint, putting crosses where I need to dig the holes for the support posts. It feels amazing to break ground on the project, and after a sweaty back-breaking few hours, I have all the holes dug.

I decide there's just enough daylight left to take a swim in the lake with Juneau, so I strip off my sweat soaked tee and kick off my work boots. I put my fingers in my mouth and whistle for my dog, who appears from his snoozing space on the porch, and together we run down the beach and splash into the cooling water. It feels amazing on my hot, sunbaked skin, and as I push out into deeper water, I allow my mind to drift to thoughts of Cam.

I was going to ask her to come and stay with me for a few weeks. I know that Don has gone to Australia for a month, so she's got some vacation time. If things weren't so weird between us, I wouldn't hesitate to invite her. She's such a great friend, and we always have a good time together. I can see us working on the deck, swimming in the lake, running the trails, and barbecuing in the evening.

But things aren't good between us. We haven't really spoken since Dallas, and I was too focused on the play-offs to reach out. I think she was too embarrassed about what happened in her hotel room to reach out to me. It's frustrating as fuck, and I make the decision it's time to sort this shit out.

As I plow back to the shore, I come to the conclusion that I need to make the first move. How I'm going to do that, I have no fucking clue. I guess first off, I should try and call her to apologize about Dallas.

I hit the beach, run back, and head straight into my outdoor shower, pulling off my soaking shorts and flinging them over the slated door. The warm water feels good after the chill of the lake, and I quickly soap up then rinse, grabbing the towel, rubbing my hair dry.

As I step out of the shower, I see Nancy rounding the corner of my cabin, and I'm greeted by a high, female squeak and a blushing redhead, her eyes impossibly wide.

"Fuck!" I shout, quickly wrapping the towel round my waist, covering my junk.

"Oh my god, I'm so sorry. I didn't mean to look at your dick," Nancy squeals, spinning around so she has her back to me. I make sure my towel is completely covering all my private parts and let her know it's safe to turn around.

"It's fine, Nancy. Don't sweat it." I chuckle, scrubbing my hand over my face.

"I'm so sorry." She gasps again, her cheeks, neck, and chest bright red with embarrassment. "I just came over to say thank you for helping me this morning and for not being a jerk while I stood there in a towel. And now I'm the jerk, looking at your ..." She waves her hand at my groin area. "... stuff."

I raise an eyebrow and smirk at her embarrassment, it's actually kind of cute. I notice she's holding a foil covered tray, and I point at it and ask, "What's this?"

"Oh, yeah. I baked you brownies to say thank you." She smiles proudly and holds the tray out to me.

"Um, I'm not really dressed for company. Why don't you come in while I dress, and we can have them with a cup of coffee?" I cock my head in the direction of the door, and she follows me inside.

As I head for the stairs I call, "Just pop them on the counter. The coffee machine is by the fridge if you want to turn it on."

"Sure thing, Cap," Nancy replies. It's a slightly over-familiar moniker for her to use seeing as we've only met twice, but I let it slide. She seems nice enough, and if we're going to be neighbors for the summer, we might as well try to be friends.

12

Cameron

I still can't believe I let Mila talk me into this trip. Once we secured Nate's silence, she felt like she had to tell Matt, so we could get the information we needed to track Warren down.

Matt looks at me with caring eyes and gives me a massive hug. "It'll be okay, Cam. Bugs is a good man. He'll step up."

I know this must be a touchy subject for Matt, especially after that puck bunny in Chicago tried to scam him with a baby that wasn't his.

As I pack a bag for my trip, Matt and Mila work together to book me a flight to Edmonton and a rental car. Matt shoots off a few texts to Warren to check if he's still at his dad's, but he's already driven to his cabin.

After a pep talk from Mila and a couple of hours in a cramped coach seat, I've lost all my earlier resolve, and also my lunch in the tiny airplane toilet. I don't know why they call it morning sickness when it happens all the damn time.

By the time the plane lands and I collect my car, I'm deep into panic mode. I grab some crackers and water from the first gas station I pass and proceed to drive toward the lake in a bit of a trance.

And now here I am, freaking out in a rest stop trying to pluck up the courage to drive the last mile to Warren's cabin. The blinking arrow on the GPS is taunting me, and I know if I don't move soon, I'll end up sleeping in my car.

"Get a fucking grip, Sawyer," I tell myself, putting the car in drive and pulling out onto the deserted road. It's twilight and even in my state of panic, I can appreciate how beautiful and quiet it is out here. I can see exactly why Warren loves it. He has so much pressure and noise in his role as captain; this must be like heaven for him.

Suddenly, a gorgeous cabin comes into view— two stories, a pitched roof—it literally looks like it's been made out of life-sized Lincoln Logs. As I park up behind a pickup truck, I can see the lake shimmering gold with the setting sun, and I take a second to gather my thoughts.

But a second is all I get before a huge black and white dog comes bounding from the side of the cabin, jumping up on the car, his massive head filling the open window. He pants his dog's breath all over me and despite his cute face, I feel my nausea return from earlier. I quickly hit the button to raise the window to save me from barfing into my purse.

"C'mon, buddy. You need to back up so I can get out," I say to the dog, who I can only assume is Juneau. He barks and backs away from my door, allowing me to open it and jump out. I let Juneau sniff my hand, then scratch behind his ear which Warren told me is his favorite spot.

"You gonna show me where your daddy is?" I ask the dog, suddenly feeling my stomach drop at the use of that title. Shit, in a matter of minutes Warren's going to find out he's about to be a real dad, not just a dog dad, and I suddenly want to jump back in my car and drive until I fall off the edge of the world.

No, it's time to pull up my big girl pants and get this done.

I take a deep breath and cross the yard to the porch, feeling like each step is taking a lifetime.

"I can do this. I can do this," I quietly chant to myself, as I ascend the porch steps and stop in front of the door. Juneau continues to bark happily behind me, charging around the yard.

I'm about to knock when I hear loud female laughter coming from inside. For a second, I think I've got the wrong cabin, but then a realization hits me right in the gut. Warren has a woman in his house—probably some lake bunny he's hooking up with for the summer. I mean, why the fuck wouldn't he? That testosterone has to go somewhere.

Jesus, I should get out of here, but before I can high tail and run, the door opens and there he is.

"Juneau! What's with the…?" he starts, coming to an abrupt halt when he sees me standing on his porch. His eyes go impossibly wide as if he's trying to check I'm really in front of him.

"Hey," I manage to squeak, waving my hand pathetically.

"Cam, what are you doing here?" he asks, blinking rapidly and shaking his head as if I'm a mirage.

"I … I need to talk to you," I stammer as Juneau comes up onto the porch and nuzzles my hand.

"You know we have these amazing things called phones that allow you to talk to people far away without actually having to travel hundreds of miles."

I roll my eyes, but then I see the owner of the laughter appear behind Warren.

"Bugs, who is it?" she asks, putting her freckled hand on his shoulder, smiling at me as if she's the lady of the house.

Warren seems to momentarily stroke out, but as he regains his composure, he introduces us. "Nancy, this is my good friend Cameron from Seattle. Cam, this is my neighbor, Nancy. We're just having coffee."

"Oh, Cameron, lovely to meet you," Nancy coos, extending her hand to me. "Why don't you come in and join us?"

Warren gapes at her—did she seriously just invite me into his house as if she owned the joint?

"Um … Nancy." He turns to her with an uncomfortable look on his face. "Do you mind if we take a raincheck on the coffee?"

I notice a burning blush creep up Nancy's pale neck as she tries really hard to keep from looking too pissed off.

"Sure." She tries to keep her irritation in check. "I hope you enjoy the brownies. You know where I am when you want to cash in that raincheck." She leans up on her tiptoes and kisses his cheek, side-eyeing me. "Thanks again for saving me."

With that, she saunters past me off the porch, flicking her curly red hair over her shoulder and doing her best to wiggle her round ass.

I continue to stare after her as she disappears round the corner, but Warren's deep, gravelly voice makes me jump and spin back to facing him.

"What are you doing here, Sawyer?" he asks. "What's so important you couldn't just call me?"

I take a deep cleansing breath and try not to freak out about Nancy. If Warren is just starting up a relationship with this woman, he certainly won't want to hear what I've got to tell him.

"Nancy seems … fun," I say, plastering a fake smile on my face. "You've worked fast getting your summer fling arranged."

As the words leave my mouth, I regret them. Warren's expression darkens, and I see his jaw ticking even under the covering of his thick dark beard.

"What the fuck is that supposed to mean?" he growls, taking a long stride to close the space between us. I immediately smell his body wash and something else. Something earthy and natural like the sand and the lake.

His annoyance is understandable. That was a shitty comment to make, and I feel immediate regret. However, I'm not going to let him get off that easily; we've always challenged each other, and I'm not going to let him crowd me.

"What? I'm just saying I'm glad you've got some company for the summer," I reply, lifting my chin and standing my ground despite my butt pressing against the porch rail.

"I've met the woman exactly twice," he begins to explain, his face mere inches from mine, his expression still cloudy. "She locked herself out, so I helped her. Then she appeared this afternoon with thank you brownies. We were just about to have coffee. That's it. She's not my summer fuck buddy."

I feel the tension leave my body at his explanation, but I'm still caged against the railing by his thick arms. The heat from his body and his annoyance are intoxicating, and I feel my nipples tighten. I've discovered that another wonderful side-effect of pregnancy is that I'm horny … like all the time. I guess that's why you should be in a relationship when you have a baby, so there's someone around to take care of that.

"I'll ask again: what do you want, Cam?" Warren's deep voice brings me back to the moment, and I realize I totally zoned out thinking about how horny I am. The zoning out has also been happening a lot more.

"Can we go inside?" I don't really want to have this conversation on the porch with the mosquitos eating us alive.

Warren seems to relax as well and takes a much-needed step back, allowing both of us the room to breathe again. He scrubs his large hand down his face and over his beard; I guess he's decided to keep his playoff look going all summer.

"Sure. Come in," he replies, seeming to remember his manners. "Juneau, come!"

Oh, something about his commanding voice makes my nipples tingle again, and I silently berate myself for being turned on. The dog trots up onto the porch and follows Warren and me inside.

I'm immediately struck by how gorgeous it is inside. We walk into a hallway with stairs directly in front, rooms to the left and right, and a kitchen at the end. Warren leads me down the corridor, and I peek into the rooms on either side—one is set up as an office with a wall of books and a desk and the other seems to be a game room with a huge TV hanging over the fireplace and a pool table.

The whole place is warm and masculine, just like Warren, and I can tell he put his all into making it perfect. I remember seeing pictures of the plot when he bought it; the house that stood on it then was nothing more than a one-story shack compared to this amazing cabin. He'd shown me more pictures after the demolition and the rebuild, and he's always said I should come and spend the summer with him.

That was all said before things got so complicated between us.

But if I thought the rest of the downstairs was quintessentially Warren, then the kitchen literally screams it. I know how much he loves to cook, and he's damn good at it. So, I shouldn't have expected this kitchen to be anything less than amazing.

"Oh, Warren. This is incredible!" I gasp as we enter the back room of the cabin. It's one huge space that spans the entire width of the building. To the left is the kitchen area fitted out in brushed steel and granite with professional spec appliances. A huge counter separates it from the rest of the room which is set up as a casual dining room with a large pine table, bench seating, and a comfortable corner sectional. A huge stone fireplace stretches up into the vaulted ceiling.

But most impressive is the wall of glass that makes up the entire back of the building. The bi-fold doors are open, but screens stop the house becoming infested with bugs from the lake. And the lake looks gorgeous—burning red with the setting sun.

"Can I get you a beer?" he asks, making me turn from the breathtaking view to where he's standing at the fridge.

I'm about to accept because we always like to share a beer, but then I remember I can't.

"I'll take a soda if you have one," I reply nonchalantly. Suddenly, I feel all kinds of nervous. "Do you mind if I sit down? It's been a long day."

"Sure, of course. Make yourself at home." Warren walks over to me and hands me a diet soda in a glass with ice, just how I like it, and my heart clenches in my chest. I feel like the biggest asshole right now.

Warren joins me on the couch, and we sit in silence for a few minutes while we sip our drinks and watch the sun disappear into the lake.

"I feel like a dick about Dallas. I'm sorry," he suddenly blurts, making me jump a little so my soda sloshes out of the glass. "I know I said we'd talk about us after the playoffs, and I'm sorry I disappeared before we got a chance to."

"Oh, okay," I reply, sweeping the cold liquid from my bare leg with my fingers. "It's my fault we didn't get to talk as well. I was so busy with Don, and then I kind of got ... distracted."

"Distracted?" Warren asks, before taking a long draw on his beer, fixing me with his green eyes. "So come on, Sawyer. What made you so distracted?"

I take a deep breath. I just have to say it before I lose my nerve. "I'm pregnant."

13

Bugs

I stare at Cameron like she's just spontaneously grown a second head. My ears are ringing with the sudden rush of blood to my head, and I'm gripping the glass bottle in my hand so tightly I wouldn't be surprised if it shatters.

"Warren, I'm pregnant," Cam repeats, reaching out to gently touch the back of my hand. "And if it's not obvious, you're the father."

I shake my head a few times to try and clear the buzzing and look at Cam: my best friend, the woman I've wanted since the day we met, the woman who's telling me she's going to have my baby. I need to fucking say something before she gets up and walks back out to her car and drives off.

"How?" I croak, my throat as dry as sand. I'm in complete shock right now, so all sorts of stupid shit is coming out of my mouth.

Despite everything, Cam snorts out a laugh. "Shit, Warren, do I really need to tell you how babies are made?"

I take a sip of beer and shake my head again. I need to move. I need to try and pace this out like when I'm trying to figure out a problem with the team.

"No, I know how *that* happens. But how did *this* happen?" I gesture between the two of us as her eyes track my movement back and forth in front of her. "I mean, I wore a rubber. I know you're on the pill because you're always moaning about the headaches it gives you, so how in the fuck did that make a baby?"

I can hear my voice getting louder and louder until I'm yelling, and I notice Cam cringe on the couch, lowering her head to avoid my stare.

"Contraception isn't one hundred percent effective," she whispers, looking up at me, her brown eyes big and scared. "And we did have sex *a lot* that night."

"I know that, but we used two kinds of contraception so shouldn't that be, like, one hundred and ninety-eight percent effective?" I shout, throwing my hands in the air, puffing out a huge, frustrated breath.

Cam's chin starts to wobble, and I know that's her cue to start crying. I've seen it enough times around the anniversary of her mom's death or when we watch one of her sappy romantic movies. Her huge eyes begin to fill with tears.

Jesus, I feel like a prick for yelling at her.

I quickly join her on the couch, but she flinches away from my touch. I persevere and wrap my arm around her shoulders, feeling her tense muscles beneath my fingers. I press my nose to her temple and kiss her hair.

"I'm sorry, Sawyer."

"This wasn't in my plan either," she whispers.

"I know. I'm really sorry for being an asshole."

I feel her take in several huffs of air, and then she sinks against my body, almost as if now she's shared this with me, she's letting everything go. My head is still all over the place, so I ask the next most important question.

"What are you gonna do? Are you keeping it?" I ask quietly. I've just got her settled. I don't want to freak her out more. But I have to know what she's planning. I can't let myself have any kind of feelings about this baby until I know if there's going to be one.

Cam lifts her head and rests it on my shoulder, looking at me with the eyes that fucking melt my heart into a gooey mess. If she tells me that she's not keeping it, I think I'll die.

"I want to keep it," she whispers in her sweet voice.

Thank fuck! I want to leap on the couch like Tom Cruise and do a happy dance, but I don't think that'll win me any points. So, I keep my celebration to myself.

"That's great. I mean, I know it's unplanned and we're not a couple, but I'm pleased," I reassure her, running my fingertip down her cheek and cupping her face.

I'm kind of surprised at myself, but I mean every word. The feeling of love I have for this baby already is making my chest ache.

"Warren, I want you in our lives—mine and the baby's," she states firmly.

I gently kiss her forehead. "That's what I want too. I'm here for you and the baby in whatever capacity you want me."

I feel her slump against me again in relief, and I hold her a little bit tighter.

"Fuck, I'm gonna be a dad," I mutter, half to myself and half to the universe, dragging my fingers through my hair.

Cameron laughs softly into my neck, and the feeling of her breath on my hot skin makes me hard. Now is not the time to get a boner.

"That's pretty much the same thought I had. It's crazy, right?" she asks. "Can we really do this?"

I pull her up, so we're face-to-face, and I fix her with my best team captain stare. "Of course, we can do this, Sawyer. We're a team. We can do anything."

A determined smile curls her lips at the corners, tucking a strand of silky brown hair behind her ear. Then she fixes me with a stare of her own.

"I'm not sleeping with you, Warren," she states firmly, pushing her hands against my chest to get a little distance.

"Hey, that's not what I mean," I protest. "I just mean we can raise this baby together. We can make up our own rules."

"Okay, that's good." The smile is back. "Do you mind if I stay here though? I haven't booked a hotel, and it's getting late. I'm so tired."

Suddenly, I feel like the worst host in the world. "Oh shit, Cam. Sure, you can stay. I wouldn't have it any other way. Do you have bags? I'll get them from the car. I don't want you lifting anything."

My mother hen routine causes Cam to burst out laughing, so much so that Juneau starts barking, as if both of them are laughing at me.

"What's so funny?" I ask, crossing my arms over my chest. I was just trying to be nice, and she's busting my balls like she always does.

Cam wipes a few tears from her eyes. "Nothing, honey. I'm sorry. You're being very sweet. I can get my bags from the car, and if you'll just show me a tub I can soak in, I'll probably head to bed. It's been a long few days."

"Sure. Why don't I get the bags and you go and start your bath?" I pull her into my arms and hold her close, once again breathing in the light flowery scent of her hair. "The bathroom is at the top of the stairs, and you can use the bedroom with the blue comforter and the view of the lake."

"Thank you, Warren," she whispers into my chest. "For everything. For not freaking out too much and for letting me stay."

"Anytime, Sawyer." I give her butt a friendly swat. "Now go get yourself in the tub."

It takes me one trip to bring in the two bags Cam has in her car, and when I bring them upstairs, I can see steam coming out from under the bathroom door and the sound of the water running.

"Cam, your bags'll be in your room!" I call through the door.

"Thanks," she calls back over the noise of the rushing water.

I quickly drop her bags into the spare room and double check the sheets are fresh. Thankfully, they're not musty, so I trot downstairs and rummage around in the fridge until I find some burgers that I can throw on the grill.

As I push some things around, I see some juice boxes in the back that my sister leaves here for the twins. Suddenly, my stomach flips, and I get light-headed. I grab the fridge door to steady myself as the enormity of the situation slams me into the boards.

I'm going to be a father.

For the rest of my life, I'm going to be completely responsible for another human being. It changes everything. I can't be reckless with my safety on the ice or frivolous with my money. I'm almost thirty years old, and I suddenly feel the weight of grown-up responsibilities weighing on my shoulders.

Taking a few deep breaths, I pull myself together and decide to take this one step at a time. The first thing I have to do is make the mother of my child some food.

One step at a time.

Cameron

I needed that bath like I needed my next breath, and as I dry off, I sweep my hand across the steamy mirror and stare at my reflection. I'm still dumbfounded that I'm growing a tiny human being inside my body. It's so sci-fi. People say you get a glow when you're pregnant, but I've yet to see it. I just seem to have a slightly green tinge to my skin, and I feel nauseous most of the time, but at the moment, my cheeks are bright red from the steamy bath.

As I look around, I'm once again amazed at how beautiful Warren's interiors are. The bathroom is gorgeous with whitewashed floorboards, and the walls are covered in tiles in a soft dove grey. The claw footed tub is under a huge picture window that looks out over the lake and there's a state-of-the-art steam shower that I'll have to check out at some point.

Grabbing a huge fluffy towel from the heated rail, I pat my body dry and wrap it around myself. At eleven weeks pregnant, I'm still not really showing, but I can tell that my body is changing. My nipples are larger and a darker brown than normal, and for the first time, my breasts are a decent handful. However, some days they're so tender, I can barely touch them. As I run my hands down my body, I feel a slight curve to my normally flat stomach.

"Your daddy took that pretty well," I whisper to my stomach. "You're gonna be a very lucky little baby." My stomach gives a loud, hungry gurgle, and it makes me laugh.

"Cam, I've made some food." Warren's voice interrupts me, and I quickly tighten the towel round my body. "Come down when you're ready."

"Okay, thanks," I call, letting my damp hair out of the elastic and shaking it out. Then I take out my moisturizer and rub the luxurious cream into my body, wincing slightly as I smooth it gently over my tender breasts. Once it's absorbed, I grab my discarded clothes and open the door, only to find Warren still standing there.

I gasp and almost drop my clothes. "Geez, Warren. Creep much?"

He looks mortified at being caught creeping outside the bathroom. "Sorry, babe. I was worried you'd gone down the drain," he stammers, turning around and jogging down the stairs.

Ugh, this could get awkward if we keep bumping into each other when we're half naked. Yet again my libido rears its horny head and demands satisfaction. With such a hot man in close proximity, I'll have to keep her on a tight leash.

Once I'm dressed in my comfy sweatpants and my baggy tee, I head downstairs to the smell of barbecued meat. The usual feeling of nausea quickly disappears, and I realize I'm absolutely starving. I can't remember the last time I kept anything other than crackers and water down, so I'm hopeful for this meal.

I find Warren sitting at the kitchen counter drinking a beer. He's laid out a feast of burgers with every possible sauce and accompaniment, a leafy green salad, coleslaw, and a jug of sweet iced tea.

"This looks so delicious!" I moan, my stomach making a really unattractive growling sound.

"I'm not sure what you can eat, but I thought burgers would be safe," Warren says, pulling out the stool so I can sit down. "I can make you something else if this isn't good. I don't know how your morning sickness is. My sister suffered really badly and …"

"Warren, relax." I laugh, holding my hands up. "You're gonna give yourself a stroke if you carry on like this for the next six months."

He takes in a massive breath and scrubs his hand down his face. "Sorry. I'm being a mother hen again, aren't I?"

"Just a bit, but it's fine," I reply kindly. "Yes, the food is perfect. Yes, I've had morning sickness so bad that I've barfed all the way from Seattle, but actually I'm hungry for the first time in ages."

"Excellent. Let me pour you some iced tea, and you can dig right in." Warren leans over and fills my glass with the sweet tea, and I begin loading up my burger. As I lift my fully loaded sandwich to my mouth and take a huge bite, I catch him staring and I stop dead.

"Whaaaa?" I ask, my mouth full of juicy burger.

"Jesus, Sawyer." He chuckles. "I've eaten with hockey players for most of my life and I've never seen anyone make a burger that fucking massive."

I chew and swallow my mouthful. "Don't food shame a pregnant woman, you D-bag," I reply, rolling my eyes.

"Wouldn't dream of it, babe. You'll outweigh me soon." He winks.

I kick his leg and chew happily on my food, moaning as I taste the vinegary pickles and the creamy mayo.

Warren continues to fix his burger, making it as big as mine, then digs in as we eat in comfortable silence, the type you can only have with someone you know so well.

I manage to eat a whole burger, a large pile of salad and coleslaw, and a juicy peach for dessert. By the time we finish, I'm so full I have to sit on the couch for a few minutes, gently rubbing Juneau behind his ear. I can hear Warren banging around in the kitchen as he loads the dishwasher, but I can't stop my heavy eyes from sliding closed as I drift off to sleep.

When I wake, the room is dark, and I can hear two different snores close to me. I shift and realize my head is resting on Warren's warm, muscular thigh. He's snoring lightly, sleeping sitting up on the couch. The other snore comes from Juneau, who's curled up next to Warren on his other side. As I shift to sit up, Juneau wakes and whines at me, but once I shush him gently, he huffs and settles down next to his master.

I check the time on my smart watch and see it's two am. Jesus, I completely passed out. I feel a shiver ripple through my body. The temperature has dropped quite dramatically, and the heat from Warren's body is no longer keeping me warm.

The urge to continue snuggling with Warren is strong, but I know I'll regret sleeping on the couch, so I gently nudge his shoulder, and he wakes with a grunt.

"Warren, we fell asleep," I whisper, trying not to disturb Juneau. "I'm cold. I'm going to bed."

Rubbing the sleep out of his eyes, Warren grumbles something and rises from the couch, grabbing my hand and pulling me up, quietly leading me to the stairs. As we ascend, I feel an overwhelming urge to follow him into his room, but I must be strong. I can't let my rampant hormones get in the way of making the sensible choice.

When we reach the landing, Warren pulls me into a sleepy hug and kisses the top of my head. It feels so safe and warm in his arms, I just cling to the back of this T-shirt and hold him.

"Night, Sawyer. No rush to get up in the morning. You sleep as long as you need," he murmurs into my hair. "I would like to talk more about our situation though."

"Sure. Good night." I let go of Warren and quickly slip into my room and close the door, leaning against it. I have a feeling tomorrow will be another emotional day, so I need to get my pregnant butt to bed.

Bugs

I deserve a fucking medal for sending Cam to bed alone. How she didn't feel my rock-hard dick pressing against her, I don't know. I lean against my bedroom door and squeeze my eyes shut, trying to banish the memories of her writhing and moaning beneath me, the smell of her hair and the taste of her pussy.

It's no good. I'm going to either have to rub one out or have a cold shower. I feel like a huge douche jerking off to Cam when she's in the next room, so I opt for a quick, ice cold shower, and by the time I climb into bed, my balls are shriveled and my libido is under control for the time being.

I lay there in the dark and think again about the fact that I'm going to be a father. I obviously need to tell my dad and sister, but that's not the sort of news I want to give them over the phone. Hopefully, Cam will agree to stay here with me for a few weeks, and we can tell them together when my family comes up for the weekend.

Thoughts of what will happen when we return to Seattle also fill my brain, making sleep impossible. Will Cam keep her own place or move in with me? Will she continue to work for the GM? What about travelling with the team? There are so many questions swirling round in my brain that before I know it, the dawn light begins to filter through my drapes.

There's no point trying to sleep now, so I throw off my sheets and sit up, scrubbing my hands over my shaggy hair. Jesus, I should get a haircut and have a shave. It'll sure as shit make working outdoors a lot more comfortable without half a grizzly bear on my face.

I decide to go for a run, then I might head into town to get some more groceries and a haircut. I need to keep busy until I can talk to Cam some more; sitting around thinking too much is always a little dangerous.

Three hours later, I've been for a run, been to the grocery store, and bought some of Cam's favorite treats and more fresh fruit and veggies. I've had my shaggy hair cut short and my beard trimmed down to a five o'clock shadow, and I've collected several bags of quick-drying cement from the hardware store. I let myself back into the house after dumping the bags of cement in the garage, calling out to Juneau, who comes skidding round the corner, jumping and sniffing the grocery bags.

"Down, boy," I command, and my dog sits his butt on the floor. "Good dog," I praise him, scratching him behind his ear as I head to the kitchen.

There's still no sign of Cam as I unpack the shopping and put it away, whistling tunelessly to myself. I assume she's still in bed, so I make a pot of decaf coffee and take her up a cup. When I approach her door, I hear the soft sounds of crying and I freeze.

I remember when April was pregnant with the twins. She cried almost constantly for the first few months about absolutely ridiculous shit like commercials on TV and finding out the date of the milk in the fridge. Pat, my dad and I were at a loss how to help her, so we usually just stood around like helpless idiots. Thankfully, I was traded to Seattle before she hit her "Rage Stage" as Pat called it, and I avoided having shit thrown at my head!

However, this woman is carrying my baby, so I need to step up and help her. If that involves her throwing things at me or crying on my shoulder, then so be it. I tap lightly on the door and wait for an answer, but all I hear is a quiet, "Go away."

"No, Sawyer. I won't go away," I say kindly into the door. "If you're upset, I want to help you. I'm coming in."

I push the door open, and at first, I can't see Cam anywhere, but I can still hear her sobbing. I put the coffee cup on the dresser and walk round the end of the bed, and that's where I find her. She's slumped on the floor, cross legged, wrapped in a towel, her face in her hands.

"Don't come in here, Warren," she sobs into her hands. "Don't look at me."

My heart stutters in my chest. I'm terrified she's hurt, or something is wrong with the baby, so I drop to my knees next to her and take her gently by the shoulders. "Cam, you need to tell me if there's something happening with the baby. Do I need to call a doctor?"

She sniffs loudly and looks up at me. "No, it's not the baby. It's me."

Again, my heart falters in my chest. "What's wrong, Cam? You're really freaking me out."

She groans and rolls her wet, swollen eyes. "I can't tell you. It's embarrassing."

I sit back on my haunches and cross my arms. "You'd better start talking or else I'm gonna call 911," I coax, freaking out but trying to remain calm for Cam's sake.

"Ugh, fine." Cam swipes her hand under her nose to wipe away the tears and snot and sits up straight. "I wanted to go for a swim in the lake, so I put my bikini on." I notice her chin start to wobble again. "But when I put it on, it's too small."

Big, fat tears start rolling down her cheeks again, and I'm at a loss as to why this deserves so much drama.

"So, what's the problem?" I laugh. "I'm sure there are some of my sisters' swimsuits in here somewhere."

Cam looks at me like I'm the most clueless asshole in the world. "That's not the point!" she cries suddenly, clambering up off the floor. "Look at me!"

All at once, the air seems to get sucked out of my lungs as Cam opens her towel, and I get a look at what she's dealing with. I've never been a breast man, and even though Cam has always been on the smaller side, that's no longer the case. Her breasts seem to have doubled in size, and the small white triangles that would have normally covered her now barely cover her nipples. Her creamy skin is lined with blue veins, and I can see her erect nipples straining against the fabric.

"Fuck," I moan, feeling my dick stand to attention and my heart rate skyrocket.

"See!" she cries. "I can't go outside with these … porno tits."

I swallow loudly and try not to stare, trying to think of anything I can to stop my dick from ripping a hole in my shorts.

"C'mon, babe. It's not that bad." I chuckle, standing up and taking a step back. I need to put some distance between us, so I don't reach out and cup her fabulous breasts in my hands.

"I hate this." Cam sobs, closing the towel, to my immense relief. "I hate being out of control, and there's shit happening to my body that I can't control. I went to bed last night looking fairly normal, and I woke up this morning looking like a bimbo."

I can't help but snort out a laugh and shake my head. "You don't look like a bimbo." I close the distance between us and hold her by the shoulders. Her silky skin feels incredible under my rough fingers, and I work my ass off to keep my eyes on hers.

"Yes, I do," she whines in a sulky voice.

Gently, I lift her chin with my finger and look deeply into her brown eyes. "No, you don't. You look fucking beautiful. Your body is growing our baby, and it's gonna get out of control. This is gonna be a long pregnancy if you freak out about every little thing. But you know what? If you want to freak out, then I'll be right here."

I can tell she's trying her hardest not to cry again, so I continue to be helpful. "Do you want me to find you one of April's swimsuits?"

"Yes, please. I really wanna go for a swim." Cam sniffles, leaning into me for a hug. When she looks up at me, I have to try to control my breathing. She really is so beautiful, even when she's swollen and snotty from crying.

"You okay now, Sawyer?"

"Yeah." She looks at me quizzically. "You cut your hair." She reaches up and runs her fingers through my short hair, sending shivers down my spine despite the heat in the room.

"Yep, I was starting to look like a mountain man." I chuckle. Shit, if she keeps looking at me like that and running her fingers through my hair, I'm going to end up kissing her.

"I liked it," Cam whispers, dragging her pink tongue over her plump lower lip.

That does it. I release her from my arms and move over to the dresser to look for the swimsuit, anything to keep my hands busy and my mind off crashing my mouth against hers. Thankfully, I find a few modest one pieces in the first drawer, so I toss them on the bed and head for the door.

"Made you a coffee. I'll be outside working on the porch if you need me." And with that I leave her and disappear into my room to change into my work gear. But before I do, I lock myself in the en suite and jerk off. This time a cold shower just won't do the job.

15

Cameron

The cool water of the lake feels incredible as I swim out to the raft that's anchored a few hundred feet off the shore. Juneau doggy paddles beside me, panting and occasionally looking over like he's checking I'm okay. It's so cute. I didn't think for a minute he'd follow me into the water, but he charged in and hasn't left my side since. It's almost as if he's keeping an eye on me for Warren.

Thinking about Warren, I feel my cheeks burn with embarrassment despite the chilly water. Jesus, I made such an idiot of myself in front of him. He must think I'm a crazy person losing my shit over a bikini. But waking up to the giant porno boobs was a shock, and it just reminded me that my body was no longer my own: it is literally possessed by a tiny alien being.

I'm not going to lie. When I saw Warren's eyes bug out of his head like a cartoon character, I did get a little thrill. I know he's told me in the past that he's a legs and ass man, but he looked like he wanted to devour my tits like they were his last meal.

As I reach the raft, I haul myself out of the water, and because Juneau can't clamber up, he turns around and swims back toward the shore. I'm glad it's a hot day or else it would be too chilly to lay here and bask in the sun. I lay down and feel the sun dry the lake water that's beading on my skin and think about the situation with Warren and the baby.

I know he has feelings for me and has since we met; however, I was in a relationship then. I remember we talked about it shortly after I broke up with Richard, and we both agreed that our friendship meant too much to us to muddy the waters with sex. But I'm not blind. Over the years, I've seen the looks he throws my way, the excuses to touch me and the offers to hang out. I know for a fact he's blown off the guys to come and watch sappy rom-coms or play board games with me on a Saturday night. And I must admit I feel guilty about that sometimes, like I'm leading him on. But over time, we've become good friends. Once we discovered we both lost our moms, we spent many an evening curled up on the couch talking about it. He's held me on the anniversary of my mom's death, and I've spent time listening to him talk about his mom and his sister.

On paper, we make a great couple. And now I know we're more than compatible in bed, I wonder what's stopping us from taking the next step. It would make raising a child much easier if we were a couple, but like I said to him before, I don't want to just become a couple in order to raise our baby.

As the sun disappears behind a cloud, I feel my skin break out in goosebumps, so I stand up and dive back into the water. It's so cold, it momentarily takes my breath away, and I tread water in order to control my breathing, then swim back toward the beach. I think I'll cook Warren a nice meal tonight, so that we can talk properly and make sure he understands where I'm coming from.

When I'm back on the beach, I wrap the towel around myself and hit the outdoor shower to wash the lake water off me. I haven't seen Warren since he dashed out of my room earlier, and as I walk through the cabin, he's still nowhere to be found. I go to my room and quickly change into jean shorts and a baggy T-shirt. I'm trying to get used to my porno boobs and just like my bikini top, none of my bras fit comfortably. I hope there's a place in town where I can pick up a few new ones while I'm out buying what I want to cook for dinner.

As I leave the cabin to walk out to the car, I hear loud rock music coming from the garage. I guess that's where Warren is hiding out and decide I should tell him I'm heading into town in case he comes looking for me. I certainly don't want him freaking out when he can't find me.

Approaching the garage, I can hear the sound of a power saw over the music. As I enter, the heat almost knocks me on my ass. Jesus, it's like a furnace in here. The weather has been so humid today, like there's a storm on the way, but it's next level steamy in the garage even with the doors ajar.

And when I catch sight of Warren, the steam factor goes up by ten. He's shirtless and slicked with sweat, his back muscles and biceps taut and bulging as he works the power saw to cut a large wooden post. He's wearing a pair of ear defenders and because his back is to me, he has no idea I'm there. Thank god because I'm standing here gawping at him like a total creeper.

The saw finally stops, and I take the opportunity to make my presence known.

"Hey, Warren!" I yell, waving my arms even though he's still got his back to me.

He whips around and pulls his ear defenders and goggles off and … Oh. My. God. His massive, muscular chest is slick with sweat that glistens in the smattering of chest hair and the happy trail that disappears into his low-slung shorts. He really is a magnificent man with a defined ladder of abs and that V of muscles at his hips that are so tempting I want to drop to my knees and lick them.

"What's up, Sawyer?" he asks, smirking because I'm sure he can see me drooling.

I shake my head to clear the images of me kneeling in front of Warren. "I'm just going into town to buy a few things, and I'll pick up something for dinner. Anything you want?"

That suddenly feels like a loaded question, but Warren sidesteps it like a pro. "I went out this morning, so the fridge is all stocked up. If there's something you want that we don't have, then by all means get it. I'll eat anything." He grabs his discarded shirt and wipes his face and chest. "Anything else you need?"

"Um, I was wondering if there's a women's clothing store in town," I ask shyly, kicking an imaginary rock.

"Yeah, I think they sell women's clothes in the general store on Main," he replies.

"Great. Thanks. I'll be back later." I spin around and leave the oppressive heat of the garage, fanning myself as I march to the car, in desperate need of some air conditioning to cool myself down.

On the drive into town, my phone rings and I see Beth's name appear on the display. I pull over onto the verge to answer, keeping the engine running so I can keep cool while we chat. The humidity is increasing and the dark clouds on the horizon definitely threaten a storm. Just perfect. I hate thunderstorms.

I hit the answer button. "Hey, Beth."

"Cam, how's it going? Are you in Canada yet?" she asks, getting straight down to business.

"Yeah, I'm here and I told him, and it was … fine." I cringe at the use of the word fine to describe how it went with Warren last night.

"Fine? I need more information," Beth replies quickly.

"He got a bit upset when I first told him, and he yelled a bit, but then we talked, and he seems really happy about it."

"He yelled at you?" she shouts. "How dare he fucking yell at you!"

"Chill, princess." I hear Nate's deep voice, and I realize I must be on speaker phone.

"Hey, Nate."

"Hey, Cam. Congratulations. I hope the Cap is treating you right," he replies.

"He's obviously not if he's yelling at her," Beth growls.

"He wasn't really yelling at me. He was yelling at the fact our contraception failed," I clarify, wanting to defend Warren against Beth's fury. "Once we talked, he was happy. We just need to sort out the finer details.

125

By the time I got here, and we talked, I was so tired I had to go to bed. Then this morning … well, we got distracted."

I hear Beth's sultry chuckle. "Oh yeah?"

"No, nothing like that. I was having a clothing crisis and the stupid pregnancy hormones got me all emotional, so he helped me. We're just friends," I explain. I certainly don't want Beth and Nate getting the wrong idea.

"No, honey. We're friends." She laughs. "I don't want to put my dick in you."

I burst out laughing at her ridiculous comment. "You know what, I'm so horny at the moment, I might just let you."

I hear Nate groan and mumble something, and I feel my cheeks heat up. "Sorry, Nate."

"I'm going to the gym. I'll leave you two to it." I hear the wet, slurping sounds of them kissing.

"Ugh, you guys, that's not helping with the horniness," I grumble.

"Sorry babe," Beth sighs breathlessly, and I feel a stab of jealousy. I've seen Nate and Beth together, and they literally can't keep their hands off each other. I wonder if I'll ever be that happy with someone?

"I'm gonna make Warren dinner tonight so we can talk, but I don't even know how to go about sorting this out."

"Just be honest with him. If you don't wanna be a couple, then figure out a way to make it work," Beth advises. "It's not gonna be easy, but if you start out with some clear rules, then you can just adapt them as you go."

"Clear rules. I like that." I'm a big fan of rules and boundaries. "Give me some examples."

"Oh, I don't know. You're talking to a woman who's in her first serious relationship in her mid-twenties. What the fuck do I know?" She laughs. "This is more Mila's area of expertise."

"I don't want to disturb her on her vacation. I'll figure it out." I sigh. "Now I have to go and buy a bigger bra because enormous porno tits are the latest pregnancy side-effect I'm dealing with."

Beth laughs. "I bet Bugs is just loving that."

"Don't even, Beth. His eyes almost fell out when he saw them. It was so awkward."

She goes quiet for a moment, and I wonder if we've lost connection. "Cam, I'm gonna ask you an uncomfortable question."

"Okay," I sigh.

"How do you really feel about Bugs?"

The question hangs in the cool air of my car, and I have no idea how to answer it.

"He's my best friend and I love him. Obviously, he's hot and sexy, and I know we're compatible in bed now …" I begin.

"So, what's stopping you?"

"I don't want him to feel obligated to be with me because we're having a baby," I blurt out.

"Honey, there's no way he'd be with you out of obligation," Beth says quietly. "He's completely in love with you."

"That's why I can't get into anything with him unless I'm sure my feelings are the same. It's not fair."

"I get what you're saying. I was the same when Nate and I started," she explains. "But I'll tell you something: if I hadn't given us a chance, I never would've fallen in love with him. You have to put yourself out there and take a risk or you'll never know."

I take a deep breath and let it out. "I suppose. I'll think about it."

"Okay, sweetie. It's our last day in Hawaii, so I've got a spa appointment, then Nate's taking me to a fabulous dinner. Take care. Love you."

"Love you too, Beth. Thank you."

With Beth's advice ringing in my ears, I drive the rest of the way into town and find parking on Main Street. It's a cute little place with lots of stores geared toward people who come to the lake for recreation. After putting money in the meter, I stroll along window shopping and make note of places I may want to visit during my stay.

That causes me to think about how long I'm actually going to stay here. I don't want to leave until Warren and I have sorted out how we're moving forward, but I do have a doctor's appointment in a week's time to have my first ultrasound. Will Warren want to come with me? Should I ask him?

There are so many thoughts swirling through my head that I don't notice the small redhead until we're crashing into each other.

"Oh shit!" she curses as her iced coffee sloshes all over her cute pink tank top.

"I'm so sorry!" I gasp as the cold coffee spills all over my feet. "Nancy?" I recognize the woman who was at Warren's cabin when I arrived.

She whips her sunglasses off and glares at me, trying to place me. "Do I know you?"

"I'm Warren's friend, Cam. We met last night," I remind her, fishing around in my purse for some tissues to help wipe her down.

"Oh, you mean Bugs. Yeah. Hi." She snatches the tissues I'm offering and begins to dab at her top. I use a few that I have left to wipe the sticky coffee from my feet.

"I really am sorry about the coffee. I'll happily pay for your clothes to be dry cleaned," I offer, feeling terrible for being so clumsy. Nancy looks pissed, but as I apologize, her face softens, and she shakes her head.

"That's okay. This is an old top anyway." She balls up the soggy tissues and throws them in a nearby trash can. "I was rushing to get home, so it was my fault too."

"Well, if you change your mind, you know where to find me. For the next few days anyway," I reply, making a move to continue down the street.

"So, you won't be here all summer then?" Nancy inquires, cocking a red eyebrow.

"I don't think so. Warren and I have some things to talk about, and I guess I'll make a decision after that. I have to go back to Seattle next week anyway. I have … an appointment." I don't really want to discuss my condition with this virtual stranger. Especially one who seems to have designs on my baby daddy.

"Perhaps we can have dinner before you leave?" she suggests. "I came up here for some peace and quiet, but to be honest, I'm already going a bit crazy for some civilized company." She laughs and I feel a little more at ease.

"Sure, why not? I'll see you back at the lake." I begin to walk away. "Sorry again about your coffee."

"No problem." Nancy waves and continues in the opposite direction.

Shit, that was really awkward. It definitely feels like Nancy likes Warren, and why wouldn't she? He's a hot sexy pro hockey player. I feel a slight sting of jealousy that she's free and single while I'm single, knocked up, and completely clueless.

As I round the corner, I come across a cute boutique women's clothing store, so I head inside in hopes of finding some new bras and perhaps a new bikini that actually fits.

16

Bugs

T he cold beer feels amazing as I drink the whole bottle in four long pulls. My shoulders and back are screaming from the exertion of the day, but I have a deep satisfaction that I got all my support posts cut and cemented in place. Hopefully, they'll be set secure in a day or two and I can get on with the rest of the deck.

Cam's been gone most of the afternoon, and I feel a little worried. She doesn't know the area, and I'd hate for her to get lost. It's been a good chance to have time to think and process though. She can be very distracting, especially with her new ... assets. I noticed when she came into the garage to tell me she was going into town, she was wearing a baggy T-shirt to hide herself. I could tell by the gentle sway and jiggle as she moved that she wasn't wearing a bra and that caused a bit of a situation in my shorts.

I also noticed her checking me out. Her eyes lingered on my sweaty torso and grazed down toward my abs. She looked like she was about ready to jump me before she stumbled out of the garage. The signals are really confusing, and I think we need to have a proper talk to set the boundaries before one or both of us fuck this up.

I'm about to get myself another well-earned beer when I hear Cam's car pull up out front. Juneau raises his head from the floor next to my bare feet and barks once.

"I know, boy. She's back." I reach down and give him a rub as the weight lifts off my chest. I didn't realize it before, but I've had an anxious feeling all afternoon, and I couldn't figure out why. I guess now I know—I was anxious because Cam was out, and I wasn't with her.

Wow. That's new. I've been in relationships before, but I can't say I've ever felt anxious when we weren't together. It must be because of the baby. Surely that's it.

But as Cam breezes into the kitchen with a big smile on her face, carrying a few shopping bags, my heart clenches in my chest, and I know it's not just because of the baby. It's because of Cam.

"Someone found the stores." I chuckle, nodding toward the bags I recognize from the little clothes shop just off Main Street. When Cam asked me earlier, I'd forgotten to mention it. It's not like it's high on my list of places to shop in town.

"Oh, I did. This cute little boutique had just what I needed," she puffs, dumping the bags on the counter and flopping onto a stool. "Jesus, it's hot out."

"It sure is. I've been sweating my ass off out there laying those support posts. Can I make you some iced tea?" I stand and move to the fridge where I already have a jug of sweet tea chilling.

"Oh, yes. That would be amazing." Cam sighs. "I thought I'd grill those tuna steaks for dinner."

"Sounds perfect. I'll fire up the grill for you, then I'm gonna take a shower." I finish pouring Cam a glass of cold tea. "So, what did you buy?"

I see Cam's cheeks turn a pretty pink as she takes a large gulp of her drink. "Um, just some things I needed," she replies, a little evasive.

"Like what? Come on. Show me!" I push, coming round the counter to stand at her side, nudging her.

Cam huffs out a large breath that blows her hair around her face. "Fine." She reaches into the first bag and pulls out several lacy bras in various different colors and designs.

Now it's my turn to blush as she holds them up in front of me, smirking at the look on my face. "I needed to buy new bras to accommodate my new boobs. Do you like them?" She waggles the lingerie in my face.

I let out a gruff choking sound and take a step back. I'm a grown ass man, for fuck's sake. I shouldn't be scared of a few bras. But knowing that Cam will be wearing them makes my dick twitch.

"Very nice, Sawyer," I growl. "I'll go and put the grill on for you." I make my way out to the porch, trying desperately not to picture Cam in her new lingerie.

After a quick shower, I dress in athletic shorts and a wife beater because it's just so damn humid. Even with the air conditioner on full blast, I still have a sheen of sweat on my forehead when I reach the kitchen. The smell of citrus and mango greets me, and my stomach growls with hunger.

"It smells incredible in here."

Cam is at the counter chopping up a mango and adding it to a large bowl. I can see the tuna steaks on a plate, marinating in lime juice and chili.

"I'm really craving chili at the moment, so if it's too hot you need to say," she replies, smiling at me. She's put her long hair into a loopy bun, and she's found my Kiss the Cook apron. It swamps her lithe body, but she looks totally cute.

I laugh. "Only you would crave chili on the hottest day of the year."

She laughs as well. "Blame the baby. I'm not in control of what I can and can't eat at the moment."

"Geez, that must suck. Want me to grill the tuna?"

"Yes, please. I'll finish up the salsa and sauté the potatoes." She points her knife at me. "Don't overcook the tuna. It'll be gross otherwise."

"Yes, Captain!" I salute and grab the steaks and the tongs and head out onto the porch to cook them.

Ten minutes later, we're sitting at the dining table, and I'm eating the most delicious meal I've had in a long time. The tuna is perfectly blackened on the outside with a good kick of chili heat, and the cooling mango salsa and crunchy potatoes are perfect.

"This is fucking awesome, Sawyer." I groan, trying not to shovel the food into my mouth like a caveman.

"It's so good." Cam is literally inhaling her tuna. "I'm so hungry."

"The morning sickness is better I take it?"

"So much better." She sighs, stopping to drink her water. "I don't know if it's the fresh air, but I haven't gotten sick since I arrived. And I sure have gotten my appetite back."

I finish my last bite and sit back in my chair, taking a long draw from my glass of water. The humidity hasn't eased up even though the sun is setting and the layer of sweat on my back is making my wife beater stick uncomfortably.

"I think we need to talk about the baby," I say as Cam finishes her meal. I see her visibly swallow her food and wipe her mouth with her napkin.

Suddenly, she doesn't look as happy as she did a minute ago. In fact, she looks really uncomfortable, and I feel like a douche for ruining our lovely meal. Cam takes another drink and looks me directly in the eye—she's ready for this conversation.

"Go for it. What do you want to talk about?"

Shit, I had all these questions in my head this morning as I lay awake, and now I can't think of a single one. I must be sitting there with my mouth hanging open like the village idiot because Cam takes charge of the conversation like I've seen her do at work countless times.

"Well, if you want to talk about the baby, I have some things I'd like to discuss." Cam gets up from the table and retrieves her phone from her purse. "I've made a list; it helps me be clear."

"Of course, you have." I chuckle. That's typical Sawyer.

"Okay, so I should tell you I have a doctor's appointment next week in Seattle. It's the first ultrasound where they could tell us the due date and perhaps the sex if we want to know."

I can see she's on a roll, so I don't want to interrupt her and tell her I don't want to know the sex.

"I'm happy if you want to come or not. I don't want to disrupt your vacation …"

"I'm gonna stop you there!" I hold my hand up. "Nothing to do with the baby or you will ever disrupt anything I'm doing." I hate that she'd think that.

Cam looks down at her phone and blushes. "Okay, sorry. So, are you coming back to Seattle with me?"

"Yes. And I'd like it if you'd come back here with me after. I'd like us to tell my dad and sister together."

"Oh. Sure. I can do that." Cam looks a little freaked out. "Jesus, I totally forgot about you having to tell your family. I have no one to tell." She shrugs sadly.

Shit, there goes the wobbly chin. I know Cam's thinking about her mom and how she's not around to help her with this. I reach over and cover her hand with mine, rubbing my rough thumb over her pulse point. She looks at me with her shiny brown eyes and smiles weakly.

"I miss her so fucking much," she whispers, chewing on her lip to stop herself from crying.

"I know, baby." I can't even imagine how lonely Cam must feel sometimes.

She takes a deep cleansing breath, removes her hand from mine, and picks up her phone again. Our moment is over; Cam is back to the business at hand.

"I think we should have some kind of contract drawn up. I'm happy for you to request a paternity test. I'm sure it's the first thing Trixie will insist you do once you tell her. And we can set out all the legal stuff in the contract. You know, like who has the baby for different holidays and where the baby will live. Stuff like that. Obviously, I'll keep living in my house, so we'll have to come up with a system for sharing time. It'll be hard during the season because we'll both be travelling with the team at the same time, so I thought I'd look into hiring a nanny. We can either share the same nanny, or you can hire your own, but for consistency, it might be wise to have the same person who'll travel between our places."

Cam puts her phone down and looks at me. I'm trying to keep my face impassive, but a lot of the information she's just given leads me to the conclusion she doesn't want to be with me.

"Right. Well. You have that all sorted," I growl. "I guess I did my job as the sperm donor, so I'll just sign whatever you want me to sign, and that'll be that." I slam my napkin on the table so hard I make Cam jump. I stand up and stalk out onto the porch and down to the beach.

I don't know why I'm so angry. Cam and I were never a couple, this was an accidental pregnancy, and we're both just trying to make the best of the situation. I run my hands through my short hair and sit in the sand, the mosquitos buzzing round my head and nipping at my skin.

I feel Juneau flop down next to me, and he whines, resting his big furry head on my knee. I can't help but smile at his attempt to comfort me, so I give him a rub behind his ear and continue to gaze out at the lake. This whole situation is so fucking confusing.

"Warren?"

I look up and see Cam standing next to me, her eyes blazing, her hands on her hips. Man, she looks pissed.

"What the fuck was that?" she demands in a tight, angry voice. "You have to understand that I'm essentially a single mom. I saw how hard it was for my mom, and I'll not put myself or my baby in that position. I have to protect myself and this baby." Her hand protectively covers her belly as she glares at me.

"Protect you from what?" I growl, standing so we're face to face.

"From all the possible ways we could fuck this up," Cam cries. "We aren't together. We aren't married. That means I have no security. I need to make sure we do the best for the baby now and in the future. I don't expect you not to meet a woman you want to marry and have kids with one day. And if that happens, what about us?"

Shit, her heartfelt confession hits me hard. I haven't even considered the future. But I guess Cam has, and yet again, she doesn't see a future with me. She sees me meeting and marrying someone else, starting a family, and forgetting about her and the baby. It hurts my heart that she'd ever think I'd do that, but I can completely understand her need to protect herself. She's just being a good momma.

"I don't expect you to stop living your life just because of this situation," she adds, more gently.

I take a deep breath and rub my hand over my face. "You're the most frustrating person I've ever met. You know that, right?"

I hear Cam snort. "Right back at ya, Cap."

"I'm sorry I got angry. I know you're just protecting yourself."

I have to lay all my cards on the table and tell Cam how I feel about this; otherwise, I'll always regret it. If she shoots me down, then so be it. At least I'll know.

"Would you consider giving us a go as a couple?" I ask quietly.

"Do you want that?" Cam replies. "And not just because of the baby. Do you want me?"

How can she ask me that? Is she blind? I reach out, taking her slender hands in mine. I've never realized how delicate her hands are; her bones feel like I could crush them in mine if I hold them too tightly.

"Cam, you know how I feel about you. You've always known," I say quietly, lifting her chin so we can look into each other's eyes. "There's no way I only want you because we're going to have a baby. It's just a bonus."

"But it's such a big commitment, we won't be able to date and get to know each other like a normal couple," she replies, nibbling her bottom lip. "We would be mom and dad almost straight away, and we'd have no time to build the strong foundations of a relationship."

"C'mon, Sawyer. It's not like we're strangers who had a one-night stand. I've known you for years, and I know plenty about you. I know you love to put M&Ms in your popcorn at the movies and that you cry at nature shows. I know that you open your presents on Christmas Eve not Christmas morning because that's what you and your mom always did. I know that you have the biggest heart and have so much love to give." I press her hand to my chest so she can feel my thumping heart. "I know that the night we spent together, the night we made this baby, was the best night of my life, and I kick myself every day for not telling you all this then."

Cam's eyes are so wide that I can see the whites all around her dark irises, and her chin is wobbling again.

A tear slides down her cheek, and I reach up to wipe it away with my thumb.

"Say something, please. I'm out on a limb here, Sawyer. Don't leave me hanging." My heart is beating so hard I feel like I've just run suicides for an hour. I'm sure she can hear it as well as feel it under her palm.

"I'm so scared," Cam whispers, licking her lips nervously.

"I know, baby. But I'm not going anywhere. I'm not your douchebag father or your shitty exes. I want to be with you." I cup her sweet face in my hands and sweep my rough thumbs over her cheeks, feeling her lean into my touch.

"If we do this, Warren, we're gonna have to take it slow," she says with her usual steely determination. "I know we've slept together and made a baby, but I want us to really get to know each other in a romantic sense. I feel if we rush into this, it'll blow up in our faces."

"Whatever you want, Sawyer," I state firmly, feeling the joy rise in my chest like birds taking flight. I can't believe she's agreeing to give this a go.

I reach out and pull her against me, kissing her hair, relishing in the floral scent. "You've literally made me the happiest man alive. But I totally understand why you want to take this slow. I'll be on my best behavior. Promise."

Even as the words leave my mouth, I know keeping my hands off Cam is going to be the hardest thing I'll ever have to do in my life.

17

Cameron

It's been three of the hottest, sweatiest days I've ever experienced; however, the atmosphere in the cabin is a little tense. Now that Warren and I have agreed to try being a couple, we don't really know how to act around each other. He's been so respectful of my boundaries and hasn't tried to pressure me into getting physical, but I feel awkward around him, and I can't figure out why.

We've exchanged polite salutations and stilted conversations over dinner, but I've been so tired that I usually go to bed by sunset. Warren has thrown himself into getting the deck finished, shutting himself away in the garage and sawing his pile of timber to size. The blare of the saw and the loud rock music wakes me at dawn every day, but I don't mind. I like getting up while it's pleasantly cool to go for a run around the lake, following the trails into the forest so I can lose myself in thought.

I guess Warren and I need to go out on a proper date; it's something we've never done, so that could be a way to kickstart this relationship. I laugh at myself for being so stupid: why didn't I think about this before?

It's so obvious. We have to start this relationship from scratch and forget for a while that we've already fast-forwarded about a million steps.

This thought is just swirling round my head when I hear my name being called. I'm running past Nancy's house, and I see her standing on the deck in her robe, drinking a coffee.

"Cam! Come on over."

I come to a stop and jog over to her, wiping sweat from my face with the bottom of my tank top. It's only eight am, and it's already as sweaty as hell. I must look like a hot mess compared to Nancy who looks fresh and rested. The dark circles under my eyes make me look like I haven't slept in days.

"Hey, Nancy. What's up?" I pant, resting my foot on her step so I can stretch my hamstrings out.

"You are crazy to be running in this weather." She laughs, sipping her coffee. "And what's up with Bugs? He's been running that damn saw for days now."

I grimace and realize that it's not just me Warren's waking with his early morning sawing.

"I'm sorry Nancy. He really wants to get the deck finished. We're heading back to Seattle for a few days so he's kind of on a mission," I explain.

"Well, he could go on his mission at a reasonable time of day." She snorts. She doesn't seem too pissed. "Hey, do you wanna come over for girl's night? You know, some wine, dinner, a cheesy movie?"

Besides the wine, that actually sounds like a fun night. I've missed having Beth and Mila to talk to about stuff, so I don't want to decline her kind invitation even though I've wanted to talk to Warren about going on a date. Perhaps we can go somewhere nice when we're back in Seattle? The date night options are fairly limited in the Canadian wilderness.

"Sounds amazing. I'll bring dessert." I laugh. "What time?"

"Seven?" Nancy replies. "Anything you don't eat?"

Shit, how can I do this without giving away that I'm pregnant? "I'm not keen on shellfish or sushi."

"Steaks on the barbecue then." Nancy waves and heads back into her house. "See you later."

"Bye, hon." I jog the rest of the way back to Warren's and feel glad that Nancy seems to be turning into a friend not a threat, like I first thought when I saw her at Warren's side.

As I round the corner onto Warren's property, I don't hear the roar of the power saw, but I do hear the deep rumbling of male voices and the thwack, thwack of a nail gun. I'm curious to see what's going on, so I continue round the back of the cabin and see Warren and an older man with a bald head and a pot belly lugging large timbers onto the frame of the deck. They talk and laugh as they fire the nail gun into the wood to secure the planks into place.

"This is coming along well," I say when there's a break in the noise.

Both men startle a little and turn to face me—the older man smiling kindly, but Warren's eyes take in every inch of exposed sweaty skin, and I suddenly feel even hotter. It makes my heart stutter in my chest; he looks hungry for me.

"Hey there, darlin'," the man says. "I'm Larry. Here to help this one get the deck finished." Larry takes his thick glove off and extends it to shake my hand.

"Hi, I'm Cam. Warren's … friend from Seattle."

Larry's eyebrows shoot up his forehead, and he gives Warren a confused look. "Oh, I'm sorry. I thought you were Bugs' girlfriend."

"Larry, for fuck's sake," Warren growls, shaking his head.

"What? You have a beautiful woman here. What else am I supposed to think?" Larry cackles.

"Nice to meet you, Larry," I say. "Warren, I'm going to Nancy's for dinner tonight, so I won't be around. Our flight is at three pm tomorrow, right?"

"Yeah, that's right," Warren replies, still looking at me like I'm his next meal.

"Okay, well I'll see you later." I wave at Larry. The men go back to their work, and I rush into the house to shower. I quickly strip off my sweaty running clothes and throw them in the hamper. I really should do some laundry before we leave tomorrow. As I've taken to doing recently, I stand naked in front of the full-length mirror and run my hands over my swollen breasts and wince a little. They're still so tender that I can hardly touch them. My hands then trail down my torso and rest on my stomach. This is almost week thirteen, and I'm positive my stomach is starting to pop out a little; when I run my hands over it, I feel the gentle slope out and in that wasn't there before.

It still amazes me that soon my belly will be massive and swollen with the baby that's growing inside me. A baby that is so wanted by me but is coming into such a fragile situation. I feel the sting of tears in my nose, and I cover my face with my hands.

God, I'm so scared. I know I agreed to try things with Warren, but the pain of my past is still so fresh in my heart. I hitch in a strangled sob and let the tears roll down my cheeks. I allow myself a few minutes to indulge in my pity party, then I swipe the tears away and look at myself in the mirror.

"You are a strong, independent woman, Cameron Sawyer. Your mom didn't raise a cry baby, and if she was here now, she'd tell you to get a grip and get your stinky ass in the shower."

Despite everything, I smile. I can hear my mom's voice clear as day in my head, and it offers me some comfort as I do what she says and get my stinky ass in the shower.

I'm working in the office on my laptop, answering several emails from agents and Don. He's sent me some amazing photographs from his vacation in Australia, my favorite being him holding a koala and looking deeply uncomfortable. It makes me snort with laughter to see him standing like a stiff statue while the animal clings to his very expensive Prada shirt. I'm sure he did it for his kids, and that makes me smile.

"What's so funny?"

I turn and see Warren standing in the doorway, filling it with his large body, holding onto the top of the door frame so his shirt rides up and gives me a sneaky peek at his rippling abs. I feel the heat spreading across my lower belly as I flood with arousal, and I silently curse my traitorous hormones.

"Just some photos of Don on his vacation." I laugh, beckoning him over so he can see. "He's in an amorous embrace with a marsupial."

Warren comes and stands behind me, and I'm immediately enveloped by the scent of his body wash and his hard-earned sweat. My arousal ramps up a hundred percent, and I attempt to hold my breath. Why the hell can't I control these feelings? My mind is telling me to be sensible and take it slow, but my body keeps screaming at me to let him touch me, kiss me, lick me, and fuck me.

His deep, rumbling chuckle brings me back. "That's one for the locker room." He laughs, pointing at the koala picture.

"Oh my god. Don't you dare share these with the team. He'll never trust me again," I scold, nudging him with my elbow.

I feel his hand rest on my shoulder, squeezing it gently. "Are you excited for the ultrasound?"

I reach up and squeeze his fingers. "I'm so excited but also a little freaked out. It's supposed to be a magical moment, seeing our baby for the first time, but what if there's something wrong?"

"It will be magical, and we're both young and healthy. I'm positive everything will be perfect." He takes a deep breath in. "I've arranged a meeting with Trixie while we're in Seattle, so we can start the process of getting this contract set up."

I'm shocked that he's agreeing to the contract. He seemed so angered by it the other night, but I must admit I feel a sense of relief that at least that's one thing we agree on.

I spin around in the office chair and stand up, putting my arms around his waist for a hug. "Thank you for understanding that I need the contact," I say, resting my cheek against his chest, finding comfort in the strong, steady beat of his heart. "I know we've going to give this relationship a go, but I'd still feel safer with everything to do with the baby in writing."

To my relief, I feel his arms wrap around me, his chin resting on my head. "Of course, I understand, Sawyer."

"Thank you," I sigh, enjoying the warmth of his embrace.

"Hey, aren't you supposed to be going to Nancy's for dinner?" Warren mumbles into my hair.

I look over the clock on the shelf—it's ten to seven. Shit! I totally lost track of time.

"Damn it!" I curse, pulling free of Warren's arms and running upstairs to change into my favorite summer dress. It's still humid and sweaty, the air is thick, and the clouds are dark and full of rain. I pray it rains soon so this heat wave breaks.

Bugs

"Bye! I won't be late," Cam calls as she dashes through the kitchen on her way to have dinner with my neighbor.

"Take an umbrella from the mud room. It's gonna rain," I shout from my place on the couch.

"Okay." I hear her shuffling around in the closet, then the back door slams as she leaves.

I breathe out a sigh of relief—not that she's gone—but that I have some time to myself to process everything. I called Trixie while Cam was out on one of her runs, telling her I needed a meeting while I'm back in Seattle. She asked me what it was about, but I decided to keep that information to myself until I saw her in person. I know how Trixie has a tendency to be dramatic, and I didn't want her screeching obscenities down the phone at me.

While I'm deciding what to eat for dinner, I check the time and decide to give Matt a call in Florida. It should only be ten pm there now, so hopefully he's free to talk. I know from Cam that Mila and Beth know about the baby, so I have an inkling that Matt and Nate know as well. I know Matt has some experience with pregnancy, and I hope he's got some advice for me.

As I click on his number and put the phone on speaker, I grab a beer from the fridge and settle back on the couch with Juneau.

"Hey, man. What's up?" Matt answers after a few rings. He sounds a little breathless. Ugh, I hope I didn't interrupt him and Mila in bed.

"Oh, you know. The usual," I say. "Making progress with the deck, swimming in the lake, found out I'm gonna be a dad. Just your average summer."

I hear Matt huff out a breath. "Cam told you then."

"Yep, hit me right out of left field," I reply. "She's decided to keep it, and we're gonna try the co-parenting thing."

Matt's quiet for a beat. "Co-parenting? So, you aren't gonna try a relationship?"

Now it's my turn to be quiet while I wonder how to explain everything that's gone down between Cam and me.

"Sort of." The words hang in the air. "We've agreed that we want to be a couple, but since then … nothing. She said she wants to take things slow, but this thing is moving at a snail's pace. Obviously, I don't wanna pressure her. I don't know what to do about it."

"How do you feel about taking it slow?" Matt asks.

I scrub my hand down my face and stare at the phone. "It fucking sucks, man. You know how I feel about Cam, even before the baby. I just want our life to start together, but I don't know what move to make next."

"Don't take it personally, Bugs. Mila told me about Cam's background, and it sounds like she's been on her own for a real long time," he replies. "That kind of independence is hard to give up, especially when you think people will eventually leave."

"But I have no intention of leaving her or the baby," I growl.

"Hey, I know that!" Matt growls back. "But perhaps Cam just needs time to see that you're all she needs. That you're in this for the long haul, for her and the baby."

"I guess. So, you're saying I just need to be patient, and she'll come around."

"No, you dick." Matt laughs. "If it was that easy, she'd be yours already. You need to work your ass off to prove that you're worthy of being her man."

Suddenly I feel like an idiot. I thought my intentions would be enough to make Cam mine. I forgot there would be more work involved. I have to prove to her I can be a good partner and a good father.

"Thanks dude. I needed to hear that." I laugh. "Jesus, I'm an idiot."

"No, you're just a man who thinks the woman of your dreams will fall at your feet."

"Fuck you, Landon."

"Fuck you back, Cap." Matt chuckles. "Are you good?"

At this moment, I really miss my Whalers brothers. "Yeah, I'm good. When are you back in Seattle?"

"Tomorrow. Coach has some things he needs Mila for, so we're flying back," he replies.

"Cool. Cam and I will be back in Seattle for a few days, so perhaps we can meet for a beer," I offer. "I know Nate's back in town for a while before he goes to Oklahoma."

"Sounds like a plan. Hit me up when you're back, and we'll arrange something. Now go woo that girl of yours."

I chuckle again and hang up. I realize I need to come up with a game plan to make Cam mine.

Cameron

"Are you sure you don't want any wine?" Nancy offers again. "I feel like a total alcoholic over here."

We've been sitting in her blissfully air-conditioned enclosed porch for most of the evening, eating steaks and cheesecake and getting to know each other. I found out that Nancy is recently divorced and works in publishing in Vancouver. She came out to the lake for the summer to finish her novel and get away from her toxic ex who still refuses to move out of their marital home.

"He's such an enormous D-bag. He's the one who cheated, yet I'm the one who has to stay with her parents until we can sell the house," she grumbles. "The housing market is in the toilet, so it's taking forever to sell."

Nancy is being so open and honest with me that I feel bad for keeping my secret. But I feel that until we tell Warren's family, it's not fair to tell someone I hardly know.

"I'm fine with the soda. Thanks." I check the time and hear the first rumble of thunder in the distance. "In fact, I should probably head back before the storm hits."

I go to stand up and Nancy rises as well. "Sure thing. But before you go, can I ask you something?"

"Of course."

"Are you and Bugs … you know, a thing?" She plays with the frayed hem of her jean shorts and casts her eyes down, looking a little embarrassed at her question.

Shit, this is an impossible situation. I have no idea where we stand, so how can I explain it to another person?

"It's complicated. That's all I can say at the moment," I reply, shrugging my shoulders apologetically. "I'm sorry."

Nancy waves her hand dismissively. "Oh, don't worry about it. I thought I'd ask. It's not every day you get to spend the summer living next to a hot man mountain like Bugs."

I laugh and shake my head. I'm not blind. I know Warren is a very attractive sexy man, but hearing him described like that is just so weird.

I hug Nancy goodbye, and we agree to go shopping together once I get back from Seattle, then I grab my umbrella and head out.

The wind is blowing strongly, whipping the trees around as I dash across the yard toward Warren's place. Suddenly there's a huge clap of thunder, a flash of lightning that illuminates the night, and the heavens open. It's the kind of rain that soaks to the bone immediately, and I let out a squeal as the cold rain drenches my dress and hair. It happens so quickly I don't even have time to put the umbrella up as I sprint as fast as I can toward the back door of Warren's cabin.

I finally make it inside, ripping open the screen door and stumbling in, dripping rainwater all over the tile floor.

"Fuck!" I mutter, my teeth chattering. The temperature has dropped, and now that I'm soaked to my underwear, I feel the chill in the air. Another loud clap of thunder makes me jump out of my skin.

I hate thunderstorms.

When I was a little girl, I'd always crawl into bed with my mom when one happened in the middle of the night. She'd hold me tight and stroke my hair, telling me stories about the cloud people who made the thunder. She described them so beautifully that I'd soon forget I was scared and fall asleep. Unfortunately, the fear I feel during storms still grips me, but I have to try to soothe myself. Usually I hide under my blanket, put my earbuds in, and listen to an audiobook.

I realize it's late, and the house is dark; Warren must be in bed. I don't want to drip water all through his house, so I whip my dress off and dump it in the dryer in the mud room. Slipping off my sandals, I creep up the stairs, but just before I reach the upstairs landing another huge clap of thunder and flash of lightning strikes, and I let out a blood curdling scream.

"What the fuck?" Warren's door flies open, and suddenly we're face to face in the dark hallway. I realize I'm standing in my underwear which, thanks to the rain, is almost transparent, and I see that Warren is only wearing a pair of dangerously low-slung pajama pants.

"Sorry. The thunder scared me." I gasp, my hands trying desperately to cover my breasts and crotch. I know that my nipples are rock hard and straining against the fabric of my bra, and it's embarrassing that it's not only down to the wet cold material.

"Why the fuck are you naked?" he growls, his eyes devouring my body in a way that makes my skin flush hot.

"I'm not naked," I breathe as a flash of lightning illuminates the hall, and I see his hungry stare. He licks his lips and devours me with his eyes.

Quicker than I can comprehend, Warren closes the distance between us in two long strides and cages me in against the wall. The heat from his body warms me and gives me goosebumps at the same time, and the feel of his breath on my neck makes my pussy ache.

"You look pretty fucking naked to me, Sawyer." He runs his nose up my neck. He seems to be breathing me in, and god help me, I feel the same need to have him inside me as I had that night at the party.

"I … I got wet," I stammer, tilting my head to the side to allow him more access to the skin on my neck. It's a major erogenous zone for me, especially when Warren grazes his scruff across it.

He chuckles gruffly against my skin and brings one of his big hands to my hip, holding me possessively. "I bet you did."

"No, not like that." I sigh as his lips replace his nose and he begins to plant soft, wet kisses along my collarbone. "I mean the rain. I got caught in the rain."

I press my hands weakly against Warren's firm pecs to try to get some distance between us, but it's like trying to move a tree. His insistent lips are working their magic, and I can feel my resolve disappearing with each firm press.

"Warren," I plead. "We agreed to take it slow."

"Fuck slow," he moans against my skin. "Stay with me tonight. Let me show you what we can be like together."

I'm incapable of words at this point, and all I can do is nod my agreement against his shoulder, and before I know it, his hands grab my ass, and I'm lifted against his hard body. He crushes his lips to mine, and I wrap my legs around his waist as he carries me into his room, kicking the door shut behind us.

I know this is dangerous. I know this contradicts everything we said, but I can't seem to control the urge to feel his lips on me and his hard cock inside me again. As our tongues slide together, I grind my needy pussy against his abs and moan into his mouth. It's a riot of sensation, and my body has never felt like this during sex. I've never felt so sensitive to touch, and it feels like all the blood in my body has pooled between my legs.

Warren sits down on the edge of his huge bed with me on his lap, and I clearly feel the hard ridge of his dick pressing against my center as I grind on him shamelessly. My wet hair clings to my shoulders, so Warren gathers it in his fist and angles my head to deepen the kiss, his other hand unhooking my bra like a pro. Such a smooth move—it reminds me of our first night together.

"Oh fuck, Cam. You feel so good grinding on my cock," he growls as his lips trail down my neck, and he slips the straps of my bra down my arms, flinging the damp garment onto the floor.

I hear him take a sharp breath in as he catches sight of my breasts in the next flash of lightning. My large brown nipples are pulled tight, and they're aching for his lips, tongue, and teeth which surprises me because of how sensitive they've been lately.

"You want me to suck those nipples, baby?" he asks as I arch toward him, desperate for some sort of contact.

"Oh god, yes," I whimper.

"I got you." And with those words I feel his soft lips close over one of my nipples, and it's like I've gone to heaven. Or at least a dirty version of heaven where the angels are huge, muscular hockey players with dirty mouths and hard dicks. His tongue works my nipple into a turgid peak, then he runs it across my chest to lavish the other one with the same treatment.

The pleasure is building in my lower belly as Warren continues to gently suck my nipples, and I feel like if he doesn't touch my pussy soon, I'll implode. Keeping one hand gripping Warren's huge bicep, I grab his wrist and slip his fingers into my damp panties where they search through my curls, finding my swollen clit. It's so desperate for attention that just one circle with his fingertip almost has me shooting off Warren's lap.

"Easy there, baby," he moans, tightening his grip on my ass. He suddenly stands and turns, depositing me on the bed, dropping to his knees and dragging me to the edge, spreading my legs.

I gasp and fling my arm over my face as Warren hooks his fingers into the edge of my panties, dragging them down my legs. He's going so slowly I want to scream at him to hurry up. I let out a little growl of frustration and wiggle my hips to let him know I need him to get a move on.

All I get in response is a throaty chuckle and the whisper of his breath on the inside of my thigh.

"So impatient, Sawyer." Warren sighs as he begins to kiss up the inside of my thigh toward his goal, holding my hips firmly to limit my ability to squirm.

"I am! You have no idea how horny I've been," I whine, lifting up on my elbows so I can look down at him, his eyes glistening in the low light of the room. I've almost completely forgotten about the storm raging outside, and I'm only concerned with the storm raging between my legs. "Please," I beg.

With a wicked smile, Warren lowers his head and sweeps his tongue from my entrance up to my clit where he works it using tight little circles. I can't help the strangled moan of pleasure that escapes me, and I reach down to grab his short hair, holding his face between my legs.

It's like I'm super-charged with erotic energy because I'm close to coming quicker than I ever have before, and soon I'm literally humping Warren's face and tongue, chasing my orgasm. My thighs clamp down on his ears, and I feel him suck my clit between his teeth as I find my release. My back arches and my thighs squeeze tighter. I'm probably suffocating him right now, but I can't stop.

"Oh god," I moan as my thighs finally release their death grip on his head, and he sits back on his haunches, wiping my cum from his lips and licking his fingers clean. It's the most erotic thing I've ever seen, and it makes my swollen pussy throb with continued desire.

Swiftly, Warren stands and rids himself of his pajama pants, which are doing nothing to hide his enormous erection. As he pulls them down, his cock springs free, and I suddenly have a rush of memories of what it feels like in my mouth and in my pussy.

"Are you ready, baby?" he asks, kneeling on the bed beside me, kissing me deeply, sharing the taste of my climax on his tongue.

"Yes, I'm so ready!" I gasp. Warren leans over and opens his nightstand drawer. "What are you doing?"

"I need a condom. There's definitely some in here somewhere." He continues to rummage around, and I can't help but giggle. "What's so funny?"

"Don't you think it's a bit late for that? I'm already knocked up."

Warren stops searching and turns to look at me, his eyes dark pools of desire. "I'm trying to respect you, Sawyer. It would be presumptuous to expect to fuck you bare just because you're pregnant."

At that moment, I remember why Warren is such a good man and such an amazing friend. He's kind and caring and always thinks about other people. I feel my chest swell with an unfamiliar feeling of love, a love that feels much more than friendship.

"I trust you, Warren. I've only had sex with you since Richard and because he cheated, I got a test. I know the organization tests you guys regularly, so if you're clean ..." I trail off my sentence when his eyes become impossibly wide, and he fists his hard cock, giving it a few rough pulls.

"I've never fucked anyone bare before," he admits, looking like all his Christmases have come at once.

"I trust you," I repeat, laying back on the bed and reaching out my hand to him.

Warren slams the drawer shut, then he's on top of me, kissing me hard as I grab at his shoulders and ass, feeling the hard-earned muscles reflexing under his skin. He positions himself between my legs, and I feel the smooth head of his cock notch at my wet entrance.

We both gasp as he slides the first few inches into me; the delicious stretch makes me angle my hips to take more and more. Warren sets a slow pace of pulling out and sliding in a little farther until I can't help but dig my nails into his ass, thrusting my hips up to take him all at once.

"Oh Jesus. That's so tight," he groans into my neck, holding himself still for a moment, his weight on his forearms so he doesn't crush me. I think he's almost afraid to move.

"Warren, you're not gonna break me or hurt the baby. I need you to fuck me hard. Please."

He lifts his head and kisses me tenderly. "Anything for you, baby."

With that, he hitches my leg up to increase the depth of his penetration, and he starts to roll his hips against me. Each thrust is deep and hard, just like I asked for, and his pelvic bone is rubbing against my clit in the most delicious way. Again, it feels like everything is super-charged, and I build quicker and higher than I ever have, joining Warren's thrusts like we've been doing this for years.

"Your pussy feels so good, baby," he groans as I feel his dick begin to swell farther inside me. "But I need you to come for me. Tell me what you need."

"Your finger ... on my clit." I gasp as Warren rolls and flips us so I'm on top. He keeps one hand firmly on my hip, keeping up the pace he's set as he puts a finger from his other hand in his mouth to wet it. I watch him open mouthed as I continue to bounce on his dick, pressing his slick digit to my sensitive bundle of nerves.

"Oh god, that's the spot," I cry, thrusting my hips against his cock and his finger, pushing my hands down onto his hard abs to help myself bounce up and down.

"Do it, baby. Come for me. Come all over my cock," Warren growls and his filthy words push me over the edge, making my pussy throb and ripple, milking his dick. I throw my head back and squeeze my eyes shut, riding the high, gasping his name.

After three more deep thrusts that just help prolong my climax, Warren follows me over, arching his hips up and groaning through his release. Once my body relaxes, I flop down onto his slick chest, the patch of hair between his pecs tickling my cheek. I feel totally spent and relaxed, Warren's fingers tracing circles on the damp skin of my back.

I can feel his heart racing under my cheek, and his cock slips out of me as I slide off him, snuggling into the crook of his arm.

"Do you need a damp cloth or some water?" he mumbles, pulling me close, nuzzling my hair.

"No. Don't move." I sigh, squeezing my arms tightly around his muscular body. I want to hold onto the moment for as long as I can before the awkward post-sex conversations start.

A distant rumble of thunder makes my body shudder, and I squeeze my eyes closed, burrowing deeper into Warren's side.

"I can't believe you're still afraid of thunderstorms." He chuckles, stroking my hair.

"Don't make fun of me," I whine, lightly swatting his sweaty chest.

Quickly, Warren grabs my wrist and pulls me on top of him, making me squeak in surprise. "I'm not," he states firmly. "It just feels good to be needed. That's all."

I look into his eyes in the darkness. "What do you mean?" I ask, my stomach tangling in knots.

"I want you to be able to rely on me, baby. I don't want you to ever be afraid to ask for anything you need." He reaches up and tucks a strand of damp hair behind my ear. It's such an intimate gesture, and I feel a tightening in my chest.

I bite my lower lip and avert my eyes. I know if Warren sees the need in them, we'll be going for round two before I know it. So instead, I push up off him and sit on the edge of the bed with my back to him. I grab one of his discarded T-shirts from the chair by his bed and pull it over my head. I know I've only got to go across the hall, but it feels weird walking around his house naked.

"Did I do something wrong?" he asks from behind me.

I stand and retrieve my underwear from the floor. "No. I think it's best if I sleep in the other room. We have a long day tomorrow, and I get stupidly tired these days."

I see the hurt look in Warren's eyes as he pulls the blanket over his naked body and reaches for his phone to set his alarm. "If you're sure. I promise to behave if you stay."

I'm so tempted to rip off the T-shirt that has Warren's scent all over it and jump back into bed with him, but I must have my sensible head on.

"I should go," I repeat firmly. "But this was wonderful." I smile and quietly leave, literally holding my breath until I'm safely in my room, letting it out in a huge huff. Leaning against the door, I close my eyes and lightly bang the back of my head against the wood.

So much for taking it slow.

19

Bugs

I t feels good to be back in Seattle. Even though I love being at home in Canada, Seattle has so many great memories for me that I consider it my second hometown. After a hot cramped flight where Cam spends most of the time locked in the bathroom heaving up her breakfast, we make it back to her house. I want to go to my place, but Cam insists on checking on her neighbor who's been looking after her cat, so that turns out to be our first stop. Luckily, the kid who lives a few cabins down agreed to feed and walk Juneau for me while I'm away, so I didn't need to put him in the kennel.

"Oh, Gatsby's been as good as gold," her elderly neighbor, Mrs. Sullivan, says as Cam fusses with her disinterested looking moggy.

"Thank you so much for feeding him, Olive. I'm happy to check him into the kennel for the rest of the time I'm away," Cam replies, reaching up to a high shelf for a tub of treats. Suddenly, the cat seems very interested and starts circling round her bare legs, making a weird yowling noise. I'm definitely not a cat person; to be honest, they freak me out. I never know what they're thinking, and this one seems particularly sneaky.

"No, no. I love our daily cuddles. It's no bother." Mrs. Sullivan gives me a quick look. "And who might this strong looking fellow be?"

"Oh, I'm sorry. This is Warren. My ... friend," Cam says quickly, dropping some of the cat's treats into its dish.

Mrs. Sullivan's grey eyebrows rise up her forehead, and she smiles. "Well, it's nice to see you with a young man at last."

Both Cam and I smirk at her remark, and I think it's cute that she's looking out for Cam.

"Um, we have an appointment to get to, but I'll be back later." Cam giggles, giving her cat one more stroke. "I notice he's running low on kibble, so I'll pick some up while we're out."

"Of course, dear. Have a good day." Mrs. Sullivan gives us both a knowing smile and heads out the back door toward her own house.

"She seems like fun." I laugh, rubbing my face where my beard is starting to grow in again.

"Yeah, she's so lovely. Her husband died just before I moved in, and she was kind of lonely. She came round my first night with a basket of homemade muffins, and she won me over." Cam laughs. "Olive loves Gatsby, and she always feeds him when I travel. It's so much better than putting him in the kennel."

"That's great." I look at my watch. "Shouldn't we go?"

"Shit. Look at the time. I need to quickly freshen up. I've still got puke breath." Cam grimaces and dashes upstairs.

An hour later, we're at the doctor's office, and I feel like I'm about to stroke out at any minute. I can't believe I'm about to see our baby for the first time; it's a total head fuck.

Cam is laying on the examination table with her shirt pushed up and one of those paper sheets tucked into her panties, exposing her slightly rounded stomach. I noticed it last night when I ran my hands over her body. She seems more luscious and curvy than before—her hips and belly are softer, and her breasts have definitely changed.

"Are you okay?" she asks, disrupting my pervy thoughts. I look over at her and realize all the fantasizing about her body has given me a semi, so I discreetly adjust myself and reach out to hold her hand.

"Yeah. Just excited," I mumble.

"Well, you look kind of horny." Cam giggles just as the doctor comes in.

"Hey there, kids," he says cheerfully. "I'm Dr. Aguilar. You must be the father." He reaches out his hand, and we shake.

"Yes, I'm Warren Parker."

"Oh, I know who you are." The doctor chuckles, opening his white lab coat, displaying a Whalers T-shirt. "Life long card carrying super fan right here."

"Well, at least I know we'll get great service." I laugh. "I'm pretty sure I'll hook you up with lifetime season tickets if we get a happy, healthy mom and baby at the end of all this."

"Deal!" We high five, and I hear Cam huff out an exasperated breath. "Anyway, back to the most important people in the room: mommy and baby. How are you feeling, Cameron? Is the morning sickness any better?"

As Cam describes her sickness and other issues in graphic, stomach-churning detail, the doc takes her blood pressure and types notes into his iPad.

"Okay, then. That's all perfectly normal for about thirteen weeks along. The sickness will ease up but keep trying to eat as healthily as you can when you can." Dr. Aguilar begins to fiddle with the machine next to Cam, and I feel my gut tightening. This is it. I'm going to see our baby for the first time. I don't think I've ever been this nervous about anything in my life. It might sound corny, but this is a life-changing moment.

He squeezes some gel onto Cam's stomach, and she grimaces slightly. "Oh, I expected it to be cold," she huffs.

"Those days are long gone. We warm it now." He laughs, reaching for the probe, pressing it firmly into the gel on Cam's belly, spreading it around.

Her grip on my hand gets tighter, and again I get that amazing feeling, the feeling that she needs me, and it makes my heart swell against my ribs.

Dr. Aguilar begins to press some buttons on the machine. Suddenly the room fills with the rapid, pulsing thump of our baby's heartbeat, and I swear to god, my own heart stops beating for a second. I hear Cam's suck in her breath, and her eyes fill with tears.

"Oh my god, is that the heart?" She gasps, looking between me and the doc.

"That's your baby with a good strong heartbeat," he replies, still moving the probe around.

"It's really fast," I grumble. "Is that normal?"

"Perfectly normal. About one hundred and sixty beats per minute."

"Fuck, that's like me after a shift." I laugh, and I see Cam frown at my use of the F-word in front of the doctor.

He only laughs and turns the monitor around so we can see it. "And here's your baby."

This time, my heart does completely stop, and my vision blurs with tears. The screen is black and white, and I'm not really sure what the fuck I'm looking at, but it's the most beautiful thing I've ever laid eyes on. The doc is explaining what everything is, and I can see Cam listening intently as tears roll down her cheeks. I reach out to sweep them away, and she smiles brightly, despite the tears, looking so beautiful I just want to devour her lips right now.

"Do you have any questions?" Dr. Aguilar asks, and I look up at him dumbly.

"Huh?" I quickly sweep my hand down my face; it wouldn't be cool for the doc to see me blubbering like a pussy.

"Do you have any questions about the scan?" he repeats kindly. He must have a lot of dumb-struck fathers-to-be in his office.

"Uh, no. Yes. I mean, everything's normal, right?"

"Yes, the baby is healthy and a good size for the end of the first trimester," Dr. Aguilar explains. "Cam's done a great job keeping herself healthy, and the baby is cooking along nicely."

"Can you tell us the due date?" Cam asks as the doc fiddles with the machine and starts to print off some pictures of the scan. "It's kind of important we have the date, you know, for our schedules."

"Of course. It really helps that you gave me an exact date of conception." I see Cam's cheeks turn bright red at his comment, and I can't help but smirk into my hand. "So, I would say you guys are going to have yourselves a Christmas baby. I'd put the due date between the fifteenth and twentieth of December."

"My birthday is the eighteenth, so that would be cool," I say, feeling a thrill at the possibility that my kid will share my birthday.

Dr. Aguilar wipes the gel from Cam's stomach and collects the pictures he just printed. "Why don't you get dressed and we can talk more in my office?" He smiles and leaves through the adjoining door to his office, leaving Cam and me alone.

"I'm fucking speechless," she blurts, her smile still lighting up her face.

It makes me laugh because her reaction to my F-bomb earlier was to frown, but now she's dropping her own. I can't really blame her. This whole experience is taking my fucking breath away.

"It's so amazing, Sawyer," I whisper, cupping her damp cheek, leaning down to kiss her lips softly. I don't mean it to, but the kiss soon deepens, and when Cam's tongue touches mine, I moan into her mouth.

I finally pull away, cupping her face and running my thumbs over her plump bottom lip. I have to stop this kiss because if I don't, I'm likely to embarrass us both by fucking her on this exam table. I rest my forehead against hers, both of us breathing heavily.

"Warren, we should go before they send in a search party," Cam says softly, and I know she's right. I stand and pull the curtain round, so she can get dressed, then we head through the door to speak more to Dr. Aguilar.

Cameron

"Oh my god! Your tits are enormous." Beth gasps when I open the door to her and Mila. She pulls me across the threshold into a hug, squishing said tits painfully against hers.

"Ow, they're really tender, Bee. Take it easy," I squeal, squirming out of her arms, but accepting a kiss on the cheek from her and then Mila as they stomp past me into the house.

"Well, they look fucking fantastic." She laughs. "I bet Bugs loves them."

So that's how this evening is going to go? I follow the girls into the kitchen where they immediately start emptying their bags, unpacking a couple of bottles of champagne and a bottle of fruity fizzy water for me.

After the scan, Warren and I went for a bite to eat, then I drove him back to his place, so he could check the house and get ready for the guys to come over. We decided that he needs some guy time, and I need a girl's night, so we can catch up and share our news properly.

Warren's seeing Trixie in the morning to discuss everything, and I'm going to spend some time at home, doing laundry and packing some fresh clothes for the rest of my time at the cabin. I have two more weeks of my vacation time left, and I intend to spend them with Warren trying to figure out how to become a couple. I hope my girls will have some advice on how I can go about that.

The loud pop of a cork makes me jump as Mila pours two glasses of fizz, and Beth fixes me a glass of fizzy water. I've already ordered the pizza which should be here any minute.

"Here's to Cameron and little Bam Bam," Beth says, handing me my drink and raising her glass. "It may not have been the ideal way to go about it, but I'm so happy for you, babe."

We clink glasses. "Bam Bam?" I smirk, remembering the character from *The Flintstones* cartoon.

Beth takes a huge gulp of her champagne. "Yeah, you know—Bugs and Cam. Bam Bam. I think it's awesome." She looks ridiculously pleased with herself.

Just then, the doorbell rings announcing the arrival of the pizza, so I go to collect it while the girls get the napkins and plates ready on the coffee table.

I'm just about to devour a slice of spicy pepperoni when Beth says, "You need to start dishing the dirt, Cam."

"Jesus, can't I eat first? Morning sickness really sucks, and at the moment I'm starving, so please let me have a slice of pizza before it comes back."

"Leave her alone, Bee." Mila elbows Beth in the ribs and smiles apologetically at me.

"What? It's okay for you to keep interrupting my very sexy vacation with Nate, but I can't ask her how things are with the baby and more importantly Bugs?"

I throw my half-eaten slice back on to my plate and take a sip of water. "Fine. I'll tell you everything. I can always reheat the pizza." I wipe my greasy hands on a napkin and promptly fill the girls in on what's happened since I left for Canada.

Obviously, Beth knows everything that happened up to the point we had our conversation on the phone, but as I recount the night Warren and I discussed our future and then what happened during the storm, they both drop their slices and lean forward to listen intently. Mila's eyes get so wide when I tell her that Warren and I had sex, I think they're going to drop out of the sockets.

Beth shrieks with glee at the news and raises her glass again, but neither Mila nor I think that it's worth toasting, so we leave her hanging, laughing at her pouty look of disappointment.

"So, what now?" Mila asks. I know she's a hopeless romantic and just wants everyone to be as happy as her and Matt.

"It seems so easy to say we'll be a couple, but it's been a little weird. It's almost like we don't know how to act around each other," I reply.

"I get that, Cam. I really do, but you guys need to get yourself out on some dates. You both need to fully commit to getting to know each other as more than friends and stop just fucking each other's brains out," Beth states, tactful as ever.

Her bluntness makes me laugh, but I realize she's right. Bugs and I need to start seeing each other as romantic partners, not best friends.

"I need help," I plead. "Please help me with this."

Beth leaps to her feet. "We need more champagne and a pen and paper. It's time to make a plan." She dashes off to the kitchen to get the fizz, and I reach into the drawer under my coffee table for the pen and legal pad I keep there.

"I really appreciate this." I sigh, handing Mila the pad when she motions for it. "I'm so terrible at dating."

"You're just out of practice. That's all," Beth replies as she returns and refills the glasses with champagne and water. "Nate gave me a real education in dating, so I'm here for you, babe. Just call me the Love Doctor."

Mila and I laugh loudly as Beth snatches the pad and pen and begins to frantically scribble her ideas down.

An hour later, the girls have made a dent in the second bottle of champagne, I've had to pee about a million times, and we have a decent list of ideas for dates and seductions I can use on Warren when we're back at the cabin.

"I'm not sure how comfortable I am skinny dipping with him in the lake." I giggle, reading through the list. "It's cold and it's not very private."

Mila and Beth snigger at my comment, and I feel my cheeks flush at the memories of how he took me last night.

"Well, when the deck is finished, you'll have to christen the hot tub instead." Beth cocks her eyebrow, and I roll my eyes at her naughty suggestion.

However, the thought of it causes a sexy tingle to dance up my spine.

"Gotta love our hockey boys and their stamina." Mila sighs a little drunkenly, and I know it's probably time we call it a night.

20

Bugs

My head feels like it's trapped in a vise which is slowly being squeezed tighter and tighter. The sun is streaming through my window because obviously I was too hammered last night to close the drapes. Thank god I made it to my room at least.

I crack open my sleep gummed eyes and groan loudly at the monster hangover that's just hit me like a puck to the temple. Damn that bottle of Jack. And the beer and the cigars that Matt brought to toast the fact that I'm going to become a father.

As I try to roll away from the sunlight, my stomach heaves and I flop out of bed, only just making it to the bathroom before I puke my guts up into the sink. When I'm done, I swill my mouth with water from the faucet and check my reflection in the mirror. Jesus, I look like hammered shit. I reach into the shower and turn the water on, stripping out of my boxer briefs to stand under the scolding spray. Initially, it hurts every cell of my body, but as I relax into it, I begin to feel slightly more human.

The smell of coffee and bacon greets me as I head downstairs, and I'm thrilled to find Nate at the stove, looking only slightly less hungover than me. I guess there are advantages to being twenty-one. I don't know what Thor's excuse is for being so fucking chirpy.

"Morning," Thor says in his cheerful Swedish accent, stuffing strips of crispy bacon into his mouth from a platter of scrambled eggs and slices of toast.

I grunt back at him and pour myself a coffee from the pot, taking it black this morning to help with my pounding headache. My stomach feels slightly less queasy, so hopefully the food will either kill or cure.

"Who's making all the fucking noise out here?" Matt growls as he shuffles into the kitchen, looking the worst of all of us. His feet are bare, his clothes are crumpled, his hair is all over the place, and he has creases down his face from sleeping on the couch cushions.

"I'm cooking breakfast for you old guys." Nate chuckles, tipping the last of the fluffy scrambled eggs onto the platter. I wrinkle my nose at the smell and continue to nurse my coffee.

"Fuck you, kid." Matt groans, fixing his own coffee and joining us at the counter. "I hope you two feel as bad as I do."

I swallow some coffee and wait for it to hit my stomach before I answer. "Worse probably. Whose idea was the whiskey?"

Matt nods at Thor who's wearing a huge shit-eating grin while he piles bacon, eggs, and wheat toast onto his plate, covering the whole lot in hot sauce. My stomach heaves again, but I swallow down the bile, grabbing a piece of toast to get myself started.

"I believe you broke out the bourbon, man." Nate chuckles, shoveling his breakfast into his mouth. "I tried to call it a night, but you guys wanted to plow on 'til dawn if I remember rightly. I ended up leaving you to it when Beth called for a goodnight kiss."

I hold my head in my hands and groan, flashes of the night coming back to me. I remember it starting with steaks on the grill and beers, then we played poker and pool while taking shots of tequila. And as talk turned to my impending fatherhood, the cigars and whiskey came out, followed by slurred advice and questions about the state of my relationship with Cameron.

"I've got a missed call from Red," Matt mutters, looking at his cell and chewing on a strip of salty bacon. "She's gonna be pissed at how drunk I got. I didn't even make it to bed." He cracks his neck and grimaces, wobbling his head from side to side.

"You guys are so whipped." Thor snorts, chugging his orange juice, shaking his shaggy blonde hair.

"Suck my dick," Matt grumbles. "You got a date for your brother's wedding yet?"

Thor shoots him a death stare and I chuckle. That's a sore subject for our huge Swedish goalie; he's flying out to Stockholm in a few days, and his Mor is still giving him shit daily about his lack of a significant other.

"I have a few leads from back in the day that I can call on, if needed," he replies, taking his plate to the dishwasher. "There are always girls ready to take a ride on Thor's Hammer."

Nate guffaws and Matt grimaces. "You can't take a fuck buddy to your brother's wedding."

As they continue to give Thor shit about his dating choices, I feel my stomach clench, but this time it has nothing to do with my hangover. When I checked my cell this morning, there was a reminder from my calendar about my meeting with Trixie.

I take a big bite of toast as the guys talk about their vacations and plans to meet up to work out and skate before Nate heads home to see his dad in a few weeks. All I can think about is how the rest of the summer will play out and the fact that Cam is returning to Canada with me for the rest of her vacation. I know we have to stop off at my dad's when we return to Edmonton tonight, and even though I'm really excited to tell my family about the baby, I'm also a little concerned that April, especially, will have a lot of questions about our relationship. And at the moment, I don't have those answers for her.

Once Matt and I force some more breakfast into our queasy bellies, we clear the kitchen and put the empties into the recycling bin. The guys hit the road with promises to come to the cabin for my summer party. I finish cleaning up and put the trash out, so it doesn't stink of rotten food when I come home again, then dress in shorts, a polo shirt, ball cap, and sneakers. I decide to give my Audi R8 a run out, so I take that into the city for my lunch meeting with my agent Trixie.

I'm still not sure how I'm going to handle this meeting. I have the information for the lawyer Cam is using to draw up our co-parenting agreement, so I just hope Trixie has some solid advice and doesn't flip out and curse at me using British slang I don't always understand.

Thankfully, I make it to the Crown & Anchor pub before Trixie, so I grab a private booth at the back and order a pint of water to guzzle before she arrives. My hangover is still lingering behind my eyes, and the smell of stale beer isn't helping. I'd have preferred to meet at O'Connell's or some place with a nice outdoor seating area, but Trixie always makes us meet in this dingy, dark pub. She says she likes their shepherd's pie and that she can get her favorite bitter.

As I finish up my water, I hear Trixie before I see her.

"Alright, love! I'll have a pint of Boddie's over at the back booth. Cheers," she calls out to the bartender as she breezes through the dark saloon toward me. Several pairs of eyes track her progress across the bar; she really is a knock-out with her Marilyn Monroe curves and cool, choppy haircut.

Trixie's an awesome agent and manager; she lives for her job and is known among the other agents as an absolute badass. She's never seen me wrong, having taken me on as a rookie when she was first starting out. If it weren't for her, I wouldn't have the career I have, so I always take her advice where that's concerned.

"Alright Bugs, how's it hanging?" she chimes, sliding into the booth and dumping her huge purse on the bench seat next to her.

"Hey, Trix. I'm good. Thanks," I reply, taking off my cap to scrub my hand over my short hair.

She squints her almond shaped eyes at me. "You look hungover as shit."

I chuckle and nod my head. "You got me. Hung out with the guys last night, and it got a bit wild."

Trixie expels a throaty chuckle as the bartender brings her pint of bitter and takes our food order— she predictably goes for the pie, and I have a garden wrap and a soda and lime.

"As your agent, I should advise you against getting pissed up during the off-season, but as your friend, I wanna know what you boys had to chat about?" She takes a sip of her bitter which leaves a white, foamy mustache on her top lip.

"Oh, just catching up," I say non-committedly.

"'Okay. I guess you're not in the mood for small talk, so why don't you tell me why you wanted to meet?" Trixie leans back in her seat and demurely wipes the foam from her lip.

Suddenly, my throat is as dry as a bone, and I pray the bartender comes back with my drink soon. I guess my face betrays how nervous I feel because Trixie's brow furrows, and she looks concerned.

"What the fuck have you done, Bugs?"

I grimace and try not to meet her angry gaze. I still can't find my voice, but thankfully the bartender brings my soda, and I take a refreshing swig.

"Did you get a DUI or spend the night in jail?" she asks, her frustration building.

"Fuck no. Nothing like that," I grumble as our meals are set down in front of us, the waitress fluttering her eyelashes at me until Trixie shoos her away.

"Please tell me you haven't knocked up some puck slut?" she whispers, glancing around to make sure our conversation is private.

I make a face at her comment and concentrate really hard on the wrap I'm about to eat.

"Jesus. H. Christ, Warren Parker, will you just tell me what the fuck is going on?" Trixie growls, and I know my time is up.

"That last guess isn't too far from it, but there are no puck bunnies involved." I take a deep breath. "Cam and I are having a baby."

Trixie looks momentarily confused, then it dawns on her. "Cam? You mean Executive Assistant to the Whalers GM, that Cam?" Her voice becomes a low whisper-shout. "You knocked up your boss's assistant?"

"Geez, Trix. Don't put it like that." I huff out a breath and take a bite of my wrap, hoping that if my mouth is otherwise occupied, I won't put my foot in it.

"Are you having a relationship? Was this planned? How did I not know about this?" She almost asks this last question of herself, and I can tell that she's mentally replaying every encounter she's had with me and Cam, trying to find the clues she missed.

"No, yes, we're … it's complicated." I shrug because there's no other way to describe what's going on with us.

Trixie pushes her forgotten lunch out of the way and pulls her cell out of her purse, opening her dictation app. "Start from the beginning. I need to hear everything."

I spend the next half an hour recounting every detail of my relationship with Cam, obviously leaving out the juicier morsels. Trixie listens, occasionally tutting and rolling her eyes. When I'm done, I drink the rest of my soda in one long swallow and wait for her to tear me a new one.

Instead, she looks at me with wide eyes. "Oh boy, you're totally in love with her."

"What?" I almost choke on my own tongue at her bold statement. "No, I mean we're ..." And then it dawns on me. I sigh and rub my hands over my face. There's no point in denying it; Trixie can see right through me.

"Yep, I guess I am," I admit quietly.

"And how does she feel?"

"That's the million dollar question. We're together, but we're taking it slow. However, I don't think she's in the same place I am."

"Well, you need to get that shit locked down, mate," Trixie states, back to being all business. "You mentioned a parenting agreement. I'll need the name of her lawyer, then I can see what terms she's offering. I want a DNA test as soon as possible, and she needs to sign a Non-Disclosure Agreement ..."

"Absolutely fucking not!" I growl, slamming my palm down, making Trixie jump. "I'm happy to sign anything she needs for her parenting agreement, but there's no way I'm making the mother of my child feel like a scheming gold digger."

"Okay. Easy tiger," she coos, squeezing my bicep which feels as tight as a rubber band. "Why don't you give me the lawyer's information, and I'll liaise with them? Your only job is to get things straight with Cam and figure out how she feels about you."

I take a deep breath and try to relax, but I'm too keyed up to sit still. I need to get out of here and see Cam.

"Look, Trix. I need to go." I slide out of the booth and throw enough cash on the table to pay for both our meals as well as a generous tip. "I'll call you when I'm back in Canada. I should have an answer for you by then."

"No worries. Take care of yourself and Cam. Call me as soon as you have news."

"I will." With that, I literally charge out of the pub with a newfound need to lock this thing with Cam down. I just hope to god she's finally on the same page as I am.

21

Cameron

The nervous butterflies in my stomach keep rising and falling like waves as I wait for Warren to arrive at my house. He texted me about an hour ago to say he wants to talk before we head to the airport this evening.

I've been charging around like a crazy person since I received the text; I've cleaned, played with Gatsby, packed more clothes for the rest of my time in Canada, ordered more prenatal vitamins online to be delivered to Warren's place, and answered some work emails.

After a quick shower, I roughly blow dry my hair and pull it into a loose ponytail. I apply light make-up and put on my favorite summer dress. As I smooth it down, I notice it is actually a little tight around the middle. When I catch my reflection in the full-length mirror, I can see the way my new curves fill out the dress like never before.

Note to self: go shopping for new clothes in bigger sizes and stretchy material.

The sound of my doorbell jolts me from my mental note making, and my heart shifts into overdrive. All this excitement can't be good for the baby.

"Come on, Bam Bam. Let's go see daddy." I rub my belly and take a deep breath. It makes me smile that I've taken on the moniker Beth came up with last night.

Warren's huge frame fills the glass panel in my front door, and my breath hitches in my throat. He's wearing stylish dark jeans that hug his incredible thighs to perfection, and his short-sleeved button-down shirt is crisp and stretches deliciously across his chest and biceps. I swear my mouth waters a tiny bit—I need to calm the fuck down, or I'll open the door and my hormones will make me jump him.

He smiles and opens the outer screen as I open the door. The warm, manly scent of him hits me square in the face, and this time I'm very aware of my mouth filling with saliva.

"Hey, Sawyer," he greets, his voice raspy and low. "Can I come in?"

I manage to drag my gaze away from his massive chest, our eyes meet, and it's like I'm seeing Warren for the first time as more than my best friend.

I see a man who shares my pain of losing a mom and knows how I take my coffee. I see the captain of the team I work for and love who leads his brothers in triumph and defeat. I see the sexy, alpha male who gives me exactly what my body needs in bed and brings me levels of pleasure I didn't know existed. And he's the man I know will do everything in his power to protect my heart and his child.

There aren't any more words left to say, so as Warren and I crash together in the doorway, our mouths devour each other, tongues tangling and searching. His huge hands grab my ass, and I'm lifted back into the house, the door slamming behind him. We stumble toward the couch, and Warren lowers me carefully onto my back, his soft lips grazing the column of my neck, causing goosebumps to break out on my skin despite the heat.

"Are you sure, Cam?" Warren growls into my ear, nibbling the outer shell, his hand running up my naked thigh, teasing the hem of my dress. "I can wait. We don't have to do this now."

"Yes. Yes, Warren. I want this. I want it now and always." I gasp, grabbing his wrist, guiding his hand under my dress so his long fingers hook into the edge of my panties. His answering moan accompanies the rough tug that snaps my underwear which he tosses aside, positioning himself between my legs.

"I've got to be inside you, baby." He groans and I reach between us to undo his jeans, frantically pushing them over his muscular butt. I need him too, in the worst way. My pussy is aching and drenched with my arousal, so there's really no need for foreplay.

"Yes, do it now. *Please.*" I hear the begging tone in my voice, and it doesn't even sound like me.

We quickly push his boxers down, and his thick, hard cock springs free, slapping against my stomach. I shift beneath him, spreading my legs wider to accommodate his hips. He reaches between us and drags the flared head of his cock through my wet folds, getting himself slippery enough to slide straight in.

And when he does, we both gasp and moan in relief, his length sliding up to the hilt.

"I don't wanna crush you," Warren moans through gritted teeth, but I grasp his ass and hook my leg over the back of the couch.

"Don't worry. Just fuck me, please." There's that begging tone again, and from the mischievous smirk on Warren's face, I can tell he likes it.

He kisses the end of my nose in a sweet, tender gesture, then he sets an energetic pace, thrusting into me, my palms on his butt to urge him on—faster and faster, deeper and harder.

Warren begins to groan into my neck, and I feel him swell inside me, like he's getting ready to come. My own arousal is building and climbing, but I'll need something extra to get me there, so I slide my hand between our clashing bodies, and I find my swollen clit, ready for attention.

Lifting his head, Warren looks at me and scowls. "From now on," he growls, "if you need anything, you tell me. If you need me to rub that hungry little clit to get you off, you tell me."

I gasp at his command and nod my head eagerly.

"I need the fucking words, Sawyer." Warren stops his thrusts and holds his cock deep inside me, rolling his hips the tiniest amount, torturing me with pleasure.

"I want you to rub my clit. I want us to come together!" I cry out desperately, moving my hands back to his ass, squeezing it so he'll start moving again.

"That's more like it." He smirks, sitting back on his haunches, grabbing my hips to pull my ass up onto his thighs. He then sets an excruciatingly slow pace while he circles his rough thumb over my aching clit. I can't do anything but lock my legs around his hips and cup my breasts to try and get some relief. I'm about to go insane with need when Warren finally shifts into high gear and resumes his thrusting pace while continuing to service my swollen bud.

"I'm close, baby," he moans, looking me directly in the eyes, his brow furrowed in what appears to be pain or concentration.

"Harder, Warren. Fuck me harder!" I gasp, and he does just that, pinching my clit between his thumb and forefinger, sending me rocketing into the stratosphere. My back arches, and I clamp my thighs and pussy around him, setting off his orgasm with a chorus of shouts and moans.

As I calm down, Warren pulls me up onto his lap, his softening cock slipping from me, his thick arms circling my body. He holds me so close and breathes in the scent of my damp skin, softly grazing his lips over my neck. It sends aftershocks of pleasure through me, and I shudder in his arms.

"You okay, baby?" he whispers, gently nuzzling my shoulder.

I pull back so I can look at Warren, his face sweaty and flushed, a stupid grin plastered across it.

"I'm better than okay." I giggle, squirming in his lap as I feel his release leaking out of me. "I'm done with taking things slow. I want us, one hundred percent, all in. Is that okay?"

Warren gently cups my face in his hands and makes me look at him; he's suddenly deadly serious. "I've waited years to hear you say those words to me, baby.

Of course, I want you, and I'm so relieved you feel the same way I do."

"I do. I really do," I declare, feeling more certain about this than I have about anything for a very long time.

The massive grin that spreads across Warren's face lights me up like the Fourth of July, and we kiss again, deeper and hungrier this time. I feel my core flare with arousal, hot and urgent, but I know we have a flight to catch so I pull away. Warren growls deep in his throat, and he doesn't look pleased that I broke contact.

It makes me giggle that he's become so insatiable and possessive in such a short space of time. I've never really been into that before, but with Warren, it feels like exactly what I need.

"There's no time for that," I scold, clambering off his lap and pulling my dress down. "The Uber will be here in half an hour, and I still have a few things to pack before we leave."

"Sure thing, Sawyer."

As I turn away, I notice Warren shuffle uncomfortably on the couch. "What is it?" I ask.

He swallows. "I wanna tell my family about the baby … and us. Do you mind if we stop at my dad's place before going back to the cabin?"

It's so cute that he's nervous to ask this of me. I mean we literally only just got together as a couple, and now we're going to do the whole "meet the family" thing. I suddenly get a bundle of tight nerves in my own stomach.

"Sure," I reply, trying not to let the anxiety overwhelm me.

Quickly, Warren pulls me back into his lap, planting a core-shaking kiss on my mouth, his tongue sliding against my lower lip, urging me to open for him. His hands cup my ass, and I can feel his arousal against my thigh as our kiss deepens.

This time I know we won't be able to stop, and as Warren lifts me so I'm straddling his lap and pushes my dress up around my waist, I don't want him to.

22

Bugs

As I turn my truck into the street where my father lives, my stomach is full of nerves. I can tell by the way Cam is nervously rubbing her palms together and the fact she hasn't really said much on the drive from the airport that she's as nervous as I am.

"You okay there, Sawyer?" I ask, trying to maintain an even tone so as not to make her more nervous.

She turns and looks at me with those big brown eyes and smiles. "I'm good. Just a little nervous." She lets out a huff of breath and squeezes my hand. "I know I've met your dad before, but I don't want him to think badly of me."

"Why the hell would he think badly of you?" I growl.

"You know why," she mutters, flashing her eyes at me anxiously.

"He'll be thrilled. You don't have anything to worry about." As we pull up to the curb, I lean in and kiss her gently on the lips. That simple contact calms me, and as I pull away, I see Cam take a deep breath and smile.

I sent dad a text before we left Seattle to say we'd be stopping by, and now I notice April's car in the drive as well. Oh well. Two birds with one stone, I suppose.

"You ready, baby?" I ask, giving Cam's hand a squeeze as we walk up the path toward the house.

She nods. "I guess."

The words are barely out of her mouth when the door is ripped open, and my redheaded nephews barrel toward us, their faces grubby with chocolate.

"Uncle Warren!" they yell, attaching themselves to each of my thick thighs, climbing me like little monkeys.

"Hey boys," I grunt as Seamus kicks me in the nuts on his way up into my arms, both boys smacking my cheeks with chocolatey kisses. Once my face is thoroughly sticky and my balls are throbbing in pain, the boys switch their attention to Cam, who's standing patiently by my side.

"Who's dat?" the boys ask in unison, fixing Cam with their mischievous green eyes.

I detach the boys from me and lower them to the floor. "This is Cam. She's my ... friend." It feels wrong saying that now, but I don't think my nephews should be the first people in my family to hear the news.

"Oh," Bryan replies, turning and yelling into the house. "Momma, Uncle Warren brought his friend here."

"Did he now." April appears in the doorway, her eyes flitting between me and Cam. "Boys, go and wash up. You got more ice cream on your face than in your mouth." The twins charge back into the house like a mini herd of wildebeest.

"Hey, sis." I pull April in a hug and transfer some of her offspring's sticky kisses back onto her cheek.

"Hi, Warren. I was surprised when dad told me you were dropping by." I see April's eyes fix on Cam. "Why were you in Seattle?"

"April, this is Cameron. We had some stuff to take care of in the city, so we thought we'd stop by on the way back to the cabin." I can see my sister's brain ticking away, a suspicious look on her face.

Then she remembers her manners and extends her hand for Cam to shake, and I feel the tension ease slightly. I've talked to April a few times about how I feel about Cam, so I hope she keeps her mouth shut and doesn't go all momma bear on us.

"Lovely to meet you at last," Cam says nervously as she shakes my sister's hand, and we follow her into the house.

"Where's dad?" I ask, dumping our bags at the bottom of the stairs and following April through to the kitchen.

"He's out back tinkering with that damn mower. Wanna drink? It's wine o'clock as far as I'm concerned." She laughs, going to the fridge.

"I'll take a beer," I say, flashing Cam a reassuring smile.

"Cam, will you join me in a cheeky vino?"

I see the panic in Cam's eyes, but she manages to think on her feet. "It's a bit early for me, but I'd love some water."

Thankfully, April seems to accept this and retrieves a beer, a bottle of water, and her wine from the fridge.

"There he is." My dad's voice fills the kitchen as he comes in from the backyard, wiping his oily hands on a rag. "And he's not alone. Hey there, Cameron. Good to see you, honey."

"Hi Mr. Parker," Cam smiles sweetly at my dad, and my heart almost bursts. He's going to be so thrilled to be a grandpop again.

"Oh shit, none of that. Call me Bob." My dad hugs Cam, careful not to get oil on her dress, then he pulls me into a hard bear hug, not being so careful. He slaps my back a few times, and I know for a fact my shirt is ruined.

"The mower giving you grief again?" I ask, nodding at his greasy hands.

"God damn thing needs to go to the scrap yard," he grumbles. "So, what brings you two here?"

"That's what I was wondering," April butts in, sipping her wine, smirking at me.

Shit, this is it.

"Shall we sit down?" I gesture to the kitchen table, and Cam and I move toward it, sitting together on the bench. I pull her toward me and wrap my arm around her waist.

"I KNEW IT!" April crows as I take Cam's hand in mine.

"Shut up, you brat." I scowl at my sister as she laughs and claps her hands. My dad just looks confused.

"What am I missing?" he asks, perplexed.

"Cam and I are together. We're dating," I explain, side-eyeing my sister who's still smirking into her wine.

My sister leans back in her chair and crosses her arms, smiling smugly. "How long?"

"It's pretty new," Cam says quietly, her cheeks blushing an adorable shade of pink.

My dad suddenly seems to catch on and he smiles broadly. "Oh, that's great news, kids."

Okay, so that went well. Now for the next bit of news.

"That's not all."

My dad and my sister share a look. "Did you get married in Vegas or something?" April laughs, rolling her eyes.

"No, of course not." I place my hand protectively over Cam's belly. "We're having a baby."

The silence seems to go on forever; both April and my dad have their mouths hanging open, their eyes shifting between Cam and me.

Suddenly, the twins reappear demanding to have some time on their tablets and that breaks the tension. Still looking shocked, April gets up to deal with the boys while my dad takes a big swig of his beer.

"Well, that sure is big news," he says eventually. Cam is as stiff as a board beside me, so I hold her a little tighter. "I take it because this is a new relationship, it wasn't a planned pregnancy."

"Not entirely," I explain. "But we're both really happy about it, and we hope you are too."

I pull an envelope out of my back pocket and take out the ultrasound image of the baby, sliding it across the table toward him.

"Here's your newest grandbaby."

My dad fixes us both with his green eyes for a moment, then they shift to the photo. I think he's going to tear me a new one for being an irresponsible douchebag. However, when his eyes crinkle at the corners and fill with tears, I breathe a sigh of relief.

"I'm gonna be a grandpop again, eh?" And with that he's on his feet, and Cam and I are enveloped in his warm embrace.

By the time April returns from dealing with the twins, dad is in full proud grandpop mode, and she doesn't get to air the opinions about this that I'm sure are on the tip of her tongue. I catch all the looks she shoots at me and Cam as we head out into the backyard to start the barbecue, but she doesn't get a chance to corner me.

Thankfully, the twins are being their usual pesky selves, so there's mostly talk of how the cabin is coming along and what the boys are up to at day camp. I keep my hand firmly on Cam's thigh as we eat, but I can still feel it bounce softly as she jiggles with nervous tension.

By the time dinner is done and cleaned away, it's time for April to take the boys home to bed.

"Walk me out to the car," April demands after kissing my dad goodbye and giving Cam a slightly frosty hug.

This is it; it's time for my lecture.

"Sure thing," I reply, smiling at Cam as she slowly heads into the den with my dad to watch TV.

My sister manages to keep a lid on it until the twins are securely in their car seats, and the door is closed. Then she turns to me with a furious look on her face.

"What the fuck, Warren?" she hisses.

"What?" I raise my hands in surrender.

"You get this girl pregnant in the first week of your relationship?" April demands. "How stupid are you?"

"Wait a minute," I growl back, losing my cool a little. "Firstly, I've known Cam for years, so she's not some puck bunny I knocked up. Secondly, we had a night together a few months ago. We used protection, but it didn't work. This was an accident, but we've been back and forth over the best thing to do, and we've decided we want to be together. I hope you can get on board with that, April."

From the slightly shocked look on my sister's face, I can see she knows she's gone too far. However, it appears she's got more to say.

"I know how you feel about her. You've talked about it enough." She reaches out and touches my arm. "I'm just afraid your feelings for her are stronger than hers are for you. Would you guys be together if you weren't having a baby?"

April's question sits in my stomach like a lead weight. She's just verbalized my greatest fear.

I swallow hard and look my sister in the eye. "Yes, I believe we would … eventually."

April seems to accept this, and she lifts up on her tip-toes and kisses my cheek. "Just be careful, little brother. You may be a big, tough hockey player, but your heart is precious to me." She places her hand on my chest. "Protect yourself, you hear me?"

"Yes," I sigh, covering her hand with mine.

Cameron

When Warren comes back into the house from saying goodbye to April, I can tell they've had words. His face is dark and thunderous, his brow furrowed in anger. I could feel the hostile vibe coming off his sister in waves all evening and it made me so uncomfortable and upset for Warren. I'm thrilled his dad is so happy about our news, but April is a different story. I know she helped to raise Warren and is protective of him, so I understand her concerns.

He's still grumbling to himself when he plops down on the couch next to me and takes my hand in his.

"Everything alright, son?" Bob asks, never taking his eyes from the baseball game on the TV.

"Yeah, just April being April." He sighs.

"Are you kids gonna stay the night? It's getting late to drive out to the lake."

Warren looks at me and I nod. I'm totally wiped out from the traveling, and the thought of driving another three hours to the cabin is not an attractive prospect. However, snuggling up to Warren in his bed sounds like the perfect end to this day.

As if reading my mind, Warren says, "Yeah, in fact we might head up now. It's been a long few days." He stands and pulls me to my feet before going over to his dad's chair and kissing his forehead. "Night, dad. Thanks for being cool about all this."

"Goodnight, you two. I'll make waffles in the morning before you go," Bob replies, smiling kindly.

"Goodnight, Bob. Thank you," I say quietly, as Warren leads me out of the room, retrieving our bags from the bottom of the stairs and going up to his room.

Once we're safely inside Warren's room, I begin to ask him what his sister said, but before I can get my words out, he's pressing me up against the door, and his lips are trailing across my jaw and down my neck.

"God, you smell so good, baby," he groans, running his large hands down my sides and around to my ass, so he can grind against me.

I feel my body come alive at his touch, and suddenly my mind is foggy with arousal. I want to ask about April and what she said to make him so mad, but all I can think about is Warren's erection pressing into my hip and the way his fingers are grazing the backs of my bare thighs.

"Warren, we need to talk about your sister," I moan as his finger hooks into the back of my panties, feeling them soaked for him.

He lifts his head and fixes me with his fern green eyes, pupils dilated with desire. "I don't wanna talk about my sister when I'm about to finger your pussy, Sawyer."

I choke out a shocked giggle at his dirty words. "Okay, sorry. But we *are* gonna talk about it when you're done … with that."

Warren laughs, his voice so raspy and deep I feel it vibrate through my chest. "You got it, baby. But just so you know, I'm gonna be doing a lot more than fingering your pussy before I'm done."

And with that, he picks me up and takes me to his bed, where we make love as quietly as possible. His mouth covers mine while I moan out my climax, my hands gripping his shoulders and my legs clamped around his hips as he falls with me.

While we lay in the afterglow, his head resting on my damp breasts and his hand gently stroking my tiny baby bump, I feel content and safe. All thoughts of April's apparent disapproval have been banished—for now.

I'm just beginning to drift off when I feel the strangest sensation in my stomach, like butterflies or bubbles. The sensation makes me flinch, and Warren looks up at me with curiosity.

"Everything okay?" he asks, that crease in his brow returning.

"I … I think the baby just moved!" I gasp, putting my hand on top of his.

Warren leaps up like he's just been slapped on the butt. "Shit! Is that normal this early?" I gaze at my man, standing naked and still slightly hard in the moonlight, looking totally freaked out, and I can't help but burst out laughing.

"I read about this. It's called quickening. It's nothing to worry about." I reach out and bring Warren back to bed, placing his hand back on my bump. He looks so curious and still freaked out, but he holds his hand gently on my belly and waits to see if he can feel anything.

"I can't feel it. Is it still happening?"

"Yes, it's like bubbles in my stomach. You probably can't feel it, but it's definitely happening." I sigh, leaning back against the headboard while Warren places his ear to my stomach to try to hear what's going on.

"Wow" is all he can say over and over again until I finally drift off to sleep, gently stroking his hair.

The next morning, Bob makes enough waffles to feed a hockey team. I guess he's used to feeding Warren, so I eat as many as I can without risking a mid-journey barf stop on the way to the cabin.

He sends us off with warm hugs and promises to come up to the cabin to check the deck. When he hugs me, he whispers, "Take care of my son. He's a good man."

"I will," I whisper back, feeling the sting of tears in my nose. I know how much Warren means to his family, and it suddenly feels like a heavy weight to carry on my shoulders. The fear of our relationship failing hits me again; not only could I break Warren's heart, but I could also hurt his family. I don't have as much at stake as he does, and that's a huge responsibility.

After filling up with gas and grabbing some supplies, we hit the road and make good time back to the lake. It's so easy being with Warren. I guess because we've always been good friends, it makes these moments easier. There's no awkward silences, and he teases me just like he always has. When we have to make an unscheduled pit stop because I'm bursting for the bathroom, he laughs his ass off when I'm in such a hurry I don't realize the door is a push and not a pull. I yank the door toward me in desperation to get to the bathroom, confused as to why it won't open even though I can see customers inside. He finally stops laughing long enough to push the door open for me, so I can run in and only just make it to the bath-room in time.

We make it back to the cabin just before lunch, and while Warren collects Juneau from the neighbors, I make us some sandwiches. As I slice the chicken, I look out of the window and see Warren and Juneau running around on the beach, the dog barking and leaping with joy at their reunion. It makes me smile at how much Warren loves that dog; his heart is so open and ready to love—it's a little scary.

I'm so distracted by the scene unfolding on the beach that I slice my finger with the knife and end up ruining the sandwiches. When Warren finally comes in, he rushes over when he sees the blood on the counter.

"Are you okay?" he asks, grabbing my hand from under the faucet to inspect the cut on my finger. "What happened?"

"You and your dog." I pout. "You were being so cute out there, I got distracted and cut myself."

Warren chuckles and lifts my hand up, slipping my injured finger into his mouth and sucking gently, never breaking eye contact with me. Despite the slight sting, the action lights a fire between my thighs, and suddenly I have to concentrate on breathing in and out.

Finally, he releases my finger from his mouth with a wet pop and kisses it gently. "There. All better," he rasps in a gravelly voice.

I swallow and lick my lips, Warren's intense eyes still holding my gaze. "Thanks," I whisper, my own voice husky with desire. "I ruined the sandwiches."

"I don't fucking care. I don't wanna eat sandwiches." And with that, Warren is on his knees in front of me pulling my panties down, and I can't even think about my cut finger anymore.

Bugs

I knew there was this thing called absolute bliss, and I'm pretty sure I've felt it before: when I lost my virginity to my high school girlfriend, when I was drafted, when I scored my first NHL goal, and when I was made captain of my team.

But none of that compares to the two weeks I've just spent with Cam at my cabin.

I've had several relationships, and they were great in many ways, but they were never so easy or comfortable as it is with Cam. And that's not to say we're like an old married couple—I can't get enough of her. It's been like hanging out with my best friend with the added bonus of having incredible sex in every room and on every surface of my home. And once on the beach as we lay under the stars.

We've slipped into an easy routine where she spends her days reading or working on her laptop, and I continue to build the deck with some help from Larry and his laborers. We run together in the morning and usually end up fucking in the outdoor shower afterward. Then we eat breakfast and begin our day, stopping for lunch which we usually eat out on the beach. Sometimes Cam goes over to Nancy's for the afternoon or video chats with Mila and Beth while I finish up work for the day. Our evenings are spent relaxing on the porch until the bugs get too bad, then we retreat inside where things heat up on the couch.

We've explored every inch of each other, and it just keeps getting hotter and hotter. I've loved watching Cam's body change. I guess because I see her naked a lot more than I ever have, I notice how her tits are keeping their new shape, and her hips and belly are becoming fuller. She moans constantly about stretch marks and her aching back, but I just kiss her cute baby bump and murmur sweet things to our little Bam Bam.

Yes, she shared Beth's nickname for our baby with me one night when I caught her talking to her stomach. I cracked up laughing because it sounds like a hockey player's nickname.

"Are you gonna be our little enforcer?" I asked her belly as we laid in bed.

"What makes you so sure it'll be a boy?" Cam asked, smirking.

"Even if it's a girl, she can be a badass enforcer on the ice," I replied seriously.

"And what makes you think I'll allow our child to play hockey?"

I looked up at her in horror. "Are you fucking kidding me, woman? Of course, our kid'll play hockey. It'll have skates on before it can walk."

Cam rolled her eyes. "Don't be ridiculous."

"You're not fighting me on this one, Sawyer," I growled, crawling up her body, taking her wrists in one of my hands and pinning them above her head. It caused her back to arch and her delectable tits grazed my bare chest. Her breaths came out in shallow huffs as I dragged my fingers through her wet folds.

"I don't want our kid getting hurt!" Cam gasped as I worked her clit with my rough thumb and pushed two fingers inside her tight channel.

"It won't get hurt. I'll always protect you both." I moaned, crashing my lips to hers, thrusting my tongue into her mouth. I quickly swapped my fingers for my cock and rolled Cam over on top of me, so she could ride me, and I could palm her perfectly jiggly tits.

Now we're waking up to Cam's last day at the cabin. Don is back from Australia and wants her back in the office on Monday. We've decided that I'll come back to Seattle with her, so we can break the news to him together. It would be a massively douchebag move to make her face that alone.

It'll also give me a chance to catch up with Trixie. She's been emailing me about the parenting contract, but so far, I've managed to dodge her. Her last email basically told me to make contact or she'll "come to Canada and chop my bollocks off," whatever that means!

"Are you okay?" Cam's voice pulls me back to the moment as she comes out of the bathroom wrapped in a towel.

I scrub my hand over my beard and push thoughts of Trixie to the back of my mind. "I'm good, Sawyer." I reach out my long arm and grab a handful of her damp towel as she passes by, pulling her so she's standing between my thighs. God, she smells incredible. I bury my face in the terry cloth that covers her rounded belly and gently kiss it while her fingers thread through my hair.

"C'mon now. There's no time for that, Cap. We have a flight to catch," Cam whispers in a breathy voice that betrays her arousal to me. She gasps quietly as I run my hands up her bare thighs and give her juicy ass a squeeze.

"You sure about that?" I look up at her with a cheeky smirk, slowly kneading her butt cheeks. Cam's face flushes with desire, and she pulls her plump lower lip between her teeth. But just as quickly, I see sensible Cam take over, and she pushes my hands away and takes a step back.

"Yes, I'm sure. Now get your butt in the shower, Cap," she huffs, pulling the towel off her head and scrubbing her hair dry.

I chuckle as I walk past her on the way to the bathroom, giving her ass a playful slap. This has been the best time of my life—living in this little bubble with Cam. But now real life, responsibilities, and consequences are about to rain down on us, and I have to admit, I'm quietly shitting a brick.

After dropping Juneau at my dad's, we catch a flight back to Seattle and land mid-afternoon. I bring up the subject of where we're going to stay while I'm in town, and Cam makes a good point that she should really stay at her place because of the cat and going back to work. I can't say I'm not disappointed that she won't be coming home with me, but I totally understand where she's coming from.

So, as we leave the airport terminal building, we agree to get our own cabs to our own places and meet up tomorrow to see Don at the Whalers offices.

While we wait in line for a cab, I pull Cam into my arms and press my forehead to hers, breathing in as much of her as I can before we have to spend the night apart.

"I'm gonna miss you tonight, Sawyer," I whisper, my hands possessively gripping her hips.

She looks up at me through her thick lashes and licks her lips. "Well Cap, you'd better give me a kiss I'm gonna remember."

With a possessive growl, I crash my lips against hers and claim her mouth, sliding our tongues together. Her fists grip the front of my T-shirt, and the thickening behind my zipper could be embarrassing once we part.

We continue to make out on the sidewalk, my hand protectively smoothing her neat little baby bump, until an annoyed cough pulls us apart, and I realize we're next in line for a cab. Cam blushes a bright shade of scarlet as I usher her into the first cab and give her one more kiss on the forehead before closing the door.

"I'll call you tonight," I call as the cab pulls away into traffic, and Cam leans out of the window and waves to me, a brilliant smile on her beautiful face.

Jesus, how the fuck did a guy like me get so lucky?

Cameron

It's so good to be home, but I must admit there's a huge Warren-shaped hole in my world since we parted at the airport. As much as I desperately wanted to go home with him, I knew the sensible thing to do was go to my own place and get my shit together. I was about to drop a huge bombshell on my boss that could have repercussions for my job as well as Warren's position as Captain. I know things were cool when Matt and Mila got together, but this is slightly different.

Once I unpack and get the laundry on, I open my calendar app on my phone and schedule a meeting in Don's diary for tomorrow morning, quickly closing the app and pushing my phone away. Don's been back in the country for a few days getting over the jet lag, so hopefully he won't check his diary until he gets into the office in the morning.

I spend the rest of the evening trying to get Gatsby to forgive me for leaving him again and catching up on some trashy TV. Warren calls as promised, and we talk more about how we're going to approach talking to Don tomorrow.

"I've also got a meeting with Trixie in the afternoon," Warren says just before we hang up.

"Oh, okay. I heard from my lawyer, and she says that Trixie's been in contact, and they've got the first draft of the contract drawn up for us to look at," I reply, feeling slightly uneasy about the whole co-parenting contract now that Warren and I are a couple.

"I guess that's why Trixie wanted to meet me then. I've kinda been avoiding her," he confesses gruffly, and I can tell he's still pissed off about the contract.

I'm quiet for a few seconds. "We still need it, right?" I ask quietly.

Now it's Warren's turn to be quiet; I can almost see him warring with what he wants and what he thinks is right for me and the baby.

"Let's see what Trixie and the lawyer have come up with, and we'll go from there."

"Okay. That seems smart," I reply, feeling both reassured and shitty at the same time. We've managed to avoid talking about it while at the cabin, but now it seems like reality has come crashing down on us. Part of me wants to tell the lawyer to get rid of the contract, but a stronger part of me keeps insisting I keep going ahead with it.

And that part sounds exactly like my mom.

Warren and I talk for a few more minutes; however, I can feel some tension between us that wasn't there before we mentioned the contract.

I just hope I'm making the right call, that this contract won't drive a wedge between us before we've even got going.

Once we've said goodnight and hung up, I get my suit out of the closet ready for tomorrow. As I hold it up on the hanger, I decide to try it on, and I'm glad I do because the skirt is now too tight, I can't zip it up, and the jacket can just about button over my neat baby bump. With a huff, I fling the useless garment back into the closet and pull out some drawstring palazzo pants and a floaty shirt that will hide a multitude of sins until I can get to the store.

My wardrobe malfunction has made me even more nervous about facing Don tomorrow, but thankfully I'm so tired from a day of travelling that once I'm in the T-shirt I stole from Warren's overnight bag and slip under the sheet, I'm out for the count.

24

Bugs

I left my phone on last night in case Cam needed me, so when the blaring ringtone jolts me out of deep sleep while it's still dark out, I'm immediately on high alert. Slapping my hand out toward my vibrating cell, I make a grab for it but only succeed in pushing it off the nightstand.

Jesus, you wouldn't think I make my living because of my excellent hand eye coordination, would you?

Eventually, I hang over the edge of the bed and retrieve the phone from the floor just as it flips to voicemail.

"Fuck!" I curse, sitting up and putting on the bedside lamp. As I scrub the sleep out of my eyes, I see it was Trixie calling, then the phone pings to indicate a voice-mail message.

What the fuck could she want at … five thirty am?

Irritated, I hit the button to unlock my phone and open the voicemail, putting it on speaker.

"Bugs, it's Trix. Where the fuck are you? Did you know you're all over the hockey blogs and sports news sucking face with Cam at the airport? Some wanker sold a saucy little video of you both, and worst of all, you can see her little surprise. Call me back immediately."

Oh shit. If Don gets wind of this before we get to tell him, he's going to be pissed. And this will devastate Cam that the news gets out like this.

Before I can even dial Trixie's number, she calls me back. "Trix, I just got your message ..."

"What the bloody hell were you thinking, you stupid sod?" she yells at me, and I hold the phone away from my ear and put her on speaker.

"I'm sorry! We were just saying goodbye," I explain quickly. "Anyway, I thought you'd be pleased that we're making a go of our relationship. It makes a pregnancy easier to explain."

"Yes, of course I'm pleased," Trixie growls. "But Jesus H. Christ, I'd have preferred to do a nice little press release with the two of you looking all cute and in love. Instead, I've got to explain you mouth-fucking her on the sidewalk while she shows off her baby bump."

"Shit, I'm sorry."

"I know you are, love. I just hope we can get to Don before he wakes up and sees this all over his phone. I suggest you get your arse dressed and go to Cam's and explain the situation, then meet me at the Whalers office ASAP."

"Yes, ma'am."

"Fuck you, Bugs. I hate getting up this early." Trixie moans, but I can hear the slight smile in her voice. "See you soon."

I know that Cam usually gets up at six am, so I throw myself into the shower and get ready at warp speed. I grab a banana and a protein shake out of the fridge and leap into my Range Rover, tapping my fingers impatiently on the steering wheel while I wait for the garage door to open, peeling out of the drive toward the city.

When I pull up outside Cam's house, I see the upstairs light on, so I know she's awake at least. I decide to check out the news before I go in there, so I know exactly how bad it is. I bring up Google on my phone and search for the story, my gut dropping when I see article after article come up with pictures of Cam and I in a passionate embrace.

"Whalers Cap kisses mystery girl."

"Parker in love."

"Is that a baby Whaler on the way?"

God damn it, and that's just a few of the headlines that pop up. Cam's going to be devastated. But this is the sort of shit I'm here to protect her from, so I need to get in there, explain this, and keep her calm.

I've not heard from Don yet, so that's at least one blessing. Hopefully, he hasn't seen it, and we can tell him before he does.

With a big sigh, I climb out of my car and walk up the path to Cam's front door, dropping her a text to say I'm waiting. A few minutes later, she opens the door, a quizzical look on her freshly washed face. God, she's so beautiful, I feel sick to my stomach that I'm about to make her so sad.

"What are you doing here, Warren?" she asks, pulling me into a warm hug, her naked body under her robe making me hard. "I missed you last night, but this is getting borderline stalkerish."

I kiss her cheek and follow her into her house, closing the front door quietly as her creepy cat swirls his body around my legs. I swear he's trying to trip me over.

"We have a bit of a situation," I mutter, rubbing the back of my neck. How the hell am I supposed to tell her this?

Cam turns around, and I can already see she's tense, so I step toward her and pull her against my body. "Apparently, someone filmed us kissing at the airport yesterday, and now it's all over the news and the internet."

I immediately feel Cam's body go rigid in my arms, so I kiss her temple and rub her back. "Trixie's all over it, so her advice is to get to Don's office as soon as possible, and hopefully, we can tell him before he sees the news."

Cam huffs out a frustrated breath, but I know I'm about to drop more fuel on the fire.

"That's not so bad. Do people really care who you kiss?" she says quietly into my chest.

That makes me chuckle despite the shitty situation. "Well, no, but that's not all they have."

Now, Cam pulls away from me and fixes me with her dark brown eyes. "What do you mean?"

I swallow because suddenly my mouth is completely devoid of moisture. "There's speculation that you're pregnant because apparently I had my hand on your belly, and you can see the bump."

God, I feel like the biggest asshole. I promised Cam I'd protect her and our baby, and I seem to have failed at the first hurdle.

Cam's eyes fill with tears, and my heart literally breaks in two as her chin quivers, and she steps away from me.

"Oh god, this is so bad," she whispers, almost to herself. "Don will be so disappointed."

"It's gonna be okay, Sawyer. Get dressed and let's get to the office. We can fix this."

Cam blinks a few times and seems to come back to herself, nodding her head, setting her mouth in a determined line. "Right, yes. Let me get dressed. Will you feed Gatsby?"

At the mention of his name, the cat yowls at me and slinks over to his empty food dish, waiting to be served.

"Sure, just hurry up."

Cam disappears upstairs, and I feed the cat, pouring kibble into his bowl while he looks at me with mild disgust. When he buries his face in his dish, I attempt to pet him, but he just growls into his food, and I give up. This cat is such an asshole. Dogs are much more friendly.

Finally, Cam reappears, and I take in what she's wearing: it's definitely not her usual business attire, and she obviously sees my confused expression.

"None of my work suits fit anymore, okay?" she snaps, grabbing her purse and her phone. "Don't give me shit, Parker. Let's go clean up this mess."

Cameron

The offices are quiet, a fact I'm so grateful for at this point. Warren parks in the players' parking lot, and we ride the elevator up to the GM's floor in silence. In fact, we've hardly said two words to each other the whole ride here. I was hoping this would be an exciting time, finally sharing our news with Don and the team, but now our hand has been forced by some dickhead with a camera phone.

As the elevator doors slide open on our floor, I see Trixie pacing back and forth in the lobby, her cell phone glued to her ear while she speaks at a hundred miles an hour.

"It'll be okay, Sawyer. We haven't done anything wrong," Warren whispers, enveloping my shaking hand in his firm, reassuring grip. He sweeps this rough thumb over the pulse point in my wrist, and I immediately feel calmer.

"I know that. I just feel shitty that Don will have to find out like this," I reply. "Having to do it this way makes it look like we're hiding something."

We make it to Trixie just as she ends her call. Her high cheekbones are bright red, and I can see her grinding her teeth in frustration.

"Hi, Trixie," Warren says, pulling her into an awkward hug. "How are things?"

"Things could be better," she huffs, pulling away from him. "Hi, Cam. I'm sorry this is happening." She reaches out and pats my arm.

"Yeah, it's not ideal. Have you heard from Don or Coach?" I ask, rubbing my hands nervously together as I make my way round my desk to turn on my computer. I notice the blinking red light on my phone which indicates voicemail messages, but despite the overwhelming desire to listen to them, I resist. It'll only be the press asking for comments about the news or shit I can deal with later.

"No, not yet," Trixie replies, continuing to pace and fiddle with her phone. "I'm hoping that's good news. I'm sure if either of them had seen it, they'd be all over you by now."

"Let me make us some drinks while we wait …" I begin, just as the ding of the elevator sounds. Then I hear Don's voice talking animatedly as he gets closer to our office. The three of us freeze and wait for him to round the corner, Warren smiling reassuringly at me and reaching for my hand.

"It's okay, baby," he whispers as he kisses my temple just as Don appears in the doorway.

"No, I will not make a comment at the moment …" he barks into his phone, coming to an abrupt halt as he surveys the scene awaiting him.

He hangs up and scrubs his hand over his face, his expression thunderous.

"So, I guess the fact the three of you are here waiting for me and it's not even seven am means there's some truth to these news stories doing the rounds this morning, huh?"

"Don, let me just reassure you Bugs and Cam were planning on telling you their news this morning," Trixie begins. "It's unfortunate a member of the public captured this private moment between the two of them …"

"Private moment!" Don bellows. "They're kissing in full view of every idiot with a fucking camera phone!"

Trixie recoils as his angry words hit her, and she nods and steps back.

I step forward and Don turns to me, his face more angry than I've ever seen it. I gently put my hand on his arm. "I'll make you a coffee, and we can talk in your office. I'm so sorry it came out like this, but it's out now. We just need to come up with a way to manage the fall out."

I see Don's features relax; I've been dealing with his occasional meltdowns for years now, and I'm pretty good at reading him. Even though he's blustering and yelling, I can see the hurt in his eyes at finding out this way. Don nods, throws Warren a dark glare, and disappears into his office.

We all seem to exhale at the same time, and Trixie's phone vibrates.

"Okay, you two deal with Don, and I'll firefight the press until you know how you want to move forward."

I give Trixie a thankful hug as she answers her phone, and I pull Warren into the small kitchenette at the back of our suite of offices.

"Fuck, he looks so pissed," Warren whispers as I busy myself making a pot of coffee.

"He's upset," I reply. "He does the loud shouty thing, and once he's calmed down, he'll be ready to listen to us. As long as he hears that we're together and having a baby within a relationship, he won't really care how it started out."

Warren pulls me into his warm embrace as we wait for the coffee maker to do its thing. He tucks my head under his chin and kisses my hair, gently sliding his large palms down over my butt. The flash of heat I feel between my legs has become an unstoppable response whenever Warren has his hands on me, but this is definitely not the time to get a lady boner.

I squirm out of his arms and rise up on my tiptoes to kiss his lips. "Less of that, Mr. Parker. We have to be serious and responsible."

Warren smirks and adjusts himself before saluting me. "Yes, ma'am. But I should tell you that it really turns me on when you get all bossy."

I can't help but laugh and slap his firm chest. "Idiot." I hand him coffees for him and Trixie, and I take Don's and a bottle of water for me. "Let's go, lover boy."

Trixie is still on a call when we walk through, so Warren leaves her coffee on my desk, and I knock on Don's door, entering when he barks that we can.

Thankfully, he seems calmer, and he even manages a stiff smile as I put his coffee on his desk and take a seat in one of the club chairs opposite.

"Right, let's pretend that shitshow didn't happen this morning," Don says, steepling his fingers, looking between Warren and me with his steely eyes. "How did all of this happen?"

I'm about to speak, but Warren steps in. "You know we've been friends for a long time, and back in the spring, we started a relationship but just kept it between the two of us."

My head snaps toward him as he tells Don a half truth. I can't believe he's trying to sugarcoat this. I know he's just trying to protect me, but I don't want to lie to Don.

"That's not exactly right," I reply quickly, holding up my hand to Warren when he tries to talk over me. "It's true that we started something in the spring, but it wasn't a relationship to start with." I can feel my cheeks burning as realization dawns on Don's face, and he stares daggers at Warren.

"I see," he growls.

"It's not Warren's fault," I interject. "It was something we both wanted but agreed we didn't want a relationship. So, we went our separate ways and carried on being friends."

"Sort of," Warren mumbles under his breath, obviously pissed that I've taken charge.

"I found out I was pregnant after the playoffs, and when I told Warren, he was so great." I reach out and hold his hand, smiling at the man I've come to care about deeply over the last month. "We decided to give our relationship a go, and we're a couple."

Don stays silent and just studies us like specimens under a microscope.

"So, let me get this right; you had a friends-with-benefits one night stand, got pregnant, but now you're a real couple."

"That's right, Sir," Warren replies, squeezing my hand. "I'd just like to reassure you that I care very much about Cam, as a friend and more, and we're thrilled to be having this baby. I understand the way the news broke is gonna cause you a headache, but we're willing to do anything within our power to put a positive spin on this for the club."

I feel my heart squeeze tightly in my chest at Warren's sweet words, and I almost have the sense that if we were alone, he might tell me he loves me. However, that romantic notion is swept away when Don speaks again.

"Cam, go and get Trixie and let's see what we do about getting a press release out."

I quickly rise up from the chair and head for the door.

"And Cam?" I turn and see Don finally smiling. "Congratulations."

25

Bugs

"**D**ude, how are your balls not sitting on Don's desk right now?" Thor chuckles, pulling his goalie mask off, shaking his sweaty hair like a huge shaggy dog.

I've met up with the guys for a pick-up game at our training rink, and I've just fired a screaming slapper straight into Thor's glove. I'm pissed at missing such an easy shot; I'm definitely distracted.

I snort and skate round the back of Thor's net. "He was ready to cut them off at first, but Cam is like a GM whisperer or something. She handled him like a champ, and when he heard our side of the story, he seemed almost happy about it."

"Well, you're a braver man than I am. As far as Don's concerned, Cam falls under the category of sisters and ex-girlfriends in the Bro Code," Thor replies, bouncing the puck on the blade of his goalie stick.

"And that is?" I ask.

"Totally off fucking limits!" Matt laughs, skating past me.

"How the fuck does that work?" I grumble. "You fucked the Coach's assistant, and that was okay with everyone."

"Hey! Don't talk about what Mila and I have like that, you douche," Matt growls, slapping a puck at me, so it bounces harmlessly off my ass pads.

"Alright, darlin'." I laugh. "Don't get your panties in a bunch."

Matt flips me off, and we get back to the game. All this sensitive talk has no place on the ice. However, the chirps and digs continue for the entire game, and by the time we're done, I've had about enough.

"C'mon on, guys. Give it a rest," I grumble as we clear away the equipment. Thor and I carry the goal toward the edge of the ice while Matt and Nate collect the pucks. "I really want this to work with Cam."

"I know, man." Thor drops his side of the net and slaps me on the back. "You've loved her for just about forever. I hope it all works out for you."

"Me too," Matt pipes up. "I'm just a huge bundle of love these days, and I wish everyone was as happy as me and Mila."

I hear Nate making gagging noises as he follows us to the locker room.

"I don't know why the fuck you're doing that, kid," I shout over my shoulder. "You're as whipped as the pair of us. Doesn't Beth wear your balls as earrings these days?"

That comment causes snorting laughter from Thor and Matt and grumbled curses from Nate.

"C'mon, let's hit the showers, then go out for beers," Thor suggests, pulling off his enormous goalie jersey and throwing it in the laundry hamper.

"Ah I can't, man. I'm heading back to the cabin tomorrow, and I wanna spend time with Cam," I reply, also throwing my sweaty jersey into the hamper.

"WHIPPED!" Nate cough-shouts into his fist before disappearing into the showers like the punk ass kid he is.

"DICK!" I yell after him, shaking my head.

"Nah, you're right. You go spend some time with your woman," Thor says, following me into the showers. "We'll really wet the baby's head in a few weeks when we come up for the party."

I arrive at Cam's place at six, just like we arranged this morning as I kissed her goodbye on my front step. I made her a decaf coffee to go and packed a bran muffin in a brown bag for her breakfast. I love having her in my home, taking care of her, and I'm sure as shit going to miss her when I go back to the cabin tomorrow.

To be honest, I've been in two minds about going back at all. We're deep into July, and I could always pay Larry and his guys to finish the deck for me and just return for the weekend of the party I throw every year.

But when I suggested this to Cam last night, she flatly refused to entertain the idea. She told me I'd earned my down time, and that I should go back, reminding me that two weeks apart is nothing when we have all the time in the world together. That sweet comment made me roll on top of her and make love to her so slowly, we were both crazy with desire by the time we came.

When I get to the front door, I see Cam sitting on her couch, so I let myself in, expecting to smell the tacos she promised to cook as she has a huge craving. Instead, I hear the sports news channel and her soft, gasping sobs.

"Hey, what's happening?" I ask as I round the end of the couch and see her hunching over her iPad, big fat tears rolling down her cheeks.

"Oh, hey," she sobs, looking up at me in a way that's liable to break my heart or have me punching whoever upset her like this.

I plop down on the couch beside her and pull her into my arms, letting her snuffle into my chest, no doubt rubbing her snotty nose all over my shirt. I rub her back in soothing circles and let her sob it out. I know from experience that I'm not getting any sense out of her until this phase has passed.

I do, however, sneak a look at the iPad she threw on the coffee table. What I see makes my blood boil, and the urge to tear someone apart is so strong that I have to ball my fists and bite the inside of my cheek until I taste blood. Cam has obviously been reading one of the many Puck Bunny Blogs that infest the internet, and from what I can read, they're being particularly spiteful and derogatory about Cam and the pregnancy. I see words like "gold digger," "abuse of position within the franchise," and "securing her place as more than the GM's assistant."

I'm finally so worked up, I can't wait for Cam to work through her process, and I hold her arms gently and move her away from my chest so I can look at her.

"Why have you been reading this fucking garbage?" I growl through gritted teeth, darting my eyes toward her iPad.

Cam looks guilty and wipes her eyes, smearing what's left of her makeup around the swollen skin. "I got an email with a link, and once I clicked on it, I couldn't stop reading."

Okay, so job number one is to find out who sent her that link and destroy them!

"C'mon, Sawyer. You know what these bunny blogs are like. Those skanks have nothing better to do than get botox and bitch about the women we choose instead of them," I whisper into her hair as I hug her again.

"I know that, but I've never been the subject of their vitriol before," Cam sobs. "I don't even care what they say about me, but it's the speculation that I trapped you or that the baby isn't even yours that's most hurtful. Trixie's press release hasn't done anything but get the legitimate press off our backs. The hacks and bloggers are still screaming for my head."

"Baby, who cares what they think? All the people who are important to us know the truth," I remind her. "And I've gotta be honest with you: I'm fucking crazy about you, Sawyer."

I notice Cam's chin begins to quiver, and the last thing I want is for her to start crying again. However,

I need to tell her how I'm completely on her side, and hopefully, I'm all she'll ever need.

I take a huge cleansing breath, cup her face in my hands, and gently stroke my thumbs over her tear-stained cheeks, making sure her eyes are on me so she can see how much I mean the next four words out of my mouth. "I love you, Cam."

Now her eyes fill with tears and the chin goes into overdrive. I have a horrible feeling in my gut that she's going to turn me down. Shit, have I just made a huge fool of myself?

But before the doubt can take root, Cam flings her arms around my neck and plants one hell of a kiss on my lips, her tongue seeking mine in desperation. I grab her ass as we fall back onto the couch, her lips raining down kisses all over my face.

"Does this mean you feel the same?" I laugh as we roll around like a couple of teenagers.

Cam pulls away from kissing me and fixes me with her deep brown eyes. "Yes, Warren. I feel the same."

And then we're kissing again, and it gets much hotter than a teenage make out session, the tacos and puck bunnies temporarily forgotten.

Cameron

After Warren makes love to me on the couch, so slowly that I beg him to take me harder, we only make it as far as the shower. In there, I take him in my mouth, driving him insane until he spurts down my throat, then he finds my swollen clit and caresses me until I sag against his wet chest, totally spent.

Instead of cooking, Warren calls the local Tex-Mex place and has every kind of taco delivered to satisfy my craving. We end up eating them in bed while watching our favorite Will Ferrell movie, laughing like idiots and reciting all the best lines. Yet again, I marvel at how easy it is to be with Warren, and I feel my heart swell with affection for him. He's so easy going, I imagine him with our child: carrying them on his shoulders as we walk together along the beach at his cabin. Or being the calm one when I lose my shit about something. Or taking them skating for the first time, being so patient and gentle. It's such a beautiful picture, I want everything my imagination promises.

However, as we snuggle down to watch the end of the movie, I have a gnawing feeling in my gut. Earlier, Warren said he loves me, I have to think really hard about whether or not I said it back to him. Damn baby brain!

I was a complete mess about the disgusting shit I'd spent the afternoon reading on those bunny blogs. Suddenly, I have a horrible realization that I didn't say it back.

"There seems to be a lot of deep thought going on there, Sawyer," Warren says, bringing me back, pressing his index finger to the middle of my forehead. "You missed the Catalina Wine Mixer bit."

I look up at him from my spot snuggled into his side, and his face is so open and handsome, full of love and affection for me, I just can't help myself.

"I love you, Warren," I whisper. "I'm sorry I didn't say it earlier …"

"Hey, I don't want you to feel like you have to say it back to me if you're not ready," he replies, gently tucking a strand of hair behind my ear, grazing his fingers down my cheek.

"I'm not. I mean, I am." I sit up and face him, holding the sheet to my breasts. "I've always loved you Warren, but now there's a whole other dimension to it. It feels so right to say it out loud. I love you!" I fling my arms in the air, and the sheet falls away.

I can't miss the smirk as Warren takes in my bare breasts, then a massive grin splits his stupidly handsome face.

"I fucking love you, Sawyer, and I think it's time I showed you again just how much," he growls, getting that hungry look in his eyes. I know what's coming, and I can't wait for him to take me again.

The next morning, Warren makes me breakfast, and before sending me off to work, I get an unfor-gettable kiss that makes my toes curl in my new com-fortable shoes. He keeps offering to stay in Seattle for the next few weeks, so I won't be alone, but I've assured him I'll be fine. I have Beth and Mila to hang out with, and plenty of work to do at the office. The agents are in and out of Don's office like there's a revolving door, gearing up for the new season, so I'm going to be run off my feet.

"Promise me, if you need anything, you'll call me first, okay?" he whispers as we hug on my doorstep.

"I promise. I've got my checkup next week, and Mila has said she'll come with me," I reply, squeezing my arms around his wide body. "I'll even FaceTime you during the appointment if that makes you feel better."

"I should be here for that," Warren grumbles, and I can see how conflicted he is about going back to Canada.

"It's just a routine checkup. I'll have plenty more you can come to. You'll be back in time for the twenty-week scan. Oh, and I'm gonna look into birthing classes, so be ready to get your breathing on when you're back in town." I laugh, loving the look of horror on his face.

"Shit, am I gonna have to watch some sort of birthing video with a baby and stuff coming out of a woman's … area?" Warren asks, grimacing.

I can't help but laugh even more at his sudden realization that me giving birth and him being there is also part of this whole experience.

"Oh, baby. It'll be fine." I pat his cheek and kiss his soft, pillowy lips again. "I'll be there screaming and cursing at you, so you'll hardly notice all the other stuff going on in my *area*."

Warren kisses me back. "Fuck, I'm gonna miss you, Sawyer." His eyes fill with emotion, and suddenly my voice fails me, my throat full of sawdust.

"It's only a few weeks. And we live in the twenty-first century. There's always Skype sex." I try to lighten the moment.

The comment makes Warren snort and pull me closer, his semi-hard dick pressing into my baby bump. "I'll hold you to that, baby." He gives my ass a slap. "Now get to work, woman."

I yelp, loving his hands on me in that rough way. "Remember to feed Mr. G before you leave and lock up." I point my finger at him along with my best bossy face.

"C'mon, Sawyer. You know how much I love it when you boss me around," Warren growls, reaching for me, but this time I manage to dodge out of his grasp and head down the path to my Jeep.

"Don't forget about Gatsby," I call over my shoulder, already knowing that my cat will be swirling himself round Warren's legs, waiting to be fed.

I slide into my seat, noticing how much closer my belly is to the steering wheel and smile to myself, giving my bump a loving rub.

"We've got ourselves a good man, Bam Bam," I whisper. "I just hope we don't fuck this up for you." Yet again, the enormity of our situation hits me, and I'm slightly overwhelmed with all the responsibility I'm taking on. I think about my mom when she was pregnant with me; she must have been so scared. For the first time, I truly understand what a huge task she took on when she decided to raise me alone, and it causes my eyes to fill with tears. She was such a great mom, and I miss her so much; I want nothing more than to share this experience with her. As more memories of her flood my brain, the tears begin to fall, and I sniff loudly into my hand.

Jesus, these pregnancy hormones will be the death of me. Warren is going to come out here in a minute if I don't pull myself together and get to work. Quickly, I wipe the tears from my cheeks and start the engine. It's time to be a grown up and get my shit together.

26

Cameron

2 Weeks Later

I hold the cold, damp washcloth to the back of my neck and moan. It's the end of July, and even though it doesn't get extremely hot in the Pacific Northwest, we're having a particularly humid spell. Even with the air conditioner on full blast, I'm still sweating like a player after a long shift. The cold washcloth and ice chips I'm constantly sucking on are helping, but I'm really struggling today.

My bump has grown a lot over the last few weeks, and I noticed it the other day when I struggled to tie my sneakers. I've always been slim and fit, so having all this crazy shit happening to my body is freaking me out. I spend most of the time on the phone to Warren, moaning about the new and weird things that are going on. He just smiles kindly and reassures me that I'm glowing—and that, to him, I'm still sexy as fuck. The first time he said that I cried for about half an hour because all I heard was that he's the *only* person who would find me sexy. In the end, to stop my melt-down, he had to whip his shirt off and make his pecs dance, which always makes me laugh.

I try to avoid mentioning the bunny blogs when I talk to Warren. I'm ashamed to say it's become a little bit of an addiction that I can't seem to kick. Ever since I received that first anonymous email containing the link, I've discovered a never-ending sea of poison out there. Obviously, I'm not the only target of their snide comments and nasty memes. It seems that any wife or girlfriend of a professional athlete is fair game to these nasty bitches. There's a particularly disgusting one about Matt and Mila, and it took all my willpower not to tell her about it. There's a puck bunny called Raven who I see at a lot of the games with her little gang of mean girls, and I know that Mila has already had a run-in with her. I really need to stop caring about what they say, but every time I read something about me being a gold digger or trapping Warren with a "fake" pregnancy, the love I feel for him cracks a little bit, and I take a tiny piece of my heart back. I want to be strong and ignore it, be secure in our love for one another, but it's so hard when he's hundreds of miles away.

Being away from Warren over the last few weeks has been a struggle, I'll admit it. We've spoken every day, and I make sure the first thing I do in the morning is send him a sideways mirror selfie so he can keep a track of my growing bump. Bless him though! All that talk about Skype sex has turned into me bitching about insomnia, bloating and swollen ankles, head-aches and the weird nosebleed I had the other day. Obviously, when he heard about that, he freaked out, and within half an hour, Dr. Aguilar was on the phone with both of us, reassuring Warren that the odd nosebleed is perfectly common, but if they become more regular or take a long time to stop, I should go to the Emergency Room.

I can't wait until the weekend when we're all flying out to the cabin for Warren's summer party. Matt has decided because there's a whole group of us going, he'll charter a private jet. This makes me feel much better because I've been worried about fitting into a normal plane seat with my ever-expanding ass.

While I've been sending him baby bump pictures, he's been sending me progress shots of the deck. It's almost finished, and he told me last night that the hot tub is being delivered and sunk into the deck tomorrow. He's so proud of it, and I can't wait to spend the weekend with all our friends admiring my man's handiwork.

"Damn it, Cam. It's like the Arctic in here," Don grumbles as he passes through my office, shivering in an overly exaggerated fashion. For a man who spends half his life in an ice rink, you'd think he'd be made of tougher stuff.

"Sorry, Don. Once this hot spell is over, I promise I'll turn it down," I apologize, puffing out my cheeks which seem to be constantly flushed at the moment.

He chuckles kindly and waves his hand at me. "Don't worry, Cam. I'll just wear my coat when I walk through here."

"Sorry," I call after him as he disappears to his weekly meeting with Coach Casey to review footage of this years' crop of rookies.

I'm just deciding if I can bear to go out into the heat to get some lunch when Trixie pops her head round the door.

"Hey, Trixie. You just missed Don."

"Bloody hell, Cam. It's brass monkeys in here!" Trixie grimaces, rubbing her bare arms that have broken out in goosebumps.

"Excuse me?" I ask, confused. Did she say something about monkeys?

"It means it's bloody freezing in here." She laughs, taking her jacket out from under her arm and slipping it on over her strappy summer dress. "I guess you're feeling the heat, huh?"

"Yes, I am." I smile politely as I try to hide the gurgle my hungry belly makes. "If it's Don you need, he's just gone into a meeting with Coach. I don't have you on his schedule for today."

"Actually, love, it's you I want to talk to. Can I take you to lunch?" Trixie looks at my belly. "It sounds like you could use a bite to eat."

I blush a deeper shade of red and slip my swollen feet into my flip-flop style sandals. "As long as it's somewhere inside, and it's got air conditioning, I'm in."

Trixie laughs. "Deal!"

We end up at a little bistro that's close to the arena, and thankfully, Trixie doesn't suggest we walk there. Instead, she drives us the short distance in her fancy SUV, and we get a table straightaway even though it's busy.

"They love me here," she explains as we're seated at a table, even though I didn't ask.

We order drinks, olives, and bread to start while we look at the menu. I really like Trixie, so we just talk companionably about the food and what we want to eat, then about how delicious the olives and bread are. However, I've known Trixie since she first started representing some of our players, and I know there's no such thing as free lunch. I just wonder what it is she wants from me.

Once we've ordered our food—a Cobb salad for her and a ricotta and spinach omelet for me—I decide to call her out on why we're here.

Trixie looks me square in the eye once and pops an olive into her mouth, chewing it thoughtfully.

She seems to chew on that damn olive for hours, but she finally swallows and speaks.

"I've been trying to get in contact with Bugs about this parenting contract, and he seems to be avoiding my calls."

She lets that settle for a minute, then continues, her grey cat-like eyes never leaving mine.

"I've had everything from your lawyer, and the contract has been drawn up according to your specifications. Bugs gave me his notes, and the contract is ready for signing. However, it feels like the pair of you are dragging your feet, and I'm just wondering why."

Trixie sits back, folds her arms over her impressive chest, and continues to stare at me. Jesus, she's intimidating, and suddenly I feel myself sweating even more.

I'm also a bit pissed at Warren for dodging her. True, we haven't really talked about the contract since we made our relationship official, but he could have taken her call and said he'll get back to her. I really don't appreciate being blindsided at work when he's not around to back me up.

As usual, it looks like I'll be sorting this out on my own.

"To be honest, Trixie, I'm not sure what to say," I begin just as our food arrives.

The smell of the cheesy, eggy omelet is actually making me feel quite queasy, so I don't start eating.

"Warren and I are in a relationship now, so I guess the need for a contract is kind of a moot point."

I notice Trixie's eye twitch, and her lips pull into a tight line. "Look, I understand what you're saying, Cam. But you need to understand that I have to do what's right to protect my client. I really like you, but I can't, in my capacity as Bugs' agent and manager, let him enter into this thing without protection. I still think the contract is a good idea. It'll save a lot of confusion and upset if things go ... tits up."

My heart sinks into my stomach, and I know that Trixie doesn't think what we have is real or that we'll go the distance. Is that what everyone thinks? I certainly read it every day on those damn bunny blogs.

"Look, I'll email you the contract. Your lawyer has approved it based on what you initially told her, but if you and Bugs want to make changes, then you need to let us both know."

I swallow hard and take a gulp of my ice water. I suddenly feel really unwell, and this restaurant is no longer pleasant and cool; it's stifling and I need to leave. Now.

"I'm sorry, Trixie. I need to go." I rise from my chair, and it falls over behind me, banging loudly on

the flagstone floor. People look up from their conversations, and I don't even care that they're staring at me.

"Shit, are you alright, love? You look a bit green
around the gills," Trixie asks, her face a picture
of concern.

"I'm fine. Just email me the contract, and I'll see
Warren looks at it this weekend." I grab my purse and
lurch away from the table. "I'm sorry."

As Trixie calls my name and struggles to pull cash
from her purse, I burst out onto the street and thankfully grab a cab that has just dropped someone off. As
I sit in the back, sweating bullets, my eyes full of angry
tears, I realize that no one believes in Warren and me.
I quickly fire off a text to Don explaining that I don't
feel well, and I instruct the driver to take me home.

I was afraid this might happen; when I'm with
Warren, he's all I need and all I can see is our love
for one another. His love for me shines so brightly
that I have no doubts about us or our future together.
However, being without him these past few weeks have
allowed those seeds of doubt to creep in. If I'm one
hundred percent honest, I'm terrified that this will all
blow up in our faces, and I'll just end up alone anyway.
At least if I take control of the situation now, like I
wanted to begin with, I'll know exactly where I stand.

Just as we turn into my street, my phone pings to
indicate a new email. It's from Trixie, and it contains
the contract and a note wishing me well and apologies
if she upset me.

As the realization of what I have to do dawns on
me, I let the tears roll down my cheeks, and I lock
down my heart to everything and everyone except the

life growing inside of me. He or she is now my one and only priority.

Bugs

"Man, this looks amazing!" I say, clinking my beer bottle against Larry's. "I can't thank you enough for helping me. I don't think I realized what a big job it was gonna be."

Larry just chuckles, his belly wobbling slightly under his sweaty shirt. "If I had a dollar for every person who called me asking for help because the job they started 'turned out to be harder than they thought,' I'd be a very rich man."

I snort out a laugh. "Well, you charged me more than a dollar, so I suspect you are a very rich man."

Larry shrugs and chugs the rest of his beer, surveying our handiwork. The porch at the back of the house now extends seamlessly into a wide deck that ends just before the beach. I installed steps down to the sand, and the rails around the perimeter come up to waist height. Tall pillars hold up the open roof which can be covered with awning for shade or protection from the rain or be left open at night so we can see the stars. One of my final jobs is to wind the never-ending lengths of fairy lights around them as per Cam's request. She said it would look gorgeous at night. I also have to put out the pots containing the plants she picked out and the long table with bench seating and the cozy outdoor couches around the fire pit. The hot tub looks awesome in the far corner, the perfect place to relax with a beer and watch the sunset. Or perhaps other, more sexy activities with my woman.

The thoughts of Cam make me happy, desperate, horny, and a little frustrated all at once. I love that she wanted to help make my home look cozy, but I've missed her so much over the last few weeks. I think that's why the deck was finished ahead of schedule. Even after Larry left for the day, I made sure he left enough little jobs for me to carry on with until he came back. I needed something to keep my mind off Cam, alone, back in Seattle.

Our daily FaceTime calls have been the highlight of each day as well as the cute baby bump pictures she's been sending me every morning, so it's the first thing I see when I turn on my phone. However, the last few days, she's not sent one and when I asked her during our last call, she looked sheepish and said she didn't feel like cataloguing her metamorphosis into a whale. Despite my reassurances that she looks beautiful, she just scrunched up her face and changed the subject.

There was a definite chill in the air during our last call, and even though I asked her countless times if she was okay, she just blamed the heat and her hormones. I have to say, if she wasn't flying in tomorrow with the rest of the gang, I'd be on the first flight back to Seattle. There's definitely something up, and when we're face to face, she'll have no choice but to tell me what it is.

"The party has arrived!" Thor booms as he steps off the small bus they hired to transport them all from the airport. He holds a keg in his arms like it weighs nothing, smiling like an idiot as I step out onto my porch. "Greetings, Captain."

I laugh loudly and feel a huge sense of relief that they're all here, but more importantly, that the bus contains my woman and my kid.

As the rest of the Whalers and their significant others pile off the bus, Thor puts the keg on the porch and pulls me into a big hug. "Don't mention her ankles," he whispers into my ear, then he pulls away and heads inside.

I'm a little confused as I greet Matt and Mila, Nate and Beth, Ford, Brett, Knox, and some punky chick he's got his arm around. Then I see Cam and I immediately understand Thor's little nugget of advice. My woman looks completely miserable, and her normally slim ankles are puffed up so you can't tell where her calf ends and her foot begins. I've heard these referred to as "cankles," but I remind myself to absolutely not use that term this weekend.

I rush over to help her off the bus while Matt and Ford help the driver unload the bags.

"Hey, Sawyer." I pull her off the last step and into my arms, her growing baby bump making it more difficult than before to hug her close. However, that's not the only problem; she seems stiff and tense, and I put this down to the long journey.

"Hey, Warren. Is the air conditioner on?" she mumbles, pulling away from me, fixing her tank top that's ridden up, showing off her belly. I notice a few stretch marks and the fact that her belly button has popped out. I have an overwhelming urge to drop to my knees and kiss her there, but I doubt she'd appreciate that.

"It sure is, baby. And I got extra fans for our room, just like you asked." I gently kiss her lips, and after a moment's hesitation she sinks into it, allowing me to stroke her tongue with mine.

"Get a room, you two!" Beth yells from the porch. "Talking of rooms, where are we all sleeping? There's no way I'm sharing. I want my man all to myself!" Nate slaps her ass, and she squeals with delight, shooting Nate a burning look.

I pull away from Cam and tuck her under my arm, walking us over to the cabin. "The couples are in the two guest rooms, and the rest of you are on inflatable mattresses in the game room and the office. You goons can sort that shit out between you."

"Hey, Cap," Knox pipes up. "Technically, I'm part of a couple, so where are Charlene and me s'posed to sleep?"

I laugh and shake my head. "A heads up to the extra guest would've been the polite thing to do, rookie. So, you're shit outta luck."

"What about your dad and April?" Cam asks. "Where are they staying?"

"Nancy offered to put them up for the night next door. I figured dad and the boys would want somewhere quiet to retreat when this lot gets too rowdy," I reply, loving how my girl always thinks of other people. "She jumped at the chance to come to a Whalers party."

I chuckle to myself when I remember how much she squealed when I mentioned it.

When we go into the house, there's a full-blown wrestling match happening on the floor of my office between Knox and Thor about whether the rookie and his girlfriend get that room to themselves. I commend the kid's balls for trying to take down our behemoth of a goalie, but I figure it's best to leave them to it.

"Don't break any of my shit!" I yell as we walk past, following everyone else down the hall into the back room. There are gasps and compliments on how well the deck turned out, and Beth and Mila are already digging around in their bags to find their bikinis.

"I think I'll take a little nap," Cam whispers next to me, and I get a definite sense that she's not happy.

"Come on, baby. I'll take you up and tuck you in."

We slip out of the room while the guys raid the fridge for cold beers. Knox and Thor finally finish with their wrestling match, and I'm pretty sure the pissed off look on Knox's face tells me who won.

I grab Cam's bag from the hall, and we head upstairs to my room, which I've made sure is frosty cold. As we enter, I break out into goosebumps, but Cam just sighs in relief and flops on the bed.

"Oh, that's good," she moans when I kneel at her feet and slip her sandals off, rubbing her swollen feet. "My feet are so big now I can't even get my sneakers on. Ooooohhh, right there."

Cam falls back onto the bed and continues to moan, which I'm ashamed to admit, gives me a semi chub.

"Babe, is it wrong that I'm totally aroused right now?" I growl, running my hand up her calf, massaging the tight muscle, eliciting another loud groan.

Cam huffs and sits up, pulling her leg away from my grasp. She looks at me and shakes her head. "I'm sorry, Warren. I'm sweating like a beast. I'm exhausted and swollen. There's no way I feel sexy right now. I just want a cold shower and a nap."

She's not the only one that needs a cold shower, I think, adjusting my deflating cock. But I completely understand, so I put my horn dog feelings away and lean up to kiss her soft lips.

"Whatever you need, Sawyer. You get in the shower, and I'll make you some iced tea." I rise to my full height and lean over to kiss the top of her head, loving the flowery scent of her hair. As I turn to leave, she reaches out and grabs my wrist.

"Warren, thank you. I'm sorry I'm being a killjoy." Cam looks up at me with the expression that melts my heart, and I sit next to her and cup her face in my big hands.

"Don't be stupid," I whisper, gently kissing her lips. "You're growing our baby in there, so as far I'm concerned you get whatever you want. If you want me to send everyone away so it's just us, I'll do that. If you want ice cream in the middle of the night, you got it. I love you, baby. This is it for me; you're it for me."

Cam's bottom lip goes berserk as her eyes fill up with tears, and she leans into me, kissing me like it's the first time. She brings her hands up to cover mine as they continue to cup her face, and I feel her wet tears on my cheeks. We stay like that for several minutes until she pulls away, and I don't know what it is, but there seems to be a wall between us that wasn't there before. Cam wipes her eyes and keeps them away from me as she stands and fusses with her bag. The moment of tenderness we've just shared is gone.

"I'll be back with your iced tea in a minute," I say, rubbing her back.

"Sure, no rush." And with that she disappears into the bathroom and shuts the door.

Frustrated, I scrub my hand over my face and suck in a deep breath. There's more going on here than her pregnancy hormones driving her crazy. I need to find out what it is before it drives me crazy right alongside her.

27

Cameron

The chilly water cascades over my body, mixing with the tears that also stream down my face. I've cried so much over the last few days I'm sure I'm dehydrated. I rub my hands over my face and hair to clear the water. My decision has been made, the contract has been rewritten, and all I have to do is tell Warren. I bark out a desperate noise that echoes around the tiled shower.

That's all.

All I have to do is crush my best friend's heart and tell him we can't be together. Back in Seattle when I was freaking out and full of doubt, this seemed like the right choice. But now I'm here, back in his arms, his lips on mine, his declarations of love ringing in my ears, it's so hard to stand by my decision.

I'm so confused.

I step out of the shower and wrap one of Warren's huge towels around my body. My waistline has pretty much disappeared now I'm on the verge of being halfway through my pregnancy. It still amazes me that there's a life growing inside me, a life I'll be responsible for for the rest of my life. It's incomprehensible, but everything in my heart and soul tells me that protecting my baby is my most important job now.

"Knock, knock," Mila's voice jolts me from my dilemma, and I pull the towel tighter around my body.

"Come in," I call, sitting on the bed, rubbing my hair dry with a towel.

Mila slowly opens the door and comes in, carrying a tall frosty glass of iced tea. She shivers as she closes the door and comes to sit next to me, placing the glass on the nightstand.

"Bugs got to talking about the deck and other man stuff with the guys, so he asked me to bring you this," she says quietly, looking at me a little too closely. "Are you okay?"

I know my eyes are puffy from crying in the shower, and I feel so overwhelmed by everything, but I try to smile and nod. However, Mila's continuing sympathetic gaze breaks me, and my smile crumbles into tearful sobs.

"Oh Cam," Mila pulls me into a hug. "What's wrong?"

I continue to sob against her shoulder, completely lost in my confusion.

When I'm all cried out, again, I reach over for some tissues and wipe my wet face.

"I'm sorry for crying all over you," I huff, blowing my nose.

"Babe, that's fine. But you're really scaring me now. What's wrong?" Mila asks again, gently rubbing my back through the damp towel.

I take a huge deep breath. "I'm going to end things with Warren."

I hear Mila gasp as she flinches next to me. "Why? What did he do?"

"Oh god, he didn't do anything," I reply quickly, not wanting her to think badly of Warren. If anyone's to blame for this situation, it's me. I'm the one who got swept away in the sex and romance and didn't keep my practical head on.

"So, what's going on?" Mila repeats gently.

"I just don't think it's fair to trap him into a relationship with me because we're having a baby. I know we slept together, but if I hadn't gotten pregnant, I don't think it would've happened again. We'd have just gone back to being friends. I feel like I've forced him into this," I explain, only telling Mila a half truth.

"Oh my god, you're insane," she cries. "Bugs has held a torch for you for as long as I've known you both, and from what the guys say, he's been into you for years. He's not trapped; he's getting his happily ever after."

I quickly stand, clutching the towel to my chest. "Do you know how much pressure that is, Mils?" I sigh. "I'm getting it from all angles; his sister hates me, the bunny blogs are constantly talking shit about me, and Trixie …" I clamp my mouth shut to stop myself from continuing with that sentence. "Look, all I'm saying is I need to start this as I mean to go on. I need to be in control of what happens to me and my baby. I can't think about Warren's feelings as well. It's too much responsibility."

Mila blows out a breath and shakes her head. "I can't say I understand it, but I guess this is your decision.

And you're right. You need to do what's right for you and the baby. Can I just ask you to do one thing?"

I nod. "Sure."

Mila stands and gently holds my biceps. "Please let him down easy."

Tears sting my nose, and I can only nod. Now I've told Mila about my plans, it's suddenly all very real. I've got no idea when I'm going to do it, but one thing I know for sure, I can't wait too long, or I might chicken out.

After Mila leaves, having sworn not to mention this to anyone, not even Matt, I slip into bed and try to take a nap. My mind swirls with every possible scenario to avoid breaking Warren's heart. But every avenue I go down ends up with me alone with the baby. I just can't see it working out between us in the long run. So, my plan is to get Warren to sign the revised co-parenting agreement which sets out a fair division of responsibilities and time with the baby. That way I'm protecting both of us. This made Trixie very happy, especially when I added a clause to the contract which states that apart from reasonable child support and a trust fund for the baby, I don't stake any claim on Warren's current wealth or any future earnings he may make.

I guess I must doze off at some point because the loud shouts and squeals of little kids wake me up, and when I look at the clock on the nightstand, I notice it's after four, and I've been napping for hours.

"Seamus, Bryan, stay on the deck!" I hear April's voice outside, so I guess Warren's family has arrived. I exhale to calm my suddenly fluttering heart and stretch my aching body. As I wiggle my toes, a clenching cramp shoots up my leg, and I swing out of bed, flattening my foot on the floor, crying out at the pain. These cramps are happening more and more.

The pain finally subsides, and I gingerly stand up, flexing the muscles to make sure the cramp has passed. As I pull on my unflattering maternity panties and floaty summer maxi dress, I feel the nerves really take flight. I'm really anxious about seeing April again, especially after Warren told me how much she disapproves of our situation. I pull my hair into a ponytail—it's dried weird because I slept on it damp—and leave my feet bare. If I can go without shoes this whole weekend, I definitely will.

"Hey, look who's awake!" Warren calls as I shyly make my way out onto the crowded deck, sunglasses securely covering my eyes. They didn't stop me noticing Warren walking toward me with his strong, muscular arms open, his low-slung board shorts showing off his washboard abs and sexy Adonis belt. God damn it, why does he have to be so hot?

"I'm glad you're up, Sawyer," he whispers into my hair, pulling me into a hug. He smells like sunshine and warm man, and I allow myself to breathe him in, feel the hard muscles of his back as I wrap my arms around him. I hope we'll get back to this one day. We were always tactile friends, and I'll really miss this if it disappears from our relationship.

We pull apart when I feel little hands tugging at my dress. I look down and see one of the twins. I still can't tell them apart. "Momma says you've got a baby in your belly," he states, looking up at me with inquisitive fern green eyes. The eyes he shares with his uncle. "How'd it get there? Did Uncle Warren put it there?"

Barks of laughter erupt around us, and Warren swoops down to pick up the little boy. "Bryan, that's a conversation you need to have with your momma." He smirks. "But yes, me and Cam are having a baby, and he or she will be your cousin."

A flustered looking April suddenly appears and takes her son from Warren's arms. "I'm sorry, Cam," she gasps, her cheeks tinged pink with embarrassment.

"You need to have the birds and bees talk with your kids, sis." Warren laughs, winking at his sister.

"Oh, he'll be getting a talking to. Believe me," April grinds out, turning away, whispering sternly in her wriggling son's ear.

"C'mon, Sawyer. I saved you some food," Warren says, taking my hand and leading me back into the kitchen where Thor, Knox, Ford, and the punky girl are playing Quarters on the coffee table.

"Ugh, I really needed that sleep." I sigh as I take a seat at the kitchen counter while Warren fusses around, fixing me a plate from the barbecue they must have had while I was sleeping.

"You slept hard, baby." He chuckles, placing the delicious looking feast in front of me. Despite my nervous belly, the baby demands to be fed, so I dig in. "I looked in on you a few times, and you were out for the count."

"It's been so humid in Seattle, I've not been sleeping," I explain, ripping into a beef short rib that literally melts in my mouth. "And Gatsby's being a real asshole.

He insists on spooning me all night, and his furry little body is like a heat pad."

Warren laughs and shakes his head. "I told you that your cat's an asshole."

I glare at him for dissing Mr. G but continue ripping into the ribs, not caring that my face is getting covered in sauce.

"Cam! Good to see you, honey." Warren's dad comes in from the deck, dropping his empty beer bottle into the large recycling bin. He comes over and gives me a side hug. "Enjoying the ribs, I see."

"Sure am," I mumble with my mouth full, suddenly a little embarrassed at how much food I'm stuffing in.

"It's all good for the baby, so keep it up." He chuckles. "I want a big, strong, bouncing grandbaby."

I swallow my mouthful. "Not too big, eh?"

Warren and his dad both pull identical grimaces, and now it's my turn to laugh. They're like peas in a pod, and it reassures me that the baby will have such a strong, happy family on its father's side, at least.

Bugs

Now that the sun's gone down, the strings of fairy lights I spent hours fitting yesterday look amazing. The party's in full swing, and my friends and family are making full use of the deck and the house. My sister's husband, Patrick, is involved in a feisty game of darts with Nate in the games room while Beth tries to hustle Thor at a game of pool. The twins have conked out on an air mattress in the office, and the rest of us are sitting around on the deck enjoying the balmy evening.

I look over and see Nancy and Brett chatting by the fire pit, and Ford and my dad are throwing a ball for Juneau down on the beach. My eyes narrow as I notice Knox and his punky girlfriend making out in my new hot tub. I need to shut that shit down right now!

"Excuse me, ladies. I have a rookie to slap upside his head," I growl, rising from my place at the table where April and Cam are sitting with me. I stalk over to the hot tub and stand behind Knox, who's currently tongue fucking his girl while she straddles his lap. I swear to god, if they're fucking in there, I'll kill the little shit.

"Hey! Rookie!" Because the hot tub is sunk into the deck, I can nudge his shoulder with my foot to get his attention. I really don't want to touch him with my hands right now.

They pull apart, the girl's lips swollen, her lip ring glinting in the light, her eyes drunk with arousal. Knox turns around, his face like thunder.

"What the fuck, man?" he barks, but when he realizes his captain is the one interrupting his little make-out session, he has the decency to look chagrined.

"Dude, that's not appropriate hot tub behavior, especially with my family around. Rein it the fuck in before I send you back to Seattle," I grumble, feeling like an old fart.

"Sorry, Cap," Knox replies. "Hey baby, shall we go find a quiet spot on the beach?"

Charlene nods enthusiastically, and they thankfully get out of the hot tub and disappear into the darkness. "Don't fuck near any of my neighbors!" I call after them as Knox smirks at me over his shoulder and grabs a handful of Charlene's ass.

I make my way back to the table. "Little punk," I mutter as I sit next to my sister. "Where'd Cam go?" I ask, noticing her empty place.

"Bathroom, I think," April replies, looking a little sheepish, taking a long sip of her wine.

"I know that look, April. What did you say?" I nudge her in the ribs, making her spill her wine.

"Fuck's sake, Warren," she whines, wiping liquid from her chin, shooting me her best pissed off mom look. "I didn't say anything. Pregnant women go to the bathroom a lot."

"I call bullshit. You have a lot of opinions about me and Cam, and I'm sure you took your chance to share them with her," I say through gritted teeth. I love my sister, but I swear if she pissed Cam off, I'll kick her ass.

April rolls her eyes and sips her wine. "I may have expressed my concerns," she says quietly.

"Fucking hell. You're such an asshole." I stand up and move inside, not before bumping against her so her wine spills again.

"Jerk!" she calls after me.

"Hag!" I yell back, going inside to look for Cam.

She's not in the main room or the game room with the others, so I head upstairs and find the door to our room closed. I knock lightly until I hear Cam say I can come in. When I enter, I see her sitting on the edge of my bed with a manilla folder in her hands and tears on her face.

I'm going to kill my fucking sister.

"Baby, what's up? What did my dumbass sister say?" I ask, sitting next to her, putting my arm around her shoulders.

She takes a deep breath and actually shifts away from me, which sets all sorts of alarm bells ringing in my head. I swear if my sister has ruined this with her big fucking mouth ...

"She didn't tell me anything I don't already know," she says quietly, fiddling with the folder in her hands.

"What's that?" I ask, tapping the folder, my voice low and gravelly with pent up frustration.

"It's the co-parenting agreement. I had my lawyer and Trixie rewrite it."

My gut clenches and I ball my fists. "Why?"

Cam passes me the folder, her hand shaking so slightly I almost don't notice.

"Trixie came by the office the other day and said she's been trying to get hold of you about signing the contract," she explains quietly, keeping her eyes downcast.

"Yeah, I had a few missed calls, but I figured if it was really important, she'd have left a message or sent me an email." I feel like a dick for dodging Trixie now, leaving Cam to deal with it alone. "I'm sorry. I should've called her back. It wasn't fair of her to come to you about it without me."

Cam shakes her head. "No, I wanted the contract in the first place." She quickly looks at me, and I see something in her eyes that makes my heart race. That wall is back again. "I asked Trixie to rewrite it so that you're completely protected."

"What the fuck does that mean?" I bark, ripping open the folder, quickly scanning the contract. As I see the changes from the original document, it dawns on me what this means.

"It's what's best for everyone," Cam replies.

"What's all this shit about splitting time between us and child support payments? Why will I need to pay child support if we're together?" I ask, trying desperately to keep a lid on my frustration. "I know we haven't officially talked about this, but I was hoping we'd move in together when the summer's over."

"I can't do it, Warren," she answers on a sob. "Beginning this together is such a risk, and I just can't put myself or my baby in that position."

"*Our* baby, Cam! It's our fucking baby!" I yell, my last strand of control snapping. I stand up and pace, running my hands through my hair, tugging at the short strands.

"I know that, Warren. But I also know that if we get into this together, and it goes wrong or we fuck it up, I'm gonna end up alone again," Cam yells back.

"Who said we're gonna break up?" I bark. "I fucking love you, Cam. I've told you that so many times. When's it gonna sink in? You can't keep comparing me to your dad or Richard. It's not fucking fair."

Cam fixes me with a blank stare that sets my heart hammering against my ribs. "It's not about them. Love doesn't always last forever, Warren. We've done this thing in the wrong order, and nobody thinks we'll go the distance; Trixie doesn't, your sister certainly doesn't. Have you read those blogs lately? Have you read what they're writing about me?"

I gawp at Cam, completely confused by her outburst. "What blogs? What are you talking about?"

"The bunny blogs," she cries. "Ever since that picture of us kissing at the airport came out, it's been non-stop. Every day there are new comments calling me a gold digger or saying that you're not the father, or even worse hoping that I lose the baby, so you'll be a free agent again!"

I can feel the blood rushing through my head as I take in everything she's telling me. As far as I was aware, all that bullshit had calmed down once Trixie put the official press release out.

"I haven't seen any of this," I growl. "Why the fuck didn't you tell me you were still reading that trash?"

"Because I was afraid you'd start to wonder if they were right!" she sobs, burying her face in her hands, her shoulders heaving with the force of her tears.

I sit down and pull her into my arms, holding her close to my chest as she sobs her heart out. This can't be the end. This can't be how we finish things. I need to fight for her, and she needs to believe that I love her, baby or no baby. As she blows her nose, Cam grimaces, rubs the side of her belly, and immediately my anger dissolves. I kneel at her feet and put my hand over hers.

"Everything okay?" I ask calmly. All this yelling is obviously upsetting her.

"Yeah, Bam Bam's just moving around." She sighs, looking into my eyes. "It's fine. It happens."

Gently, I rub my hand over her baby bump, moving to the floor between her feet so I can press my ear against it. I feel the slight movement under my cheek as the baby rolls over, and my heart clenches in my chest.

"Please don't do this, baby. Please don't end it like this. I love you," I beg. "I don't care what anyone says. We know what's real."

I feel Cam sob again, her hand gently stroking my hair. "I'm sorry. I can't. Please sign the contract. It's the right thing to do—for our baby."

I feel the prick of tears in my nose and the back of my throat. I can't believe this is happening. I can't lose her, especially over the bullshit other people are laying at our door. But I'm scared to push her in case I hurt her or the baby. I swallow the dryness in my throat and quickly wipe my hand down my face, sweeping away the wetness. Cam needs a strong man, not a fucking cry baby.

I sit back on my haunches and fix Cam with a look that makes her avert her eyes from me. As hard as I'm trying, I can't keep the hurt from them. She's put me in an impossible position, and I don't know how to fight for the woman I love if she doesn't love me back.

"Let me look over the contract and speak to Trixie. If I'm happy with it, I'll get it signed." I rise to my feet. "I'll sleep on the couch tonight. Might as well start as we mean to go on."

"Warren ..." Cam cries, but I'm already turning away from her and storming out of the bedroom, slamming the door.

I need to speak to Trixie and see why the fuck my life has just imploded. And then I need to get drunk.

28

Cameron

"I can't thank you enough for this." I sigh as Nancy drives me to Edmonton, so I can catch a flight back to Seattle.

"No problem, babe," she replies, joining the freeway which is quiet at this early hour.

I feel like a coward, leaving the cabin at the crack of dawn, but after a sleepless night, I had to get out of there. When I couldn't sleep, I went online and booked a flight, then I messaged Nancy, hoping she'd still be awake. Luckily, she was, and she agreed to drive me to the airport.

"Is everything okay?" she asks. "I didn't see you again after Bugs evicted the rookie from the hot tub."

"Yeah, I just came over a bit tired, so I went to bed," I reply quietly, wringing my hands in my lap.

Nancy glances at me. "I don't want to pry, and you can tell me to mind my own business, but it seems like more's going on. I mean, you called me in the middle of the night asking for a ride. I take it this is more of a moonlight flight than a planned departure."

I let out a heavy sigh, something I've done countless times in the last twenty-four hours.

"I kind of broke up with Warren, so I thought I should give him some space."

"What?" Nancy screeches, swerving slightly in her lane.

"Jesus, I'd like to get to the airport alive!" I cry, gripping the arm rest and bracing my legs in the footwell.

"Sorry, sorry," Nancy apologizes. "But seriously, girl. What the hell? That man is fine, rich, and he loves you. What's the issue?"

Jesus! I just can't explain this to yet another person.

"It's just the right thing for me to do," I mumble, and I hope my short answer gives Nancy the message that I don't want to talk about it anymore.

"Okay, as long as you're sure." She reaches over the center console and pats my hand. "Just make sure you take care of yourself and that little baby."

I swallow the tears back and smile over at her. "Thank you."

After a hot, uncomfortable flight in economy, I make it back to Seattle in one piece. I've had my phone off since I got to the airport, but now I'm waiting on the sidewalk for the next taxi, and I anxiously turn it back on.

As I suspected, my phone blows up with texts, voicemails, and emails. I still feel like an asshole for sneaking out like I did, but I just couldn't cope with all the questions and awkwardness. Judging by the noise last night, the party raged on into the small hours, and I could hear Warren shouting drunkenly until the very end. I have no idea if he told anyone about what happened, so I took the coward's way out.

I climb into the taxi and use the time to look at the messages. There are several from Mila asking if I'm okay and then asking where I am. Lots from Beth and Nate asking the same thing. I have to admit, I expected hundreds of messages from Warren, but when I've been through them all, there's just one voicemail message from him.

With a heavy heart, I hit play and press the phone to my ear.

"So that's it then?" Warren's angry, slurred voice makes me flinch. "You just leave and don't say goodbye? I thought we were friends above everything else, and you pull this shitty move on me. Fuck! I guess you've made your choice. I'll send the signed contract to your lawyer. Just make sure you let me know when your doctor's appointments are because I will be there. I know you don't want me, but I will be part of this baby's life, so you'll just have to deal with that."

The message ends, and I realize I'm not breathing, so I take a huge gulp of air and release a strangled moan, causing the driver to glance over his shoulder. I bite the inside of my cheek to stop myself from crying and stare out of the rain-streaked window. Thankfully, the humid weather has broken, and the Seattle rain perfectly matches my current mood. I want to believe that I've done the right thing; my rational, practical side tells me that I have. So why does my heart feel like it's shattering into a million pieces? God, I need my mom so badly. The pain of her loss feels so fresh I can taste it, but I don't know if it's also mixed with the pain of losing Warren. I cover my face with my hands as the tears refuse to wait until I get home and I quietly sob for the rest of the ride, ignoring the concerned looks from the driver.

Bugs

"Drink this, son," my dad says as he takes a seat next me on the sand, handing me a steaming cup of black coffee. He also tips two painkillers into my palm to help ease my crippling hangover.

I smile at him and dry swallow the pills, grimacing at the bitter taste as they crawl down my throat. I chase them with a sip of hot coffee, burning my tongue, but I welcome the pain. It reminds me that I'm not dead, that Cam didn't cut my fucking heart out last night, and then stomp on it this morning when she left without even saying goodbye.

My dad found me passed out on the deck this morning, sprawled out on one of the couches, damp from the morning dew. He dragged my drunk ass into the outdoor shower which he turned on hot to warm me up, bringing me a towel and clean clothes. When I was dry and dressed, that's when he dropped the bomb that Cam was gone.

"I know you're hurting," he states in his quiet, calm way, patting me on the back.

"I don't understand what I did wrong," I reply, looking over at my dad. He's always been my fucking hero, and I pray he has the answers I need.

"I can't answer that, Warren." He looks at me with an apologetic smile. "Only you and Cam can sort that out. But my guess is, you did nothing wrong. It sounds to me like Cam is a frightened woman who's spent most of her adult life looking after herself."

"But I want to look after her. I need to look after her and the baby. I've made that very clear to her," I reply angrily, putting my cup down in the sand, raking my hand through my hair.

"I know you have, son. But you need to look at this from Cam's point of view. Her mom died when she was ...what ... eighteen? She was barely an adult, and she suddenly had to look after herself and make all these huge decisions. That has to have molded her and affected how she responds to people helping her. The only person who loved and cared for her ended up leaving her at the most vulnerable time in her life. No wonder she's scared."

"Why are you defending her?" I suddenly yell. I thought my dad was supposed to be on my side.

"Hey, don't yell at me!" he barks. "You're not too big for me to beat your ass."

"Sorry," I mumble, feeling seven years old again. My dad very rarely uses his pissed off voice, and he's never laid a finger on me in punishment, so I know there's no real danger in his threat.

"I am on your side." He reaches over and pats my knee. "I just want you to see past your hurt and anger and realize that this can't have been easy for her. She's doing what she thinks is right and at the moment that means she wants to concentrate on her and the baby. It doesn't mean she won't come back to you, son. You may just have to be patient. My advice is be there for her as a friend and as the father. Try to put your romantic feelings on the back burner for now."

Jesus, this guy is like Yoda. And even though his advice stings, and it doesn't get me what I want, I know he's talking sense. I need to play the long game with Cam. It's just going to hurt like hell for the time being.

29

Cameron

6 weeks later

"Cam, get me Coach," Don barks through the intercom. "I want him in the viewing room in ten with Parker and Landon."

"Sure thing, Don," I reply, my stomach still clenching at the mention of Warren's name. In the weeks that have passed since the weekend at the cabin, things are still tense between us. When I returned to Seattle, I spent days crying and second-guessing myself. I couldn't bring myself to call Warren. He was so angry, and I knew he'd need time to calm down. So, I sent him a calendar notice for my twenty-week scan, so he'd know when it was and left it at that.

I squirm uncomfortably in my office chair, Bam Bam kicking furiously against my bladder, making my need to pee extremely urgent. I push up from the chair and waddle quickly to the little bathroom in our suite of offices, only just making it in time. The baby's been using my bladder as a squeeze toy all week and

I've had a few near misses, but so far, I haven't embarrassed myself.

When I return from the bathroom, Don is by my desk, looking expectant.

"Is Coach ready to meet me?" he asks, cocking an eyebrow when I look at him in confusion.

I return his look, wondering what he's talking about, and then his pre-bathroom emergency instruction returns to my baby brain, and I click my fingers.

"Sorry, Don. The baby needed a bathroom break. I'll call Mila now," I apologize. Shit, my memory is totally shot, another wonderful side effect of pregnancy.

"No problem, Cam. When does your maternity leave start again?" he asks, smirking.

"Not for ten more weeks," I reply. "But my replacement will hopefully start by the time we have the first away series. You need someone to travel with you; it also gives me plenty of time to train her up."

"That's great. But I still need to see Coach, stat!"

"Yes, of course. On it!" I grab my cell phone and call Mila, giving her the message before dropping into my chair. I'm officially entering beached whale territory, and every day I get more immobile. But no matter how uncomfortable I get, I know that Bam Bam is healthy and growing strong. It gives me a little thrill every time he or she wriggles around, even when it wakes me in the night or makes me feel like I'm going to barf. It's a constant reminder of the little miracle I'm protecting.

Physically, Dr. Aguilar says I'm right on track and everything is perfect. My twenty-week scan was amazing, and I looked at the 3D image of Bam Bam sucking its thumb with tears in my eyes. It got super awkward when Warren grabbed my hand and squeezed it, tears filling his green eyes. In that moment, we put all our bullshit behind us, and we were mom and dad to our baby. We shared the experience, but then it passed, and it was back to being awkward as fuck.

As we left the doctor's office, Warren handed me an envelope.

"I signed the contract," he said matter of factly; all the emotion from earlier was gone. "Your lawyer has a copy, but I thought you'd want one too. I also set up the trust fund. The paperwork for that is in the envelope."

I took it from him, our fingers brushing briefly during the exchange. It took everything in me not to react to the spark that passed between us.

"Thank you," I whispered, holding the envelope to my chest. "I'm sorry again about how this went down."

"No need," he huffed. "It was my mistake. I saw something that wasn't there."

"No, Warren, that's not ..." I began, taking a step toward him, but he backed away.

"I have to go," he said. "Call me if you need anything ... for the baby."

"I will," I whispered again, watching him leave, my eyes filling with tears.

And since then, that's pretty much how we've been with each other. Warren spent most of August at his cabin, only coming back to Seattle for doctor's appointments and team stuff. I spent the time throwing myself into work and trying to avoid my friends. It got to a point where I dodged Mila and Beth so much, they performed an intervention. They showed up at my door one Saturday morning with pastries and sympathy, ready to drag my sorry ass out of solitude.

They listened as I spilled my guts and cried into my cinnamon roll. Like the good friends they are, they offered their support and advice but never their judgement. It was so awkward because we're all in the same friendship circle so there's no getting away from the drama. In that moment, I decided to take myself out of it, and from then on, I avoided the places I knew the guys hung out, and I declined invitations that weren't just the girls. It was hard enough having to see Warren at our baby appointments; I didn't want to drag all our friends into it as well.

However, as Training Camp started this week, I have no choice but to deal with Warren and the rest of the guys on an almost daily basis. To give them credit, none of the guys have been off with me or given me shit about what I did to their Captain. I'm keeping a low profile and am just thankful that, at twenty-seven weeks pregnant, I'm no longer able to travel with the team if a flight is involved. That's why I've already hired my temporary replacement, and she'll start in a few weeks when the pre-season kicks off.

Thinking about my maternity leave reminds me that I have to see Annabel in HR, so with a huff, I push up out of my chair, slip on my shoes, and trudge to the elevator. Bam Bam kicks furiously as I wait for the elevator to arrive, and I gently rub the side of my belly, smiling to myself.

"Keep squirming, kid," I whisper, loving the bond I already feel to my little surprise.

Bugs

"Do you see the hole in your defense?" Coach Casey states, aiming his laser pointer at the big screen. He pauses some footage from the practice game we played yesterday against our farm team. I can clearly see that Nate and I are miles apart, and the hot shot center is about to slip between us. My memory repeats the play, and I remember that little punk faked me out and hit a screamer right through Thor's five-hole.

"Yes, Coach. Nate and I will tighten that up when we do drills this afternoon," I reply, not even bothering to make excuses. With Don sitting there as well, there's no point. It just makes me look like a dick, and I'm sure Don thinks that about me anyway.

We continue to go over game footage, and I try my best to concentrate, but my mind keeps wandering. It's been awkward as fuck between Cam and me, even though I'm trying my best to be the bigger man. I took my dad's sage advice on board and did my best to keep my feelings out of our interactions.

Even though I decided to spend the rest of the summer at the cabin, I still flew back and forth to Seattle to attend all her appointments. When I saw our baby on the 3D scan, I felt my heart burst with pride and love for the weird little alien on the screen. It was sucking its thumb, curled up all cozy, and I couldn't help reaching out of Cam's hand, needing to share this incredible moment with her.

Apart from that, we've just skirted around each other, making polite small talk about the baby and the new season. And I have to admit, I fucking hate it. We feel like polite strangers, not best friends, and I miss her so much. It's not even the physical side of the relationship I miss the most, but I'd be lying if I said I didn't wake up most mornings with a painful boner and a deep ache in my balls. I don't think I've beat off this much since I was a horny teen, and I refuse to look elsewhere for relief, despite Brett's offers to take me cruising for bunnies.

I've also been avoiding Trixie. When everything blew up, I called her and tore her a new one for confronting Cam the way she did. She just yelled back at me, using all those British curse words I don't quite understand, but I got the gist.

"For fuck's sake, Bugs," she barked. "If you'd just called me back, I wouldn't have had to do that."

"She fucking left me, Trix," I grumbled. "She broke up with me, and I feel like my goddamn heart's been ripped out."

"Oh love, I'm sorry." Trixie sighed. "But I'm not sorry that I did my job and protected you."

"And it's my job to protect Cam and my baby, and now I'm gonna have to do that from the fucking bench."

"I think it's for the best, Bugs."

"Then why does it hurt so fucking much?" I yelled, hanging up on her.

And now I can add Trixie to the list of women I'm avoiding, along with Cam and my sister. I made sure

April knew exactly how her comments and actions had added to the stress that Cam had felt before she left. She also tried to convince me she had my best interests at heart, but by then, I'd had a gutful of people interfering in my life.

"You okay, Cap?" Matt whispers as Coach Casey turns on the lights and starts talking to Don about something. Shit, I totally zoned out.

"Yep, all good," I lie, standing from the auditorium style seating and following Matt outside.

"You seem really distracted," he replies as we walk towards the players' lounge to load up before this afternoon's practice game. "There's no way you'd let that little shit from the farm team get past you."

I huff out an exasperated breath and scrub my hand over my head, enjoying the feel of my freshly buzzed hair. I let it grow out over the summer, and when I came back to Seattle, Beth told me I looked like a grizzly homeless man. She insisted her business partner, Andre, come over and "deal with my situation" as she put it. If only all my situations were as easy to deal with.

"I miss her, man. I miss her so fucking much I can't breathe. I can't concentrate, and all I think about are all the little moments I'm missing because we're not together," I explain as we stop outside the lounge.

"I know, but you can't force her into being with you." Matt slaps my back. "She'll come back. You guys are meant to be. Everyone thinks so."

I bark out a laugh. "Everyone except the person who matters the most."

"Have faith, brother. You'll get your woman back."
Matt pushes open the door to the lounge.

My quads are burning, and my lungs feel on the
verge of collapse as I complete what feels like a million
burpees. This is the worst part of Training Camp—the
physical tests that make me want to die. I've already
run the 5k on the treadmill, hooked up to heart moni-
tors and breathing machines, and now I'm in the gym
completing standing jumps onto taller and taller plat-
forms, pull ups, sit ups, rope work, and now burpees.

I've already witnessed some of the rookies puking
into the garbage cans Coach dots around the place, and
Brett has had to see the physio because of his dicky hip
flexor. On the whole, as I wipe sweat out of my eyes,
I see a strong team ready to take another run at the
Stanley Cup this season.

My main concern is Knox. He's no longer the
rookie, but he still acts like a punk ass kid. I've been
keeping my ear to the ground over the summer, and I
have to admit, I've heard way too many rumors about
out-of-control partying and whoring around. I've definitely squirrelled away plenty of details to share with
Coach when we have our pre-season meeting where
he shares his ideas for the lines with me. He's one of
the best wingers I've seen come up in a long time, but
he's at risk of losing it all if he doesn't watch his ass
and take this seriously.

"Okay, Bugs, you're done. Good hustle," Coach says, slapping my back. "Hit the shower, and we'll talk on Friday when I have the preliminary lines mapped out."

"Yes Coach," I gasp, bending over to catch my breath, sweat dripping from my face onto the mat. I'm getting too old for this shit.

Once I cool down on the bike, get a stretch out from one of the athletic trainers, and take a shower, I head out to the players' parking lot. Matt offered to have me over for dinner, but I'd rather just order in some Thai, watch some game footage, and have an early night.

But as I walk through the parking lot, I notice Cam standing by her Jeep, her hand on her hip, and her phone pressed to her ear. I can hear her shrill voice, but I'm too far away to hear what she's saying. As I get closer, I notice her Jeep is leaning weirdly on the driver's side, and I know for sure she's got a flat tire.

"I can't hang around for two hours waiting for a tow … No, I can't. I'm six months pregnant," she replies to whoever is on the other end of the phone.

"Hang up the phone, Sawyer," I say as I come into her line of sight.

"What? No, I need a tow," she hisses at me. "Sorry. No. I was talking to someone else," she says into the phone. "I still want the tow, but can't you speed it up?"

God damn stubborn woman. I reach out and pluck the phone from her hand which earns me an angry growl. "Hi, this is Warren Parker. I'd like you to come and tow my colleague's Jeep as soon as possible," I say to the operator on the other end of the phone. "I'll leave the keys with the security guard at the parking lot, and I want the tire changed, a full service and valet, and then I want it delivered back to Ms. Sawyer's home address by seven am tomorrow morning."

"Yes, Mr. Parker. The tow truck will be there in thirty minutes." I give the operator my credit card details so she can charge it all to me, then I hang up and turn to Cam.

I don't expect her to fly into my arms, but I sure as shit don't expect her to look as pissed as she does.

"What the fuck was that?" she cries, snatching her cell phone out of my grasp. "I'm not a completely helpless damsel, and I don't need you to swoop in and save me!"

"Well, fuck me for trying to help," I yell back, my voice bouncing around the underground parking lot. "I'm sorry if I don't want the mother of my kid standing around in a dark parking lot for two hours waiting for a tow."

"I was dealing with it."

"Yeah, it looked like it," I scoff, rolling my eyes. "Give me your keys, Sawyer, and I'll take them over to the security guard. Get your stuff, and I'll take you home."

"Ugh, you're so annoying," Cam grits out, slamming her keys into my palm, grabbing her purse off the hood before stalking off toward my SUV.

I can't help but chuckle to myself at her reaction to me helping her. It's very different from the last time this happened. Jesus, that seems like a million years ago. So much has happened since then, it's almost like we're different people now.

Perhaps we are.

30

Cameron

I sit in Warren's luxurious SUV, fuming at the knight in shining armor bullshit he just pulled. Yes, I'm on my way home and not standing around a cold underground parking garage, and yes, my Jeep will come back to me fully repaired, serviced, and valeted. But I'm still pissed that he felt the need to go all alpha male on me. I had it under control. I didn't need him to rescue me.

As we drive through the drizzly Seattle streets toward my house, I can't think of what to say to him. We haven't really spoken, and this feels so uncomfortable I can't stand it. I'm the one that put us here, so I should be the first one to speak.

"Thank you, Warren. I'm sorry I yelled at you," I say, squaring my shoulders. "That was really kind, what you did."

"No problem," he replies casually. "I wouldn't leave you stranded."

"I know." I take a deep breath. "And thank you for sorting out the trust fund. I logged in and saw how much you put in there. It's too much. I want you to take half of it back."

"No fucking way," he growls, flicking his eyes to me because we're at a stop light. "That money means you'll never have to worry about saving for college or a first car or anything."

"Those things you've just listed do not need that much money," I argue.

"It's done. The trust is locked until the kid turns eighteen, so I can't change it now anyway." Warren pulls away from the light and turns into my street, parking outside my house.

He kills the engine and turns toward me, his handsome face cast in shadows, but it doesn't hide the need I see there.

"There's nothing you or our kid is ever gonna want for, baby," he tells me in a low, gravelly voice, his hand stretching across the center console to gently stroke my belly. I flinch slightly at his touch, but just as quickly the warmth of his hand leaks through my blouse, and I relax into his touch. "God, I miss you."

At that moment, I don't know if he's talking to me or the baby, so I put my hand on top of his and squeeze it. "I miss you too," I whisper, overwhelmed by the tenderness of the moment, the scent of him filling the car and my own emotions surging through my system.

Warren's eyes flick up to meet mine, and I see the love shining out of them. It's intoxicating, and I can't seem to stop myself from leaning into him. My lips whisper over his and my hand runs up his neck, over his short hair, causing a whole-body shiver.

"I miss you," I sigh before pressing my lips fully to his, using my hand on his neck to tilt his head to the side as our kiss deepens. The rumbling groan that escapes him urges me on, and his tongue runs across my bottom lip. While we kiss, Warren keeps his hand firmly on my bump, but I'm desperate for him to move it lower, the ache between my legs pounding along with my heartbeat.

"Please, Warren. Touch me," I beg as my lips mark a trail across his scruffy jaw.

"Wait, Sawyer. Stop!" he growls, pulling away from me, scrubbing his hands over his face.

"Why did you stop?" I gasp, putting my fingers to my swollen lips, my very unflattering maternity panties flooded with desire.

Warren looks at me, confusion and pain written all over his face. It's no wonder; one minute I'm dumping him, and the next I'm begging him to touch me.

"What happened? I thought you didn't want this," he asks, his brow furrowing.

Suddenly, I'm overwhelmed with shame and guilt. I can't believe I literally jumped his bones after making it very clear I didn't want to be in a relationship with him.

My cheeks burning with embarrassment, I quickly turn and open the door, needing to escape the confines of the car, but Warren reaches out to grab my wrist. I turn back and see his serious expression.

"You need to figure out what you want because I can't keep doing this. You either want me or you don't."

My eyes sting with tears at his ultimatum, and I look down at my belly. My feelings are so conflicted between allowing this man into my heart fully, allowing him to love me and our baby. Or closing myself off to the possibility of more pain.

"I'm sorry, Warren," I say as he releases my arm and I slide out of the seat. "I didn't mean to confuse you. Just forget this happened."

He simply nods. "If that's what you need." And then he starts the engine as I slam the car door. I watch him drive away, and yet again I'm full of conflicting emotions.

The next morning, I wake up after another shitty night's sleep. My brain would not switch off, the feeling of Warren's lips and hands on me replaying in a constant loop in my mind. And it didn't help that Bam Bam was doing a gymnastics routine in my womb all night.

I have a busy day today; Don is hosting his preseason brunch in the players' lounge. It's where he sets the tone for the season ahead, welcomes new members of the team, and mingles with everyone. I've spent the last few weeks organizing it, so I need to be on top form today. Don will not be happy unless everything is perfect.

I shower as quickly as I can. I don't do anything quickly these days, and head downstairs where I find my car keys on the doormat. As promised, the garage returned my Jeep and pushed the keys through the mail slot. I peek outside and see my red Jeep sitting on my drive, shining in the morning sun, with what appears to be four brand new tires. Along with my keys, there's a detailed breakdown of all the work they carried out, and I'm a little ashamed to say I've let my car maintenance slip over the last few months, hence yet another flat tire.

I stand there clutching my keys and think about the moment Warren and I shared last night. As confusing as it was, it felt so right to be in his arms again. He's the kindest, most generous man I've ever met. He does so much for other people and the love he already has for his unborn child is clear to see. There's never any doubt about how he feels about the people he loves; I see it when he's with his family and his teammates.

With absolute clarity, I know what my mom would say about him. I can hear her as if she were in the room.

"You grab that wonderful man with both hands, Cammy, and never let him go. Love like that comes around once in a lifetime."

Releasing a sigh, I grab a banana and a bottle of water and shove it in my purse. I don't have time to deal with these feelings at the moment. I've got a really busy day, so I push them to the back of my mind, and I'll deal with them later.

Bugs

I pull into the players' parking lot and turn off the engine of my Audi. I feel like shit after spending most of the night tossing and turning, staring at the minutes as they ticked by until the sun came up.

My encounter with Cam has thrown me into turmoil. I was so shocked when she kissed me, I got completely lost in the moment. Lost in the smell of her which has become my own personal brand of catnip—I can't get enough of it. I mean, she's always smelled great, but since she got pregnant, she seems to be pumping out all kinds of pheromones that just drive me nuts.

But as good as the kiss was, as amazing as it felt to have her lips and hands on me again, I had to pull away. I know Cam, and I know when she feels vulnerable, and there's no way I'm the kind of guy to take advantage. That would make me an incredible douchebag, and it would also end up hurting us both all over again.

I need Cam to choose me with all her heart. I need to be her first choice, not someone she's settling for. It took every ounce of willpower I had to pull away from her last night, but I know myself. If I hadn't, we'd have ended up in bed together. I know for sure that's what my dick wanted. However, he doesn't do my deep thinking these days, so I made sure to make the right choice and drive away.

I can't keep making a fool of myself, so I'm taking my dad's advice and playing the long game. I know Cam is confused and terrified of being hurt, so I don't want to force her hand. I intend to back off, keep my distance, and wait.

I take the elevator up to the Coaching Floor and find the reception area already bustling with players and coaches waiting to go into the large auditorium we use for team meetings and reviewing game footage.

"Hey, Cap," Thor greets me with a bro hug and a handshake. "Geez, you look like hammered shit."

"Thanks, man," I scoff. "Didn't sleep well." I look around and see the rest of my line just as they head into the auditorium, laughing like they don't have a care in the world.

"C'mon, big guy. Let's find a seat," Thor says, pushing me forward as people move toward the doors.

We filter in through the double doors, and I see the guys have snagged a row of seats near the front, Nate's long legs stretched out in front of him as he laughs at something Matt is saying.

"Hey, Cap. Nice of you to join us." Matt chuckles. "I thought, as captain, you're supposed to be the first to arrive and the last to leave? Maybe I should relieve you of that title if you're not up for it."

I flop into my seat and flip him off, really not in the mood to deal with his shit today.

"Oooohhh, someone's got their panties in a bunch today." Ford laughs, slapping me on the shoulder. I shrug him off and keep my eyes fixed on the podium. I hear Ford and a few of the other guys chuckle, but I just keep my eyes facing forward.

"Dude, are you okay?" Matt whispers, catching on to the fact I'm not my usual self.

"Yeah, I'm fine. Just not in the mood for their juvenile shit today," I mumble, thankful that Don chooses that moment to enter the room and head to the podium.

The general chatter of the room dies down as people see him waiting, and after a few death stares from Coach Casey, everyone shuts up so he can address us.

"Good morning Whalers family, and welcome to a new season, and what I hope will be a Stanley Cup winning season," Don begins, and his words rouse rambunctious cheers and whoops from the assembled players and coaches. I manage a slightly limp fist bump with Matt, but as Don continues, my attention is drawn to Cam, who sneaks in and stands near the end of my row, her iPad clutched to her chest. She's dressed in a cute yellow dress that hugs her chest and drapes down over her baby bump. She looks so fucking beautiful, plump with my baby, it makes me hard looking at her like that.

However, I feel a twist in my gut. The room is packed, and there's not a free seat in the place, but I'll be damned if I'll let a pregnant woman, my woman, stand while I lounge on my ass.

As quickly as I can, I hunch my huge frame over and sneak to the end of the row, grabbing Cam's hand and pulling her back toward my empty seat.

"What are you doing?" she hisses as I drag her in front of Don and deposit her in my chair, taking a seat on the floor in front of her. I ignore the sniggers coming from the guys behind me.

I turn to her and whisper, "You're pregnant. You're not fucking standing through this thing."

I return my attention to Don and notice that he's stopped speaking, and his frosty gaze is fixed on me. Sweat breaks out on my forehead, and I prepare for him to tear me a new one for interrupting his speech.

However, a huge grin splits his face, and he says into the microphone, "Our Captain, Warren Parker everybody, living proof that chivalry isn't dead!" Then he begins to clap, and the entire room erupts into applause, cheers, and chants of "BUGS, BUGS, BUGS."

Jesus, this is embarrassing, but I quickly stand and take an awkward bow, noticing the shy smile and pink blush on Cam's face. That makes my humiliation totally worth it.

"Okay, okay, take a seat, Cap. Let's get this thing done, so we can dig into the delicious brunch Cam has organized." Don laughs, bringing the room back to an acceptable level of civility.

As Don begins to talk again, I feel Cam's foot poke my lower back, and I quickly glance over my shoulder to see her mouth the words "Thank you." I simply smile and wink, returning my attention to our GM so I know what the hell I'm supposed to be doing this season.

Cameron

Don's pre-season speech was a huge success. I can still hear the players and coaches talking about it as I mingle around the lounge, making sure people have everything they need. I manage to keep a happy smile on my face, even though inside I'm still confused after last night.

I'm so thankful to Mila for helping me out with this event. I know she has a lot on her plate already, organizing Training Camp and the upcoming season, but this is her second season, so she's much more clued up than she was last year.

"Cam, this is amazing," Mila enthuses, stuffing a forkful of fluffy omelet into her mouth, groaning and rolling her eyes with pleasure. This year I hired the chef from Don's favorite brunch spot to cater the event, and the food is unbelievably delicious. I've already polished off a plateful of Eggs Benedict and smoked salmon while everyone else enjoys the Bellinis and Bloody Marys.

"People are enjoying themselves, which is the main thing," I reply, scanning the room to make sure everything is running smoothly.

I feel Mila bump against me. "Are you okay, girl? You look a little zoned out."

I smile, hoping it reaches my eyes. "I'm just tired. That's all. Bam Bam was doing somersaults all night." I give my bump a rub and feel either an elbow or a knee poking against my palm.

Mila gives me a sympathetic look. "That was sweet of Bugs to give you his seat earlier," she says, smiling at me.

At the mention of his name, I feel my shoulders tense up. I need to unload some of this turmoil, and I know that Mila has my back. As much as I know she doesn't understand my reasons for breaking up with Warren, she's never judged me for it.

"Can we have a girl's night tonight? Maybe see if Beth's free?" I ask, hopeful that some time with women who've taken the risk and given their hearts to their men will inspire me to be brave.

Mila smiles and rubs my arm. "I'm on it, babe." She pulls her phone out of her pants pocket and starts tapping away on the screen, putting it to her ear. "Beth, get all your best pampering stuff and order some pizzas and ice cream. We're having a girl's night at your place. Yes, Andre can come. Okay, perfect. Love you."

She fixes me with her huge smile. "Bring your jammies. We're having a sleepover."

I can't help but laugh and pull her into a hug, thankful to have such good friends.

"Ooft, take it easy, Cam. Your bump's crushing me."

The rest of the day rushes past in a blur. The brunch is a huge success, and I'm thrilled when so many of the players and coaches approach me asking where the food came from, and I happily hand out business cards from the restaurant.

I spend some time chatting to the chef while he packs up the kitchen, and he kindly offers me a meal on the house whenever I want which I happily accept. I'm never one to turn down a free meal. By the time I finish packing up the event, everyone except Mila and Don have left.

"Cam, thank you so much," he says as we wander back to our offices. "That was the perfect way to begin this season. I really think we'll do it this year."

"I think so too, Don." I lower my gaze to my baby bump and feel a sting of sadness that I'm going to miss so much of the season.

"Is everything alright?" he asks as we enter our office suite. "I don't want to pry, but I've noticed things with you and Parker have cooled off."

I swallow and feel my cheeks heat with embarrassment. "I kind of broke up with him over the summer," I reply quietly, flicking my eyes to meet his.

Don frowns and rubs his chin. "I'm confused. What happened?"

I huff out a breath and prepare myself to retell the story yet again. The problem is every time I tell a new person the reasons why I broke things off, I feel more and more ridiculous. And once I'm done with this recount, I know for certain that I've made a huge mistake.

"Cam, honey, I can see from your face that you're not one hundred percent invested in this break up," Don says, cocking his bushy eyebrow.

"You know what, Don," I sigh. "I don't think I am either. I just don't know how to get him back."

Then Don laughs. He laughs so loudly a few people walking past our office look in to see what's going on. In the end, he laughs so hard, he has to bend over, his big hands splayed on his thighs.

"Hey!" I whine, slapping his shoulder. I've finally had enough of his gleeful laughing. "What's so funny?"

Don finally stands up and wipes the tears from his eyes. "You were in the auditorium today, right?" he asks.

I scowl at him, wishing he'd hurry up and get to his fucking point. "Yes, you know I was."

"And you saw the captain of my hockey team get up during my welcome speech and give his seat up for you in front of all his teammates?"

"Yes?" I phrase the word like a question, but I have an idea where he's going with this.

"Cam, he's completely head over heels in love with you. It's clear as day and every single person in that auditorium saw him declare it to you with his actions." Don shakes his head. "You just need to be honest with him and tell him how *you* feel. Men aren't that complicated. We're kind of like dogs."

Now, I'm the one laughing my ass off at Don. I've never known him to dish out relationship advice, and I'm so touched that he chose to impart his wisdom to me. However, the laughing soon gets the better of me, and I have to excuse myself to hit the bathroom before I make a puddle on his expensive rug.

As I head home to pick up the stuff I need for the girl's night at Beth's, I think about all the advice I've been given since I ended things with Warren. It swirls around my brain, making a tornado that could quite easily carry me away. I quickly shake my head and focus on one thing—Warren. His heart, his soul, his kindness, and his compassion for other people. His body and the fact that no man has ever made me feel the way he does when we're together. The fact that he's my best friend in the whole world, and I miss him like I'd miss a limb.

By the time I get to Beth's apartment, I'm ready to admit I want to be with Warren. I'm completely terrified by this decision, but I know if anyone can help me, it's my girls.

"Come in, come in," Beth cries, answering the door, already dressed in a unicorn onesie with some kind of lumpy oatmeal looking stuff all over her face.

"Thanks," I gasp. "And can I suggest you get an apartment on the ground floor? Climbing those stairs almost killed me."

"Oh babe, I'm sorry," Beth says, grabbing my bag and ushering me down the hall to her sitting room.

"It's fine. Just carrying around all this extra weight is really slowing me down." I laugh, finally able to take a deep breath. It's so frustrating that I get out of breath doing the simplest things now. I've run a marathon for fuck's sake, and now I can't even climb a few flights of stairs!

"Oooooh, you look gorgeous, Cam. You're glowing!" Andre coos, leaping to his feet, wearing a unicorn onesie that matches Beth's.

"That's because I just busted a gut climbing the stairs. It has nothing to do with the baby." I chuckle, accepting a hug from Beth's extremely tall business partner. Andre and Beth have a hair and makeup business which has become even more successful since they did a movie recently.

Andre runs his hand over his smooth brown scalp which shines like polished wood. He always looks flawless, even in a unicorn onesie. "Baby girl, you look incredible. Accept the compliment."

"Thank you," I reply shyly, accepting a glass of something pink and frothy from Mila. When I look at her, she's also wearing a unicorn onesie. "Ummm, are you guys in some sort of unicorn cult?"

Beth cackles mischievously and reaches into a bag, producing another one. "If we are, then so are you."

"Oh god," I moan, rolling my eyes, grabbing the garish pink garment and disappearing into the bathroom to change.

When I return, the teddy-bear soft onesie enveloping me in a comforting but slightly embarrassing hug, my friends are sitting around the low coffee table, digging into pizza and ranch dip. I stand for a short while and watch them laughing and talking, Beth and Andre regaling Mila with stories from their time on the movie shoot. I feel so blessed to have such great people in my life. After spending so many years alone, I finally have the security I had when my mom was alive, and it feels really good.

"Hey, there she is." Mila giggles, taking in my appearance. "You look so cute."

"Come on. I look like a pink sparkly narwhal." I pout, trying to hide my smile. This causes my so-called friends to dissolve into peals of laughter, and Mila pops up and comes over to hug me. "I love you," I whisper, suddenly overcome with emotion.

"I love you, too," she whispers back, kissing my cheek. "Come on. Let's eat pizza and pamper ourselves."

As I lower myself down onto the couch and accept a huge slice of pizza and a napkin from Beth, I allow its cheesy goodness to soothe me.

"So, what's the plan?" Andre asks as he elegantly dabs the grease from the surface of his slice.

"Plan?" I reply through a mouthful of cheese and dough.

"Yes, your plan to get Bugs back," Andre sasses, rolling his eyes, which today are his own natural light brown. He normally wears extravagant contacts depending on his mood or his outfit. "I assume that's why we're here—to formulate the grand gesture to win him back. I take it you bitches don't read as many romance novels as me."

Beth sniggers and we all fall about laughing as Andre pulls a notepad and a flamingo pen from his bag ready to take notes and set our plan into motion.

32

Bugs

"**P**arker! Get your head in the fucking game," Coach Casey shouts as he skates toward me. "My four-year-old granddaughter could've made that shot!"

I growl under my breath and wipe the sweat out of my eyes. He's not wrong. I'm playing like shit. It's been over a week since Cam and I kissed in my car, and other than a few brief conversations that were purely professional, we haven't talked properly since. I know I made a promise to myself to wait for her to come to me, but the waiting is fucking killing me. I haven't slept properly, going over every moment and conversation in my head, trying to identify the point at which my life turned to shit.

The guys have been great, trying to cheer me up with visits to O'Connell's and dinners at their houses. Thor even made me a traditional Swedish dish of pickled herring, and I almost puked my guts up, much to his amusement. But I just can't drag my ass out of this funk.

After Coach rips me to shreds about my wrister, I skate off to the bench, leaning over the boards to squirt some Gatorade into my mouth and sulk. A couple of the rookies side-eye me from the bench and I realize I'm setting a shit example for them. I'm the fucking captain. I should be leading these men, not sulking like a little bitch. As I turn around, Matt skates up to me, plowing to a stop and spraying me with ice.

"Fucking douche," I bark, wiping the water droplets from my visor.

Matt just chuckles and barges me into the boards. "C'mon on, Cap ..." he begins.

"I swear to god, if you tell me to cheer up and snap out of it, I'll beat your ass like a redheaded stepchild," I shout, my voice echoing way too loudly around the rink. My outburst elicits a few nervous laughs from the rookies, but when I turn around and glare at them, they quickly rise and head down the tunnel.

"I wasn't!" Matt growls back. "Coach asked me to tell you that we have some pre-game shit to do in the GM's box this afternoon, so we need to be in our game day suits and ready to go by three."

I lower my eyes and feel like a dick. Matt's been nothing but an amazing friend, teammate, and brother to me through all this shit, and he doesn't deserve to be at the sharp end of my frustration. I hold my fist out for him to bump and offer him an apologetic smile.

"Sorry, man. I'm so fucking tired," I offer, shaking my head to clear the fog. "I don't know how I'm gonna get through one shift tonight, let alone a whole fucking game."

"I know you miss her, brother. I remember when Mila ran off to New Orleans, I was out of my fucking mind. But you said you wanted to give her space, that was your idea, so you need to let it play out." Matt slaps my shoulder. "C'mon, let's shower and get some lunch. We need to get our naps in before the GM's thing this afternoon."

We skate to the gate, and I huff out an exasperated breath. That's the last thing I want to be doing before our first exhibition game against the Winnipeg Warriors. These high roller events are bad enough, but the fact that I'll probably have to spend an hour or so in the same room as Cam just makes it all the more tortuous.

So, once I've showered and carb loaded in the players' lounge with my linemates, I drive home and try to nap. I lie in bed and try to shut my brain off. A pre-game nap has always been part of my game day ritual since I played in the Juniors, but today I just can't seem to get there. I keep glancing at my phone, taunting me from the nightstand, tempting me to call Cam so I can tell her I want her back.

However, that's not an option. I've made it very clear where I stand; I want her and the baby, and I want us to be a family. It's her turn to think about what she wants, and as much as it pains me to wait, I have to back off and let her come to me.

Eventually, my eyes slide shut, and I drift off to sleep, only waking again when my alarm sounds at two o'clock. I groan and rub my face, thankful for the few hours of sleep I got. However, I need to get moving, I have shit to do.

Cameron

"Seriously, girl, you need to stop pacing," Mila moans. "You're giving me motion sickness!"

I turn to her and drag my fingers through my hair, pulling the strands slightly. "I can't help it. I pace when I need to think. I'd normally go for a run, but ... hello!" I gesture to my large baby bump and grimace.

"Look," Mila replies, standing up and lightly holding my upper arms. "It'll be fine. Everything is in place. All the preparations have been made. You'll do great. It's not like you're in the dark about Bugs' feelings for you. At least that's a sure thing."

"I know that. I'm just scared," I say quietly, pulling my bottom lip between my teeth. "You guys were pretty drunk by the time we came up with this idea."

"Oh pfft." She waves off my concerns. "It's a fucking amazing plan, and it will definitely prove to Bugs that you want to be with him too."

"I hope you're right," I huff. "If you're not, I'll be humiliated in front of all those people, and I'll hold you, Beth, and Andre completely responsible."

Mila squeals and jumps up and down in front of me. "I can't wait for this! I've literally never been this excited!"

"You need to get out more." I laugh, holding her arms to halt the bouncing because it's making me feel queasy. At least that's what I think is making me feel sick.

I check my watch and notice it's time to head over to the GM's box for the reception Don has organized for a local kid's charity. He always opens up his box for local charities during the home exhibition games; it's such a lovely gesture. This year he asked me to pick three of the charities, and this first one is one of mine. It helps children who have lost a parent to cancer, and it's very close to my heart. The San Francisco chapter helped me when my mom died, and I'll be forever grateful for the support they gave me.

As we enter the arena, I hug Mila goodbye, and she heads toward the locker rooms to put the main part of our plan into motion while I walk along the deserted concourse toward the GM's box.

My nerves are completely frazzled by the time I arrive, and as I push the door open, I spot Warren immediately, already sitting on a couch surrounded by kids who are hanging on his every word. Matt is talking to the parents, and Don is schmoozing with the woman who runs the Seattle chapter of the charity.

"Ah, here she is," Don pipes up as I enter the suite. "The lady who made all of this possible."

I feel my cheeks burn with embarrassment as all eyes in the room fix on me, and I wave awkwardly, waddling forward as everyone turns back to their conversations.

"Hi Melanie," I extend my hand to the woman from the charity. "I'm so happy you could all make it. We have a really special treat for the kids. We'd like to invite them to sit on the away team bench for a private warm up session before we allow the other fans in."

"Oh my gosh, Cameron! That's so generous." Melanie gasps. "The kids are going to be so thrilled. Can I tell them?"

I laugh, so happy that I could help make this happen, but also feeling the nerves take hold because it's almost time to execute the final part of my plan. "Sure, go for it."

"Kids! I have a wonderful surprise for you." Melanie claps her hands to get their attention. "Ms. Sawyer has arranged for you to sit on the away team's bench and watch the Whalers warm up before anybody else comes in. Isn't that amazing?"

The kids go completely mental, but I don't miss the puzzled looks shared between Matt and Warren. While the kids jump around and talk to their parents excitedly, I go over to them.

"Sorry to spring this on you, but could you go to the locker room and suit up?" I explain, trying not to meet Warren's eyes. He knows me so well; he'd sense something fishy was going on. "We had to wait for word from the Warriors Coach to move their warm-up time, so it was all kind of last minute."

"Sure thing, Cam. No worries," Matt replies, smiling at me because he's privy to the details of my plan and is probably more excited about it than Mila. "C'mon, big guy. Let's go."

"I don't understand what's going on," Warren grumbles as Matt drags him away. I'm so freaked out now, I have to wipe my sweaty palms on my maternity pants and concentrate on my breathing. Thank god I've already started watching YouTube videos on calming breathing during childbirth.

"Everything in place?" Don asks, making me jump slightly.

"Yes, it's all good, as long as Mila does her part." I still can't believe Don went along with this harebrained scheme when Mila brought it to him. But he's an old romantic at heart, and he just wants to see us happy.

"Okay kids, are you ready to get right up in the action?" Don asks, turning around to address the room.

"YES!" the kids and several of the parents yell, following Don out of the suite toward the rink. Before I go with them, I go out onto the balcony that overlooks the ice and notice Mila putting out the goodie bags for the kids on the away team bench. I whistle down to her, her head snapping up, and I give her a thumbs up which she returns. Even from this distance, I can see the huge grin on her face, and her joy at what's about to happen just makes me even more nervous.

33

Bugs

"**W**here the fuck is everyone?" I grumble as Matt hustles me into the deserted locker room, ripping his suit jacket off and throwing it in his cubby.

"Must already be out there," he replies, continuing to undress, a great big shit-eating grin on his face.

"What's got you grinning like an idiot?" I ask, pulling my pads out of my cubby.

Matt just chuckles and continues to dress. "Just loving life, man. Just loving life."

I'm not sure I like this cheerful, happy version of Matt. When we first met, he was all growly and pissed off, and I'd take that version of him at the moment.

As we continue to dress, I notice there's no warm-up jersey in my cubby.

"For fuck's sake!" I explode. "Where's my fucking jersey? If this is some prank bullshit, I'm really not in the mood."

I shoot a look over to Matt and notice he's all geared up but minus his jersey as well.

"Don't sweat it, Cap. I'll go and find Mila. She'll know what's happened." Matt clomps off up the tunnel in search of his woman, and I sit on the bench and quickly tape my stick. This day is just going from bad to worse; I'm still exhausted, and now I'm pissed off at the equipment team. I have a feeling if anyone looks at me the wrong way on the ice tonight, they're gonna get their asses handed to them.

"Cap, got your jersey. Let's hustle! The kids are waiting," Matt calls from the tunnel, so I sigh and stand up, my skates adding several more inches to my height. I need to shake this mood off before I go out to hang with the kids. I don't want to scare any of them.

When I emerge into the tunnel, I see Matt disappearing onto the ice, and Mila is standing there holding up a jersey for me.

"So sorry, Bugs." She smirks, handing me the warm-up jersey and taking my stick while I pull it over my head.

"No worries, Mila," I reply, slapping a smile on my face even though I know it doesn't reach my eyes.

"Have fun out there," she calls after me as I trudge toward the ice, pulling my bucket on my head and jumping onto the ice, taking off at full speed for a circuit. Then I cruise past the away team bench and high five the kids and their parents, all of them now wearing their souvenir jerseys and beanies.

I also notice Cam and Don standing behind them. Cam's eyes are darting all over the place, and she's gnawing on her thumb nail. I've no idea why she looks so worried; this charity event is a huge success as far as I can see, so she should be proud of herself.

"You ready to hit some pucks at Thor?" Nate asks as he skates backward past me.

"Sure am, kid," I reply, pushing away from the board and picking up a puck on the end of my blade, bouncing it up and down a few times before dropping it on the ice. When I look up to see what the others are doing, I notice that all the guys are standing on the blue line, several of them smirking into their mitts.

"Come on, Whalers. Let's get warmed up," I shout, but no one moves. Damn, has my foul mood ruined my standing as captain? Are these assholes staging a coup?

"I'm afraid we can't do that yet," Coach says, skating up beside me. I turn to him and frown.

"What's going on, Coach?" I ask. "You're starting to freak me out."

Coach Casey also chuckles into his fist and winks at me—he actually winks at me. What the fuck is going on?

"Okay, boys. Let's show our captain his message," he shouts, blowing his whistle.

"YES, COACH," the entire Whalers team yell in unison, spinning on their skates so their backs are now facing me. I look along the line, wondering why the hell I'm looking at all of their asses, but then my eyes catch the back of their jerseys. Instead of their name and number I can see words written in large yellow letters against the navy blue of the jersey.

"What the fuck?" I ask under my breath as my brain tries to process what I'm seeing.

Written on the back of each of their jerseys are the words CAM LOVES BUGS.

I feel my breath hitch in my chest, and my heart begins to pound as I try to process what the hell is going on. When I look over to Coach Casey, he grins and unzips his Whalers hoodie, showing me the front of his T-shirt, which also bears the same message. I shake my head and look over toward the bench where all the kids and parents have their backs to me; they also wear the message on their jerseys.

Suddenly, I hear Cam's sweet voice over the PA system. "I wanted to make a grand gesture. I feel like I owe you that. Plus, I was talked into it by Beth, Mila, and Andre, so you can partly blame them for this." Her husky chuckle echoes around the arena, and I see several of my brothers laughing along, in particular Nate and Matt who are obviously in on this little stunt.

"Anyway, I want to tell you something, and I want to make sure you hear me loud and clear." Cam clears her throat, and I feel my own throat close up with emotion. "I love you, Warren Parker. I think I always have: first as a friend and then as something more. I'm sorry I was so scared of your love, but I've been looking after myself for a really long time, and it was hard to accept that you wanted to raise this baby together."

I look over at my team, expecting to see the guys laughing and chirping on me, but most of them are looking around with sappy grins on their faces.

"But I know that you do, and I want that more than anything. When my mom died, I locked away a part of my heart so I would never again feel so hurt by love. But you've made me realize that I can't live or love with a piece missing. So, I'm giving it to you, baby. I trust you with heart, and I give you every piece of it. I've lived without a family for so long, but then you came into my life. You are my family, you're home to me, and I love you so much. Please forgive me for being so stupid." On those last words, Cam's voice breaks, and I can hear her soft sobs.

"Go and kiss your woman, Cap, before I do!" Knox yells, and suddenly all the guys are banging their sticks against the ice.

"Back off, rookie!" I growl, skating toward the MC booth, where I see Cam struggling to her feet so she can meet me at the gate.

"Not the rookie anymore," Knox chuckles, but I suddenly don't give a shit about his smart mouth. I need to go and claim my woman. Getting my hands and mouth on her is all I care about.

As I skate up to the gate, Cam appears, her beautiful face streaked with tears, her bottom lip quivering out of control. I plow to a stop and rip my helmet off my head, dropping my gloves to the ice.

"What are you doing, Sawyer?" I ask quietly, cupping her sweet face in my hands. "You could've just texted me."

She smiles, her whole face lighting up, the dark circles under her eyes the only evidence that she's been as troubled as I've been. "I felt like I owed you more than that, baby. I'm so sorry ..."

"Shhhhhh, no more apologies. Just kiss me."

And with that, we crash together, my arms circling her back, hers around my neck, our tongues tangling, and I really don't care that we're being inappropriately R-rated in front of a bunch of kids. I feel like a fucking superhero! With my woman and my baby back in my arms, I can do anything.

EPILOGUE

Bugs

Christmas Eve

C am is a week overdue and as miserable as sin. I can't really blame her. She's uncomfortably big, and I feel partly responsible for that, with my giant man genes and all. Thankfully, we've got a four-day period over the holidays without an away game, so I'm primed to take her to the hospital when our daughter decides to make an appearance.

Yes, we found out that we're having a girl, and I couldn't be more thrilled. Cam cried when we found out, scared that I'd be disappointed, but I can't wait to have a badass little girl who has her mom's good looks and my hockey skills. We both decided that we'd like to know the sex. Cam is all about being in control of things, so when she agreed to move in with me, she wanted to know what color to paint the nursery. In the end, we settled on a yellow color scheme with plenty of cute accessories, although Cam had to rein me in when I wanted to have a hockey theme.

However, that was shot to shit when we had the baby shower. All the guys were invited and along with the items we'd registered for like a diaper genie (still no clue what that is), bottles, and bibs, we got plenty of novelty gifts. Thor proudly presented Cam with a gift bag, and when she reached inside, she pulled out a cute little baby sleeper suit. As she opened it out, her face dropped, and she shot Thor a look that made my balls shrivel.

"What's up, baby?" I asked, reaching over to take the tiny garment. As I read the message on the front, I burst out into loud barking laughter. "Seriously, man?"

"What's so funny?" Mila cried, so I turned the baby sleeper around to show the room, and everyone laughed, several of the guys slapping Thor on his huge shoulder. The garment had a hockey stick shooting a puck on the front with the words "Daddy slipped one past the goalie." To give her her dues, by the time I'd finished showing everyone, even Cam was giggling and blushing.

It's been amazing living with Cam. She's settled in, and it's all been so easy. The only sticking point is my relationship with Mr. G. That damn cat is definitely plotting my death. I sometimes wake up in the night to find him squatting on my chest, his amber eyes fixed on mine, growling menacingly. By the time I wake Cam up, he's jumped over and curled up next to her, purring and looking smug. Let's just say, at this point, we tolerate each other.

"Anyone else for nog?" Nate calls from the bar as he pours himself another glass.

"Ugh, no thanks," Mila moans, rubbing her stomach. "I've eaten so much I can hardly move."

With Cam ready to burst, we decided to invite everyone to our house for Christmas Eve dinner. My family flew in yesterday and currently Pat and the boys are playing PlayStation in the game room, my sister is taking a nap, and my dad is fanboying all over Thor who happens to be on his NHL dream team.

"I'll take one," Knox calls from the recliner where he's set up camp.

I cough. "Take it easy, rookie. Pace yourself."

"Not the fucking rookie anymore," he grumbles under his breath as Nate hands him another small glass of egg nog.

"Don't worry, dude. He still calls me kid." Nate laughs, patting Knox's shoulder and flopping onto the couch next to Beth, who immediately snuggles into his side.

It fills my heart with joy to see so many of my brothers happily settled with their women. I guess we need to get Thor loved up next. His mom is on the verge of arranging a marriage for him.

"Ooooohhhhhh," Cam moans, clutching her side, her beautiful face scrunching up in pain.

"Babe? What's happening?" I ask quickly, putting my arm around her.

"I've been having cramps on and off for the last hour. I thought it was indigestion, but it's getting worse." She looks at me with huge brown eyes. "I think this is it."

It takes a few seconds for her words to sink in, then I'm leaping to my feet, my plate of pie falling onto the rug.

"Shit! It's happening? It's time?" I yell, looking around the room at all the shocked and slightly amused faces of my closest friends and family.

"It's okay, Warren," Cam replies calmly, pushing up off the couch. "My bag is by the front door. You haven't had a drink. All we need to do is drive to the hospital. We've got lots of time." She takes my shaking hands in hers and kisses me tenderly on the lips. It immediately calms me, and I pull my sorry ass together. She needs me, and I can't let her down.

"We're having a fucking baby!" I cry, fist pumping the air. "C'mon, Sawyer. Let's go. And you assholes, don't drink my bar dry while we're gone." I point my finger specifically at Knox as Cam pulls me toward the door, accepting kisses and hugs from Mila, Beth, and my dad.

By the time we get to the front door, I'm almost hyperventilating, looking around for my car keys while Cam stands patiently with her bag and her pillow. As I flap about like a headless chicken, I feel Cam's soft fingers stroke down my arm.

"Baby, breathe," she coos, cupping my scruffy face, kissing my lips softly, gently pushing her tongue against mine, soothing my frazzled nerves. When she pulls away, she smiles sweetly. "Okay, now let's go because I don't really want to give birth to our daughter in the car."

Sawyer Jayne Parker comes screaming into the world at two minutes past midnight on Christmas Day. When we found out we were having a girl, we agreed to honor both our moms by using their names: Cam's mom's last name and my mom's first name. I've already made up my mind that my little girl will go by SJ. I just haven't had the guts to tell Cam this yet!

Speaking of Cam, my woman is a superhero. She works through her labor like a fucking champ, staying calm and controlled even when Dr. Aguilar tells her things are moving much quicker than they expected.

I, on the other hand, am a total mess. At one point, I have to make an excuse and leave the room so I can pull myself together. As I take a walk through the waiting room to get Cam some more ice chips, I see several huge hockey players lurking around, along with Beth, Mila, my dad, and April.

I can't help but feel grateful for their support, then I take in what they're wearing, and my laughter echoes around the room.

"Have you guys had novelty jerseys made for every stage of my relationship with Cam?" I laugh, accepting bro hugs from the guys and warm hugs from the girls.

"Come on, man. They're awesome!" Nate chuckles, turning around so I can see the back of his jersey which reads SAWYER'S HOCKEY UNCLE. Beth and Mila's jerseys are the same except they say SAWYER'S HONORARY AUNTIE and April's says SAWYER'S

AUNTIE. My dad proudly shows off his jersey which reads SAWYER'S GRANDPOP.

"I'm so proud of you, son," my dad whispers as we hug. "Now go support that amazing woman. She needs you."

After spending a few minutes updating everyone on how things are going, I head back in, suddenly feeling empowered knowing my best friends and family are here to support us.

It helps me rein in my own anxiety, and I support Cam to the best of my ability. When Dr. Aguilar tells Cam it's time to push, I have to rip my shooting hand from her death grip and swap over because I'm sure Coach will have something to say if I go back to work with my hand in a cast.

But when I lay my eyes on the squirming, red-faced baby the nurse places on Cam's bare breasts, I'm a goner. She wriggles and blinks up at Cam, her perfect little bow lips working in a sucking motion.

"Hello, Sawyer," Cam sighs, her face serene while she shares this first moment with our daughter. "It's lovely to finally meet you. We're gonna love you so much." She leans down and plants a soft kiss on her head.

She looks at me and smiles so big, I can't help but smile back, wiping tears from my face.

"Can I tell you a secret?" Cam whispers into our baby daughter's perfect ear. "You have the very best daddy in the whole world, and he will love us both so much. He can sometimes be a bit of a goof, and I'm sure he'll be ridiculously overprotective of you, but it's all because he has the biggest heart."

Cam and I share a look, and I know for a fact that this woman holds my heart in her hands and always will.

"Do you want to hold your daughter, Cap?" she asks softly, grimacing uncomfortably at something the doc is doing.

Suddenly, I feel completely unsure of myself; what if I drop her or crush her in my big mitts?

As if reading my mind, Cam whispers, "You won't hurt her. Just support her head."

"Try skin on skin," the nurse suggests. "It helps with bonding and comforts the baby."

I quickly whip off my shirt, and I don't miss the way the nurse's eyes widen, and Cam and I make a somewhat awkward handover. Then SJ is squirming in my arms, nuzzling against my pec, gripping my finger so tight I think my heart will literally explode with the love I feel for her.

"Wow, little girl. That's some grip you've got there." I chuckle quietly, her unfocused eyes blinking up at me. "That's a good start to becoming a kickass hockey player." I shoot Cam a look, and she smirks at me; I'm sure this argument will continue for many years to come.

I lean down and smell her hair. It's the weirdest thing but she smells like the perfect mixture of me and Cam, but somehow also totally unique. It's a smell I'll never tire of; I'm hooked.

As I look at my two beautiful girls, I know I'm the luckiest man in the world, and I know for certain they're all I'll ever need.

The End

Having It All—A Seattle Whalers Romance

Book 5

Returning from France after working away, Lana takes a spare room in her big brother Matt's new house. Only problem is he's a super protective hockey player for the Seattle Whalers. She's come home with a business plan and a broken heart, but there's something more sinister lurking in the dark.

The huge Whalers goalie is the last of his four brothers to settle down. No matter how hard he tries, he only seems to attract gold-digging puck bunnies who are after his big ... stick. Can the Swedish giant find true love with a woman who makes the best grilled cheese sandwich he's ever tasted, but who's completely off limits?

PROLOGUE

Lana

Paris, France

I'm trying not to hyperventilate. I need to get my breathing under control before I pass out and miss my window. I've planned this down to the minute, and I can't fuck it up by fainting like a damsel in a black and white movie. I've spent the last six months being that girl, and I'm done.

It's time to get the fuck out of Dodge. Well, not exactly Dodge, more like the plush apartment in the Notre-Dame-de-Lorette district of Paris. A city that had once been my dream, where I attended Le Cordon Bleu and worked in a rustic Parisian Bistro as a sous chef. However, now it is my nightmare. A place where I'm trapped in a gilded cage with a monster.

I tiptoe into the walk-in closet and carefully move the ottoman into place so I can reach the bag I stashed away on the top shelf. Being barely five feet tall, I still have to stretch almost beyond my limit to retrieve the duffel, but finally my fingertips brush the shoulder strap. I grab it and pull the bag down into my arms. However, I underestimated the weight of all my essential belongings, and it knocks my tiny frame off balance, causing me to jump down from the ottoman with a loud thump.

I drop to the floor and freeze, my heart in my mouth, my breathing on the cusp of becoming a noisy gasp.

Shit! My eyes frantically scan the bedroom through the closet door, and I see the figure on the bed, but thankfully, it doesn't seem to be moving.

Hopefully, I haven't underestimated how drunk Etienne is; he got pretty loaded after service tonight, and when he came home, he was staggering and thankfully too drunk to start anything. When he finally passed out, face-down on his fancy four poster bed, I was pretty sure he was passed out until morning.

Once my panic is under control again, I stand up, holding my bag to my chest. I've had to pack light; I can't risk Etienne realizing I've gone until I don't come home from my service at the bistro at midnight, by which time I'll be back on American soil.

Thinking about home brings tears to my eyes, and I spend a moment thinking about all the reasons I have to leave. Actually, the snoring bastard in front of me is the only reason I have to go home. If I leave him and stay in Paris, he'll find me and worm his way back in, like he always does. I need to break away, so going back to America is my only option at this point.

Picking up my boots and coat, I sneak out of the bedroom, avoiding all the creaky floorboards in Etienne's classic Parisian apartment. I quietly choke down a glass of orange juice and the croissant I would normally eat for breakfast, leaving the plate and glass in the dishwasher. I know Etienne will check what I had for breakfast, so I want him to believe I went about my morning routine as normal. I've packed one set of chef's whites and my knife roll, the items I would normally take to school, so he'll have no cause to be suspicious when he finally crawls out of bed.

I take one more look around the apartment, looking at all the perfection and beauty. But I finally see it for what it is: a prison.

Quietly, I slip out the front door and walk quickly down the three flights of stairs. I can't risk using the noisy, ancient elevator. I don't want any of Etienne's neighbors to see me leave in the middle of the night. His family owns this whole building so many of the residents know him personally.

Ha! That's a joke. I thought I knew him. What the fuck did I know?

I creep through the marble foyer and exit onto the street where I'm immediately drenched by the cold January rain. God, winter in Paris is fucking miserable. The freezing rain soaks through my light jacket as I hustle down the cobbled street toward the Rue des Martyrs, where I catch a taxi.

"*Gare de Lyon, s'il vous plaît,*" I say to the driver as we pull into the light traffic. I'm heading to the train station first as I need to get rid of my phone. One of the first clues I had that Etienne was a bad guy was when my best friend Zac found a tracker app hidden on my cell. I was furious and mortified, but yet again, I let him talk his way out of it, let him convince me it was for my protection as I left the bistro late at night. And like a fucking sucker, I bought his bullshit.

It was Zac's suggestion that I go to the train station to dump my cell and use a burner until I'm back in the States. He's obsessed with shows like CSI, so he's picked up plenty of tricks like this one.

So, when I arrive, I pay the driver and hop out, walking quickly into the terminal. My heart is thundering in my chest, and my palms are sweaty as I look around for what I need. At this time, the terminal isn't very crowded, and I feel like I've made a huge error in judgement, but then I see what I need, and I stride toward the ticket booth.

There are two people in front of me in the line and one of them has a large rolling suitcase with an open pocket on the front. I carefully reach into my jeans and pull out my cell, palming it to keep it hidden. I've already put it on silent, so as I step closer to the woman in front of me, I put my own bag on the floor and bend over, close to her case.

Shit, if she catches me tampering with her case, I'm likely to get in a lot of trouble, so I have to be quick and careful. I swallow the dryness in my throat and try not to pant as I rummage around in my bag and covertly slide my cell phone into the open pocket of her suitcase.

I nervously stand up and expect to see the woman looking accusingly at me, but instead she's talking animatedly to the man in the ticket booth.

Thank god, I've done it. Now I just need to get another taxi to the airport, and I'm on my way home. And my cell phone? I've got no idea where that's going, but I'm sure Etienne will be hot on its trail when he finds out I've left.

As I get farther and farther away from the life I've built in Paris, the more afraid I get. Etienne's been my entire life for the last year; he made me rely on him, love him. He controlled every facet of my life, and I wonder who I'm going to be without him.

I guess going back to the US is the only way I'm going to figure that out.

I just hope my brother doesn't mind me showing up unannounced on his doorstep. I've now got a fifteen-hour flight to Seattle to figure out what I'm going to say to him about why I've suddenly walked out on my life in France. There's absolutely no way I'm going to tell him the truth. He'd literally fly to Paris and kill Etienne if he knew what's been going on.

And when your big brother is Matt Landon, massive, badass center for the Seattle Whalers ice hockey team, believe me when I say he could rip Etienne to pieces with his bare hands.

Yes, I need a believable story, and I need one fast.

Read Thor and Lana's story–
Coming January 2022

AUTHOR
BIO

Emily began reading romance novels in 2019 and became instantly hooked. She was inspired to write her own during the 2020 lockdown and first self-published it on Wattpad. With the help of Instagram, she gained a loyal following and eventually secured a publishing contract. Emily is a recent but enthusiastic follower of the Dallas Stars and in particular the delicious Tyler Seguin. She loves an espresso martini, dirty-talking alpha heroes with tattoos, and a lazy Sunday breakfast. Emily lives with her husband and extremely old feline fur baby.

www.emilybunney.com

INSTAGRAM
@emilybunneyauthor

TWITTER
@ emilybunneyaut1

FACEBOOK
https://www.facebook.com/emilybunneyauthor

BUNNEY'S BEAUTIES FACEBOOK GROUP
https://www.facebook.com/groups/967087900382369

CPSIA information can be obtained
at www.ICGtesting.com
Printed in the USA
BVHW031344161021
619102BV00006B/129

9 781644 502723